WALDEN WEST

WALDEN WEST

AUGUST DERLETH

Woodcuts by GRISHA DOTZENKO

The University of Wisconsin Press

A North Coast Book

The University of Wisconsin Press
114 North Murray Street
Madison, Wisconsin 53715

3 Henrietta Street
London WC2E 8LU, England

10   9   8   7   6   5   4   3   2   1

First published in 1961 by Duell, Sloan and Pearce

Printed in the United States of America

Portions of this book appeared earlier in the
following magazines: *Prairie Schooner, The University
of Kansas City Review, The Spokesman, Shenandoah,
The Passenger Pigeon, Decade.*

Library of Congress Cataloging-in-Publication Data
Derleth, August William, 1909–1971.
Walden West / August Derleth; woodcuts by Grisha Dotzenko.
280 pp.   cm.
"A North Coast book."
Originally published: New York: Duell, Sloan and Pearce, 1961.
ISBN 0-299-13590-X (cloth)   ISBN 0-299-13594-2 (pbk.)
1. Derleth, August William, 1909–1971—Homes and haunts—
Wisconsin—Prairie du Sac. 2. Derleth, August William, 1909–1971—
Biography. 3. Prairie du Sac (Wis.)—Social life and customs.
4. Authors, American—20th century—Biography. 5. Country life—
Wisconsin—Prairie du Sac. 6. Prairie du Sac (Wis.)—Biography.
I. Title.
PS3507.E69Z477   1989
818 '.5209—dc20
[B]   92-50264

for the people of Sac Prairie,
living and dead

WALDEN WEST

AN EXPOSITION ON THREE RELATED THEMES.

I. On the persistence of memory.

II. On the sounds and odors of the country.

III. Of Thoreau: The mass of men lead lives of quiet desperation.

Contents

Prologue   xv
In the mid-continent of America   3
The House of Childhood   4
*There was always in childhood that hour when the street-
    lights came on*   12
The Blacksmith Shop   13
My Grandmother Derleth   16
The first awareness of night   20
Two Nuns   21
    Sister Mary Anaclete   22
    Sister Mary Isabelle   23
I have often thought that the sounds and odors of night   25
Nature and Miss Annie   26
Walk on a spring evening   31
My Grandmother Volk   32
Of mornings . . . the musk of the Wisconsin   36
The Harness Shop   39
High over Sac Prairie soar the purple martins   44
Joe Lippert   47

Matt Schmidt   51

The process of renewal   53

Frieda Schroeder, Thoreau, and Emerson   56

Josephine Merk   59

H. P. Lovecraft   64

Quiet Houses   66

   Mr. and Mrs. Holmes Keysar   67

   Miss Jenny Baker   69

   Miss Ella Bickford   72

   Louis Cooper   77

   Reverend John Thilke   82

   Erhardt Kindschi   83

Sometimes spring rode into the village   84

The Park Hall   85

Mike Weinzierl   88

Ehl's Slough   91

Beau Wardler   97

*Quite early in life I fell into the habit of making a daily
excursion*   101

Father Aloysius Schauenberg   104

A great part of the delight of the song sparrow's threnody 111

Carrie Patchen   112

*Not long after I had made the decision to remain in Sac
Prairie*   116

Miss Poosey Lachmund   117

The voices of the wind are endless in their variety   121

Holidays   122

Of winter nights the voices of the trains   125

Billy Ynand   127

The Spring Slough was the magnet   132

Four Women   135

   Millie Pohlmann   135

   Helen Hahn   137

   Helen Merk   139

   Minna Schwenker   141

Thursday was stock day in Sac Prairie   145

John Kleinlein   146

The most gracious singer   151

Old Mrs. Block   152

Nothing more arresting comes out of the woods   158

The Electric Theatre   159

Early in the summer mornings the veery's harp   163

Rich Monn   164

No nocturnal voice seems lonelier than the whippoorwill's   169

The Trautmann Sisters   171

No winter is ever so long   177

Louis Karberg   178

If there is one winter voice informed with wildness   184

The Canning Factory   186

I wait every April   190

The Buchenau Women   191

The choir of the frogs   196

Old Parr   197

Oh, the smell of the grass   201

Lolly Denham   202

When I was a child   205

Mrs. Opal Kralz   207

When I did not walk into the marshes or the hills   212

Sam Schroeder   213

Sometimes, walking through the marshes   218

The Lueders Sisters   220

Many evenings ... I used to sit in the harness shop   225

Ethel Sholl   227

The ways of snakes   231

Mrs. Mae Bowman   232

There is a time when spring's new leaves are just opened   234

Kate Fleeson   235

Among the varied voices   239

Dr. Herman Flemburg   240

There are afternoons in late autumn   242

Mrs. Miles Keysar   243

The essence of autumn   246

Meta Meyer   247

What is it about hawks   255

Nicholas Kenyon   255

Sometimes of evenings   259

Innombrables sont nos voies
et nos demeures incertaines.

     —*Pluies*, ST.-JOHN PERSE

I wished to live deliberately, to front
only the essential facts of life, and
see if I could not learn what it had to
teach, and not, when I came to die,
discover that I had not lived.

     —*Walden*, HENRY D. THOREAU

Prologue

A TIME came three decades ago, when I found I must choose between going out into the wider world or traveling widely in the microcosmos of Sac Prairie. I had been away from Sac Prairie scarcely half a year, immured in a city at editorial work, and I could ill bear separation from the village, the river, the hills, and the lowlands among which I had put down roots and with which I had come to terms of a sort; I walked the streets of the city many nights to assuage nostalgia for these familiar places, and I found nothing in the interminable round of concerts, plays, and parties to balance their loss.

When the opportunity came, I went back to Sac Prairie without regret. It did not matter that for a while my parents thought me a failure; they had endured before; they were patient enough to endure again. So I set about to write so that I might afford the leisure in which to improve my acquaintance with the setting and the inhabitants—hills, trees, ponds, people, birds, animals, sun, moon, stars—of the region I had chosen to inhabit, not as a retreat, but as a base of operations into a life more full in the knowledge of what went on in the woods as well as in the houses along the streets of Sac Prairie and in the human heart.

WALDEN WEST

✳✳✳ 3 ✳✳✳

IN *the mid-continent of America, Sac Prairie, Wisconsin, is no longer a young village, having grown well into its second century, and its land is older still. It lies on the edge of the great driftless area, on a fertile, outthrust paw of land in a fine unbroken curve from west to north pushing out to west by south—a small village, with two centers, upper and lower Sac Prairie, one of the oldest settlements in Wisconsin, where it came into being on the Fox-Wisconsin waterway on the site of the great village of the Sac or Sauk Indians.*

The Wisconsin River is its eastern edge; to the west and to the north the undulant prairie rolls in a succession of slowly rising terraces to the foothills and the bluffs; in the south, the bottoms border the river to the Ferry Bluff range in the southwest. Across the river is the soft line of the moraine where the glacier stopped. It lies in a setting of great natural beauty, in a kind of valley, with the slow river flowing broadly past, surrounded on all sides by low, wooded hills—near on the east, far on all other horizons. In its valley are the rich farming lands of south central Wisconsin; along the river are marshes sheltering birds and other wild creatures long lost to more urban centers; and in the streets of the village there are still to be found a multitude of people who pursue their own individual ways by many a devious and solitary path through life, people who are by ancestry German, French, Scottish, Irish, English, Yankee, Hungarian, even Slovakian, who are Freethinkers or Roman Catholics or Protestants, who live their lives in no way differently from lives spent in countless other villages, in many an un-named Sac Prairie within the country's borders.

A country to be explored, to be learned anew by a walker in its lanes and byways, in its streets, its houses, its environs, a walker bent upon knowing the least bird as well as the least fellowman, an explorer of past time as well as of today, determined to know the patterns of the world of which he himself was an integral part by choice, determined to seek and find, yet knowing that what every man knows about himself and his world is but the most infinitesimal part of knowledge, and what he can know about someone else and someone else's world is even less than that.

The house of childhood is long gone from the street where it stood in Sac Prairie, but it still stands in memory—a little, one-story ground-hugging house, set close to the lane that passed by west of it in lieu of sidewalk which was to come later, sheltered by huge, century-old soft maples and some younger red cedars and hackberry trees, a little house of white-painted siding, and too few windows, its front door opening abruptly from its south wall, and its back door to the east, on to a snug little verandah, walled in to the south by a bedroom ell, and on the north by a short wooden fence running along the raised wooden sidewalk to the summer-kitchen, which shut off the north winds in winter, and which summered us from spring to late autumn—a place to eat and bathe away from the main house. On this porch the sunlight pooled warmly on the coldest winter day, and from it ran, a little way east and then north among grape arbors, a wooden walk that led still farther north across the garden to the home of my Grandmother Volk and my Great-uncle Philip, my Grandfather Volk's brother, whom she had married a quarter of a century after my Grandfather Volk had died, and who was, on my mother's side, the only grandfather I knew.

It was a snug, cozy house, in the shape of a compact L, standing with its base to the south, with a little kitchen at the north end, then a small dining-room, then a somewhat larger "front" room—in those days, in Sac Prairie, the sitting-room or parlor was always called the "front" room—dominated by a large coal stove, red with heat in winter, off which opened the bedroom which my sister and I shared with our parents. The house had a piano in it—sometimes along the west wall of the dining-room, sometimes along the

north wall of the front room. All the openings to the rooms were at their northeast corners, so that a kind of passageway seemed to run along the east wall of the house to that point at which the front door opened out into the spacious lawn, where, under one of the old maples, sat a lawn swing, and, at that same point to the left, the door opened into our common bedroom.

A huge clump of bridalwreath stood at the northwest corner of the house, where its fragrance poured into the kitchen on spring days. East of the bedroom stood an old-fashioned pump, and south of it a sturdy black ash tree grew, and there beneath it our dog

Fido had his house, from which he ran to the south through the lawn for half a block on a chain attached to a long wire, so that he commanded a wide range. Gardens stretched eastward and into the northwest, toward a woodshed, a henhouse and yard, and the two-holer from which we were afforded a leisurely view of the street and such passersby as ventured along it while any of us was occupied within. My father was a man for gardens; while my mother was much given to ferns and other potted plants, with a special predilection for geraniums, which abounded in Sac Prairie at and for two or three decades after the turn of the century, my father was strictly partial to tomatoes, potatoes, cucumbers, peppers, turnips, parsnips, carrots, onions, lettuce, radishes—in short, anything which could be eaten. He had a strictly utilitarian view of a garden and held it all his life, without a single variation, begrudging to the last any space taken up in his precious spaded land by flowers or purely decorative greenery, which did not, of course, include parsley, dill, sweet basil or similar herbs, which could be flavorsome and thus useful.

The gardens surrounded the grape arbors on three sides. There were always plenty of grapes. While Grandmother Volk had a huge back-door cavern arbor of Clintons, my father was partial to Concords, Niagaras, and Delawares, most of which he came by hereditarily from Great-grandfather Peter Damm, who had built the house and lived in it, selling most of the land for blocks around it, piece by piece, until his death precipitated our move into it when I was in my fifth year. My sister and I could eat as many grapes as we liked; those that were left were turned into jelly, jam, grape juice, and wine, since Father's love of garden products was superseded only by his determination that nothing he raised should ever go to waste—if it could not be eaten fresh, it must be canned, pickled, juiced, made into preserves of one kind or another, so that our small earth-walled cellar which lay under the trapdoor in the kitchen floor was filled to bursting with bushels of potatoes, crocks of sauerkraut, tomato jam, tomato sauce, pickled cucumbers, watermelon rind, beans, apples, and everything to which Mother could turn her hand, and it was small wonder that Mother seldom found time but in winter to sit down to the piano to play *Red Wing* and *Moonlight Bay* and *Down by the Old Mill Stream*, which were songs intimately associated with her courting days, and which remained lifelong favorites even after the piano was gone from the house which came after that little house eight years later.

I loved that little house—perhaps because it represented a kind of snug security; I loved everything about it, from the great rose trellis which covered the east wall of the bedroom ell to the soft maples which spread their great limbs and their aromatic leaves like a shelter designed by nature specifically for the house which stood for most of every day in their cool shade. I knew every corner of it intimately, I lived in it intimately, from the bed in which I slept to the summer kitchen before which, on the broad board walk, I frequently played—customarily, with the assistance of all the youngsters in the neighborhood, acting out some drama like *The King of the Golden Isles*—and I sallied forth from the house only in distinct patterns—to visit Karl Ganzlin and go fishing with him at Dickerson's Slough, from which we seldom had sense enough to return before dark, worrying our mothers into near witlessness; to visit Grandfather and Grandmother Derleth and the blacksmith and wagonmaking shop across the street from their house, three blocks south and one east, the shop where Father labored at an unvarying salary of $75 a month; to go down town, particularly to the corner across from the general store where Aunt Virginia Derleth worked, and from which she was bound to come bearing a sack of candy for her watching nephew; to go across lots to the harness shop to meet Hugo Schwenker and go with him to the river and up along the islands, to explore the ponds and Ehl's Slough; or, nearer home, to spend hours at Grandmother Volk's or to go around the block to play with Vernon Accola in the shed south of the Accola house.

The world of childhood was thus a place which radiated from this nucleus, to which all radii led back into that cozy home circle. Occasionally there was an unusual diversion—I was sent down town for groceries, or to Buro's corner saloon for a half gallon of beer, which the families of German background in Sac Prairie took with their meals, for in those years Sac Prairie was so predominantly German that most children in the village learned to speak German before they were even aware of the English language; this was true also of my family, though at that time the Derleths were entering upon their seventh decade in Sac Prairie, having come to America from Zinl, Bavaria, in 1839, and to Sac Prairie in 1852. But home, this snug little house, already very old in those years, was the center of all the world.

From that center I looked down the street to the grain elevator and the Milwaukee Road depot, at the adjoining stock yards, and Shumow's junk yard, a place of undeniable magic, where almost anything could be come upon, in particular the wonderfully colorful comic pages of Winsor McKay, *Little Nemo in Slumberland*, wantonly discarded by unfeeling readers, and carefully salvaged by me with the connivance of the Shumow boys; I looked north to the Reformed Church and the park across to the east of the street; I looked west along the lane which reached out to the prairie west of town under a row of streetlights, lemon yellow of evenings, opening up every twilight a world of sundown and afterglow, new moon and evening star, filled with unlimited promises of memorable tomorrows. The Milwaukee Road tracks ran east of the house, beyond the gardens and the lawn, on the last two miles of the spur to Upper Sac Prairie, and two trains a day went up and down there—one at noon, and the other, more magical, in the evening—trains which inevitably drew me to the depot a block away, where I sat with one-armed Beau Wardler, the mailman, and Mike Weinzierl, and Rich Monn and all those others who were drawn to watch the trains come in and go out, who took on a little of life from the hurry and bustle of move-

ment surrounding the coming and going of the train, the living and
the dying shuttling past, the clanging bell of the locomotive, and
its blasts of steam, the shouting of the brakemen, and all the activity which spoke for life just out of reach of those who waited
upon it at the depot, other than in this vicarious participation at its
perimeter.

People fascinated me, second only to books. I was interested in
everything which took place around that little house, all things that
fell to eye and ear and so to heart—except, alas!, apart from fishing
and hiking and swimming, the very things boys were expected to
be interested in—baseball, football, and the like, all of which seemed
to me dull and tedious and certainly not worth my time, though
I was early given to rollerskating, while I contrarily resisted my
parents' desire to buy a bicycle for me, partly because I preferred
to walk, partly because I had never managed to ride one successfully; I fell off either the one side or the other with remarkable
clumsiness, and decided finally that I would be brave and sacrific-
ing and go through the rest of my life without a bicycle, substituting books therefor, a decision I never regretted, not even in
those later days when Raymie Geier and I went out to fish in
Lodde's Millpond, he riding his bicycle for those four miles, and I
walking either beside him or lagging behind, lugging a pail of
sunfish—we never caught less.

And among those people, there was no one more shadowy and
yet more real than my Great-grandmother Gelhaus-Wesle, who
lived with Grandmother Volk, and was already quite old, retreating from life even as I was advancing into it. Two generations
stood between us, and though she was a stout, heavy woman by no
means insubstantial, she had only a shadowy existence for me
which grew in proportion to the years which passed after her
death, as I learned more about her. She had a firm, square face,
with unwavering eyes and a mouth that made as straight a
horizontal line across her face as her nose made a vertical, a face
filled with character, the character that comes with tribulations and

fortitude in the face of trial and care, of which she had had her share, having been left as a young woman to raise a family of five when her husband, my Great-grandfather Arnold Gelhaus, went into the Union forces in the Civil War and vanished without trace after his discharge in Washington—just as, thirty years later, her daughter, my Grandmother Volk, was left to raise six young children at the death of Grandfather Adam Volk, after six months in the state prison at Waupun for manslaughter, his Prussian temper having led him to kill a man in a duel not long after Wisconsin had outlawed duels.

She was a kind, patient woman, and I fear I must often have seemed woefully obstreperous to her, as children often do to the very old. As a child I always thought of her in semi-hibernation; she did not seem to come out often from her room in Grandmother's house, and when she did, it was only to be seen for a little while and then to retreat again; but this impression doubtless grew out of my being so little aware of her save as someone who belonged to Grandmother Volk and her house, who in turn belonged to Mother and Father and the small world which surrounded the house of childhood which was its center, someone who had come into this world from that other, the hill country west of Sac Prairie, where as Katherine Hugobach she had become the bride of Arnold Gelhaus and had gone to live in a log house beside a spring on a hill above the White Mound valley, from which he was so soon to walk jauntily away to be lost in the chaos of the war between the states, leaving her to pioneering and raising her family, and later to marry the young school-teacher who was to instil in her and her children the love of learning and of books which came down through the generations, burning the more strongly in my grandmother because she had been too pitifully poor in her widowhood to give her children the education she longed for them to have, the education Mother was determined her children would have, no matter what sacrifices might have to be made.

That little house in the near north end of Sac Prairie—that is, close to the center of town, between the churches and near the parks, but north of the dividing line three blocks south—was the heart's home and the body's security; but of course this was so because this was the place where my parents were—my father, a strong, handsome man, who taught me how to fish and tried to teach me a certain handiness with tools, and was impatient at my ineptness; my mother, who was a beautiful woman with a good figure, snapping eyes, and chestnut brown hair which was very slow in after years to grey—these two who made the little house that looked out upon the prairie more than a house, more than a home, a haven of security and comfort, where discipline was firm but never too obtrusive, a man and a woman who lived for their two children not only out of love for them but because circumstances forbade their having any more, and indeed, only the persistence of her will to live had spared Mother to live with her children after my sister's birth.

One day in 1914, when I was five, an itinerant photographer happened along and somehow persuaded my normally cautious mother to let him take some pictures—so he caught the old house forever, with my sister on one side of one of the maples, myself on the other, and Mother standing in the doorway—there it is in that one fading photograph, none other was ever made, the house which was once the home of Great-grandfather Peter Damm, who worked in an iron foundry and could whistle like a bird, talk to the birds, encourage them to answer, a short, bearded man, and of his wife, Barbara, who started bread dough and kept it going and sold "starters" and eggs, and died under a scalding bath in this very house. And then he induced Mother to let him take a picture of the children in the lawn swing—my sister in a neat cotton dress and black stockings, her hair bobbed, sitting with her hands lax in her lap and looking a little shyly toward the camera; and I beside her, bright, eager face gazing out at the world, curious, unafraid, lips slightly parted, eyes direct and interested, arms loosely crossed on my legs, above the twice patched knees of my overalls, hair a little long, looking as if at any moment I expected something strange and wonderful to take place, with an expression of adventurous expectancy on that eager face—someone from whom I have grown far, someone I knew and loved long ago, receding inexorably in time together with that cozy little house of my childhood.

❀ ❀ ❀ ❀ ❀

THERE was always in childhood that hour when the streetlights came on—on the edge of evening, at the beginning of night, when darkness had not yet taken all the village and the afterglow still burned saffron or cerise, copper or old rose, magenta or emerald or mother-of-pearl along the western rim; they came on in a soft flowering, unfolding against that western heaven all along the street, arched over the crossing on wires often invisible in the twilight. They reached out toward the prairie and into the sky, with the dark trees lovely around them, somberly beautiful on heaven, and somehow they came to represent a kind of freedom, for I never saw them come on at this hour without a lifting pleasure, and I never looked down that street toward the afterglow and the prairie beyond without a sense of adventurous expectancy, as if that moment and that hour must signal the approach of an adventure profound and stirring, not of the flesh, but of the spirit. It was, as it were, a desire for flight, for fulfilment, an unheeded impulse to be gone from the mundane, to fly down the avenue of dusk after the retreating day into spaces less alien, for at this hour it always seemed that though house and tree, leaf and blade, stick and stone somehow belonged to man, yet man was alien on this earth and only tolerated there by the vast and cosmic bounty of nature or Providence. There was always an inarticulate longing, a yearning for unknown experience, a romanticizing which permitted complete if momentary identification of the self

*with those lemon lights, the ever-recurring afterglow, the evening
star, and the trees dark on heaven, an identification and a sub-
mergence in this moment and the unalloyed beauty of this hour
between day and night.*

*This was a mysterious and beckoning borderland; none could
say what might emerge in it, what voice might rise, what adventure might come. And it presented its fascination daily, save
on those evenings of overcast sky, when something of its beauty
was made more sombre and something of its enchantment went
out of it. I suppose that it is possible to adduce any number of
reasons for this attraction, beauty being in the eye of the beholder
alone and predicated upon countless determining factors unknown
even to the beholder; and I have no doubt there was and is a
relationship between this sense of adventurous expectancy and
the spiritual isolation which is the common heritage of every
individual; but reason and explanation cannot alter the exhilara-
tion and wonder so integral a part of that hour between the day
and the night, that hour when the creatures of darkness briefly
know their brethren of daylight, that hour when the soul and the
body become fleetingly aware, one of the other.*

The blacksmith shop where my father worked at shoeing horses
and manufacturing wagons and sleighs, together with my Grandfather Derleth and, until his untimely death in 1918, my Uncle
Charlie, was an old building when I first became aware of it. It
had been built in 1852-3 by Great-grandfather Michael Derleth,
a locksmith, silversmith and goldsmith, who found little need for
his trade in this pioneer country to which he had come out of
Philadelphia, after leaving Bavaria in 1839. It was a building of
limestone, with a long L of sheds out behind it for lumber storage.
Its north half was given over to the smithy and was always redolent
of the coal fire burning on the hearth and the smell of horses
and sometimes the acrid pungence of burning horse-hooves, when

the red hot shoes were affixed to them. The south half was the shop
in which sleighs and wagons were turned out, all painted red
with black lettering—"A. Derleth & Sons"—later "Son"—and this
was sweetly fragrant with the smells of wood shavings, which
always seemed to cushion the stone floor.

It was a place of magic for a child just beginning to venture
away from his native hearth. I lived then in the house where I was
born—"the first house" which we left to go to that so-loved house
where Great-grandfather Damm had lived—and the old shop was
just around the corner from my natal place. Across the street
from it stood the house of my father's parents, and a shed in which
Grandfather Derleth kept his old horse, Ben, and another in which
was his buggy—and later his first car—and upstairs in which he
kept a cornsheller I used to long to be permitted to work—and had
to, later on, when I no longer desired to; and when I had com-
pleted my initial ventures into the world beyond our doorstep—
to Grandfather Derleth's house, where Grandmother Derleth
fluttered around her first grandson, and where Aunt Virginia,
then one of the belles of the village, danced attendance on her first
nephew—I made my way to the high-ceilinged blacksmith shop
and was entranced with the strong odors that rose all around, the
unfamiliar smells that tantalized me and drew me from forge to
lathe, past the flying sparks starring the region of the anvil where
Father or Uncle Charlie pounded a piece of red hot iron into
shape, past the sizzling pungence of hot iron being dipped into the
bath beside the forge, to the long piles of lumber out in back,
where I counted dozens of caverns and thought it a privilege to
play.

I suppose it was, as Mother insisted, too dangerous a place for a
child to be. I was entranced by the shop—by the farmers and their
talk, the men sitting around on the benches in front of the shop,
not all of whom came to have their horses shod or to buy a wagon
or sleigh or have a wheel repaired or a runner patched, men who
sat talking of weather, crops, prices, and political matters beyond

my understanding—men like old man Keller, the butcher who had a small shop half a block away, who came regularly shouting to my grandfather that if someone would get a pail of beer, he would furnish fresh, hot bologna, free; or old Dr. Von Hiddessen, who had brought me into the world, invariably popping out of his house two doors north of the shop in time to be in on the lunch; or the lonely men who came just to sit and take the sun and listen, and seldom said anything, sometimes whittling, men for whom a place was always kept, as were they expected guests of the establishment.

Grandfather Derleth gentled me. I suppose that firm, authoritative man with his keen eyes and his fierce autocracy and his broad shoulders, with his great arms and hands, saw in me a successor to the line in the blacksmith shop, though he knew long before he himself surrendered the reins that the shop must pass with the advance of events, and even his son would no longer be able to make it pay, for cars began to come upon the scene, and he met the challenge by sending Uncle Charlie to Chicago to learn all about them, thinking of turning part of the shop into a garage for Sac Prairie, and selling cars, but Charlie's sudden death in the midst of his plans curiously stayed his enthusiasm and stilled his hope, and in his apathy he watched the old shop decay and pass. He took me in hand whenever I came to the shop, and often, to get me away, got out old Ben, and some fishpoles and angleworms, dug up previously and put away against just such an occasion, and drove out to Lodde's millpond with me to fish away the hours of a summer afternoon.

He used to fill me with his wisdom, which was all on the conservative side of the ledger, but sound, for he preached honesty and honor and truth, he spoke of the value of money and the need of man to work, which were lessons I never forgot, lessons my father had already absorbed into his credos for living, and which I accepted as well and never found need to challenge or alter even when I learned how painful the truth often is.

But it was while I was in his charge that the dangers of the blacksmith shop made an indelible impression upon me. One of the areas of the shop I liked best was the musty storage room at the top of a broad open stairs along the south wall of the north section, stairs that started up behind the place where the horses stood to be shod, and ended in the dark mystery of the gable storage room, to which Grandfather often took me at my urging. One summer day when I was four, after a tour of this enchanting place, Grandfather bent at the head of the stairs for me to climb on to his back; but I sprang up and vaulted over, hurtled over the stairs, fell upon the handle of a machine, and came down upon the sharp ends of a row of iron bars, which cut not only the scalp but deep into my skull, making scars I carry today.

Unconscious and bleeding, I was carried to Grandfather's house, where Grandmother Derleth and Aunt Virginia put me to bed, called the doctor, called the priest who came and at the doctor's grave behest administered extreme unction. There I lay unconscious for two days and nights, until at last I woke to the fairy tinkling of a music box in which was lost forever the enchantment of the blacksmith shop, for all the rest of my child-hood a forbidden place.

My Grandmother Derleth was a short, quick-moving woman, neither thin nor fat. Her fine, greying hair was drawn to a tight bun at the back of her head. She looked small beside my grand-father, who was a big man, broad-shouldered, and tall, as befitted a blacksmith and wagonmaker; the top of her head came to his chin. She was shorter and smaller than any of her children—Charlie took after his father, and so did Joe and George, though George and my own father had something of their mother in them. Even her sole surviving daughter, Virginia, was taller than she, thinner and more angular.

She lived quite apart from Grandfather Derleth's world of

business; she never concerned herself with the affairs of the blacksmith shop; her world was one of flowers, vegetables, herbs, and
she had a flourishing garden of the kind that then prevailed in
Sac Prairie—one of camomile and sweet basil, of sweet william,
thyme, sage, roses, daisies, asters, canterbury bells, mint geranium,
sweet marjoram, cosmos, borage, clematis, geraniums, and all
those flowers once so common to small town gardens and since
fallen away, forgotten. In the spring her round beds of squills
were blue mounds of bloom, sometimes defying the snow; it was
a joy to look upon them, for they would be blue a long time
since, after the squills had faded, the grape hyacinths came bluely
after. Later on, tulips shone there, and then the foliage plants came
into their own while blossoms burgeoned in the rest of the garden—narrow strips along the sidewalks and around the stone
smoke-house, where each year the quarters and halves of hogs
and cattle butchered against winter gave portions to the smoke
for seasoning.

   She was a plain, simple woman, perfectly content to work hard
all her life and well pleased with the success of her garden and
her kitchen. I learned to take delight in groundcherry sauce served
with rye bread and black coffee, which was invariably produced
every evening I stopped at the house in later years with the
paper—at first *The Milwaukee Journal*, later *The Capital Times*—
my grandfather having been first a Democrat, then a Progressive
Republican, following the banner of the elder Senator La Follette
—and I can still savor this delight in a day when the groundcherry
is a rarity in Sac Prairie, where once it was a garden staple, as
common as the potato or the tomato, its cousins. The rye bread
was home made; I do not remember ever seeing "bought" bread
in Grandmother Derleth's house.

   I always enjoyed this ritual tremendously. The moment I
entered the kitchen by the back door (the only time I ever used
the front door of my grandparents' home was on the occasion of

a funeral), my grandmother bustled up from her chair, for they liked in their old age to linger over supper, they liked to stretch out that hour of the evening, which was usually sundown, the "Dämmerung," when the day drew away visibly beyond the windows at the table, which opened to the west, and twilight invaded the roomy kitchen. She asked whether I would not like *eine Tasse Kaffee,* but she had already taken it for granted that I would; she brought out cup and saucer, the dish of ground-cherry preserve, a slice of rye bread—caraway or plain—poured the cup of coffee, and sat down again, facing the west, between her husband, who sat on her right, and her oldest grandson on her left. The table was pushed up to the window-sills, and where I sat I had a view not only of the sunset and afterglow, but of the street-corner, for my grandparents' house occupied a corner of the block, and I could on occasion see familiar figures passing by—Fr. Schauenberg or old Mrs. Williams or Margery, who first shook the foundations of my heart, or fat Miss Ursula Baier, who lived in one part of the house where I was born, two doors to the west of the house where I sat watching the day fade and die away, as my grandparents had watched every day go by for years.

I customarily ate in silence, save occasionally to murmur how good the little supper was—and no matter how much I ate, it never seemed to diminish my appetite for supper when I reached home soon after—at which Grandmother Derleth would smile, pleased, as much as to say she knew what boys liked, and she did. Grandfather Derleth sometimes glanced out the window, but most of the time he sat regarding me with grave eyes, as if openly wondering how I might turn out, whether I would he honest and forthright and as outspoken as he; sometimes he glanced at the headlines in the evening paper and made some comment, but since he subscribed to the conviction that papers, magazines and books were not to be brought to the table, this was not often; he

usually waited until the table had been cleared. Then he would
put on the green-shaded light suspended above the table, pull it
down, and go patiently through the paper from first page to last,
announcing his conclusions about news and editorials to the
silence, and chuckling at *Everett True* and *Out Our Way*.

They ate sparely. The coffee, rye bread, and groundcherry
sauce served to me was no less and no more than they themselves
had—bread, sometimes with butter or jelly, sometimes with bacon
grease, sometimes dry; coffee—and rarely a little meat of some
kind, usually ham, bacon, cold pork or dried beef. They were
not given to fancy dishes, but only to simple fare. Grandmother's
groundcherry preserve was a favorite which occupied the same
place in my esteem as Grandmother Volk's raisin pie and Aunt
Annie Ring's *Datsch*—cut up pancakes served hot with cold black-
berry sauce poured over them—Mrs. Schwenker's macaroon
kisses and Mother's raised doughnuts, prune whip pie, banana
cream pie, coffeecake, and elderberry syrup.

Their evening meal was perhaps their most ritualistic, though
they themselves never thought of it as such, and it was so only
in their later life, when the affairs of the smithy and the wagon-
making business had declined before widespread automation, and
Grandfather was no longer bound to eat in haste so that he could
hurry back to the shop, where the work often went on till midnight, and sometimes through the night, when someone urgently
needed something—as, one winter night, Clarence Denzer determined to wait at his grandfather's place for a new sleigh of his
own, and Grandfather Derleth, Uncle Charlie, and Father worked
all night to make the sleigh, so that Clarence could drive home in
it next day.

For a long time this ritual was part of my existence, and I suspect my grandparents looked forward to my participation in it
as much as I did. It always seemed to me a ritual purely of sensory
pleasure, indulging the sense of taste, for little conversation marred

it; there was a kind of communication without words—I understood my grandmother's occasional glances and smiles, I knew what passed through Grandfather's thoughts as he looked upon his namesake and oldest grandson. Grandmother valued my responses to her food and her flowers, but my grandfather was only tolerant of my opinions, since to his mind I was still too young to have any very sound opinion, but he could not prevent my having pronounced ideas, and he knew it and wholly approved my manifest direction away from conformity, for which he never had any respect, his view of conformity being on a par with what he thought of compromising one's ideals, a thing to be done only when some greater benefit to one's self could be wrung from such compromise or conformity.

No memory of them both is more vivid than this mind's eye picture of them at their evening meal in old age, engraved like an intaglio on a wall along one of the corridors of memory, two old people seen always in the roseate glow of sundown, caught forever by memory's brush on a canvas only death can fade.

❀   ❀   ❀   ❀   ❀

THE first awareness of night was a world of darkness bounded by a streetlight's glow, the barking of a distant dog, the stars, trees, dim houses. The sense of being enclosed by the night, of being protected, as it were, by the darkness, is ancient. It is related to the desire to be shielded or made cozy in a small space, which, psychiatrists tell us, stems from the security of the womb, and an unrecognized desire to return to it in flight from a dreary round of responsibility inevitable in adulthood. If so, then the night is another kind of womb, and the seeking of it another kind of return. I suspect its relation is rather to the primitive in man, and to his primitive age on earth, when caverns and overhung ledges and deep forests offered man the only kind of security he knew. But this is a speculative thing, at best; what every man

knows about himself and his world is but the most infinitesimal
part of knowledge. What he knows about someone else and some-
one else's world is even less than that.

All my memories of my parochial school years are informed
with affection for the nuns who labored so untiringly to fill their
charges with learning, and at the same time instill in them something of their own discipline and set them on the paths of Christian thought and the timeless Catholic teachings with which they
were imbued. They were, in a sense, substitute mothers, and it is
quite possible that we were, some of us, for some of them, the
children they would never bear. It was never my experience to
know any Dominicans at St. Aloysius who were anything but
kind—firm, yes, but always kind, sympathetic, and understanding
—who were not only what we expected of teachers but also what
we had come to expect from mothers.

Sister Lioba wept when an epidemic of spinal meningitis took
four children forever from the primary grades, and led prayers
for the repose of their souls, and tried not to see the empty seats,
which in those days were bolted to the floor in the old red brick
schoolhouse on Madison Street, and could not be easily removed.
She dried our tears and gave us comfort in equal amounts as
knowledge, and for me she developed that especial sympathy
which older people always feel for that one child who is more
sensitive than most children and quicker to grasp knowledge—and
thus also more vulnerable to the slings and arrows of life and
destined to know pain with swift intensity as readily as ecstasy
in the joy of living among the birds and the beasts of air and
earth, the mountains and the valleys, and the lilies of the field.

And Sister Xavier sought gently to turn me toward a vocation
in the priesthood, but I knew even then that such privation and
discipline were too binding for me; and so I was not intended to

serve the children of God in this fashion. Sister Lioba eased the way from home into the world of school and by extension, the world beyond; Sister Xavier filled me with respect for learning and books, but there were two of the nuns at St. Aloysius who did more—Sister Anaclete and Sister Isabelle—the one in my fourth grade, the other in my seventh and eighth grades, and each of them stands for all time at the perimeter of my days.

Sister Anaclete was the epitome of gentleness and patience. She was fair, and she was young—she could not have been much over twenty when I came into the fourth grade—and she was beautiful with a completely feminine beauty which was enriched by humility. All of us in the three grades which were her charge loved her, and I remember that when, in the recesses of my mind I thought of angels, each angel wore the face of Sister Anaclete, and walked as Sister Anaclete did, and talked as Sister Anaclete did, which was not surprising, for it was impossible to imagine that *any* angel could be superior in any way, not more gentle, not more comely, not kinder nor more patient.

But none of these attributes was Sister Anaclete's special attribute for me, for it was she who opened up to me the world of creative art. In addition to the regular course of studies, Sister Anaclete taught watercolor painting. She herself was a highly competent artist; it was a source of never-ending wonder to her charges that this should be so, that a nun with so much already in her favor, should also be so skilled an artist. Sister Anaclete would erect her easel before the class and, as if by magic under her hands, a landscape would take form and glow from the paper on her easel with such effortlessness as to challenge us to emulation.

Alas! I was not much of an artist. My hand was clumsy, my patience short, and though I warmed to what I liked—and I liked landscapes, as if already at that early age the contours of the land that was Sac Prairie beckoned to me—I could not recreate it, I could not catch it on paper, try as I might, and all Sister Anaclete's patience and guidance could not prevail against my shortcomings. But Sister Anaclete, by her example, was proof that it could be done, and taught me that the sights and scenes I loved were inside as well as out, that the entire world, in fact, lay within the small compass of the brain, and that the fire of creative talent coupled with artistic discipline could bring all into being before one's eyes—not only in water colors, but in music, which Sister Anaclete taught and played, too—and in words.

I did not seem to have much talent for music either, much as I loved it, and the selections Sister Anaclete played were several removes from the pieces my mother most frequently played on the piano in the old house of Great-grandfather Damm where we lived then—*Red Wing, In the Good Old Summertime, In the Shade of the Old Apple Tree*, and similar sentimental melodies. Nor was Sister Anaclete given solely to hymns and liturgical music. She had a wide appreciation of good music, and this, too, she communicated to us, however unwillingly some of her charges received it. I have no doubt Sister Anaclete took a dim view of such musical abilities as I gave evidence of—I could hardly carry a tune, and my voice could certainly not be described as an asset even to the school body in song. Since mine was not alone in this incapacity, it offers ample proof of Sister Anaclete's remarkable patience and endurance.

But words were left to me, and by the time I got around to use them, I had moved into the final grades of parochial school and was being taught by Sister Isabelle, who was in many ways what Sister Anaclete was not. She was a tall, sturdy woman, pronouncedly masculine in her manner, with keen, brown eyes that gave the unvarying impression that she knew just what every one of us in her two grades was about at every moment of the time we were in the room. She was a strict disciplinarian who expected the best from her charges and in turn did her best to exact it; and, as such, she inspired either marked dislike or a strong liking—there were never any half-way, milk-sop reactions to Sister Isabelle.

She taught in a cramped little room in the southeast corner of the second floor. Those of us who had survived the first six grades, took our seventh and eighth in this room. There was no nonsense about her, but she had a fine sense of humor, and she was scrupulously fair—if a student had earned commendation, he got it, and if he merited punishment, he got this, too—and some of us did, particularly the eighth-grader who was wont to break into her cash-box and remove its contents, thus sending her into her role of avenging angel, which she played to the dramatic hilt, though, as a rule, she seemed to us a little harder on the girls, as if she expected more of them.

Sister Isabelle's instruction was not confined to the classroom. She led us into the fields and woods when each spring she took her classes on a hike to a long abandoned chapel beside a brook more than two miles from St. Aloysius, near to Roxbury, east of Sac Prairie—both classes and Sister Isabelle straggling along the highway until we came to the brook, and then following the brook up toward Roxbury and the chapel half way to that hamlet. Sister Isabelle knew the trillium, the small white wood violet, the May-apple; she knew the scarlet tanager and the rose-breasted grosbeak and the pewee; she knew oak and black alder and hard maple, and to all of us who were not Philistines, she communicated this knowledge as eagerly as the most prosaic problem in arithmetic that ever came directly from a textbook, she sitting on a boulder or in the grass or on a fallen bole with the music of the birds ringing in her ears and the hushing of the wind in the trees and the murmuring of the brook in the shallows praising the day. And she raised no cry of outrage if someone slipped a garter snake into her lunchbox, but accepted this as part of nature—a little more base, perhaps, being human.

Her discipline was in itself inspiring and it inspired me with great and lasting effect. The nature lore she communicated was enriching. Nor was she wanting in her ability to carry to her charges the subjects she taught. And her physical courage was tremendous, particularly, we all thought, when she informed Father Schauenberg one morning when he came for instructions in catechism, that she would rather he did not interrupt at that time since she was in the middle of an important lesson. Her tall, full figure commanded respect and obedience, and filled us all with comforting security. Under her wing we were indeed as safe as were we on the Rock itself, and no injustice would be worked upon us, and no wound inflicted without permission she would not give.

But for me, Sister Isabelle did far more than anyone else. She read my first story—a poor thing about violent death and detection. She may not have liked its subject, but if so, she did not say as much. But she liked the way in which it was done and she liked the spirit which moved me to venture it. She encourged me. No one could have done more. Of my watercolors and my essays in music, Sister Anaclete took a tolerant but dim view; of my words, Sister Isabelle spoke well and with warmth and kindness and made me believe that in that world of creativity to which Sister Anaclete was so devoted, I too, in time, might play a small part, one enough to satisfy my modest needs.

❊ ❊ ❊ ❊ ❊

I HAVE often thought that the sounds and odors of night are important in relation to some memory—sometimes forgotten, lost in the past of childhood or youth, but none the less carrying its own meaning to the complexity of bone and flesh and blood which is every man. Perhaps it is good and wholesome to know the source of each emotion, but such knowledge is not necessary to its enjoyment. Keys and clues present themselves, but no explication can any longer alter one's enjoyment of such sounds and

*odors as come to have an added meaning because of fortuitous
events of childhood or youth. What is locked in memory is tribu-
tary to meaning, it may even be essential to enjoyment, but it
alters in no aspect a single facet of the world outside any human
being.*

Miss Annie Maegerlein, a middle-aged spinster, was the instrument of my introduction to nature. Miss Annie was not a nature-
lover herself, though she was not antipathetic to the birds and
beasts which lived on her acres; but, learning of my childhood
interest in reading, she contributed to it in the only way she
knew—by clipping for me from the pages of the Milwaukee
Journal, to which she subscribed, the daily Bedtime Story of
Thornton W. Burgess, with delightfully graphic illustrations by
Harrison Cady, setting forth the adventures of Mother West
Wind's neighbors on the Green Meadow, in the Old Briar-Patch
and regions adjacent thereto, enabling me to make the acquaintance of Peter Rabbit, Johnny Chuck, Unc' Billy Possum, Hooty
the Owl, Grandfather Frog, and a host of others, all of which
were subsumed into my personal relationship and became an
intimate part of the world of that boy of seven or eight, which
I was then, and led ultimately straight to Thoreau by way of
Ernest Thompson Seton and John Burroughs.

Miss Annie seemed very old to me then, and she never seemed
to grow any older. She must have been in her middle forties at
that time, and when I last saw her, approaching her eightieth
year, she seemed very much the same to me, which was only
natural in that the same span of years existed between us, and
the same relativity was maintained throughout that time. She was
somewhat pinch-faced, but not forbiddingly so. Her eyes were
warm, though her lips seemed always formidable, for she spoke
incisively, without any doubt about her conclusions, and she had

a habit of snapping her mouth shut after she had spoken, with an air of daring someone to say her nay. She was rather a short woman, well proportioned, and much given to religion. Being a devout Catholic, she attended Mass daily—and I have no doubt that on certain holy days of obligation, as well as on Sunday, she very probably went to Mass more than once; for in a very real sense, her religion was her life to her, once the foster-parents whom she cared for had died.

She saved the nature stories every day, carefully cutting them from the *Journal,* and when on Saturday evening I presented myself at her door across the street from my home, she gave them to me with a certain pleasure in being able to convey to someone else so much joy at so little expense. Very often she included a good moral story cut out of some religious magazine or other but, while I accepted these and gravely thanked her for them, I usually discarded them, for they were largely wearisome pap, concerned with the dull doings of nauseatingly good little boys and girls, the like of which I never encountered in life and whose very existence I doubted even then, before I was old enough to know positively that such creatures never existed outside the imaginations of the hacks who ground out this slop. Besides, I was already then reading my fill of a much better grade of fiction in a similar vein in *The Young Catholic Messenger* and later, in the novels of Father Finn. Against the moralities which Miss Annie was in the habit of ringing in on me, the doings of Reddy Fox and Danny Meadow Mouse and Peter Rabbit seemed far more realistic; moreover, there was in these facilely done little tales a *feeling* for nature which shone through the obvious mechanics of the stories, and the promise that some of these adventures might be experienced by me as readily as by Farmer Brown's boy, who occasionally played a role in the Burgess saga.

I read these stories avidly. Quite apart from filling me with curiosity about nature and giving me a feeling of intimacy with birds and animals, reading them had other happy side-effects. It destroyed forever any impulse to hunt and kill either bird or animal, though, strangely, it did not diminish in the slightest my pleasure in fishing. It impressed upon my youthful mind the continuity of nature, which I learned to witness in the turning of the seasons, and taught me that of all aspects of life, nature alone offered the only constant, the only permanence even though the seasonal changes symbolized the inevitable changes which must come to me in my own seasons.

Miss Annie was for me inextricably bound about with these stories by Thornton W. Burgess. I suppose, actually, being their source, she was for me as much a character in them as Sammy Jay or Jerry Muskrat or Farmer Brown, though in a certain severity of manner she was unable to alter, she seemed more akin to Farmer Brown than to any of the animals. She was kind to me, and therefore she always seemed to me a kind woman. I endured her lectures on religion stoically, for, after all, there was always the reward of the Burgess stories, and the lectures, which might not do me any good, certainly did me no harm; they were delivered with such earnestness that I knew Miss Annie really *cared*, and I was just as flattered at this attention whether or not her well-meant words went into one ear and out the other with the speed of her delivery, for, after all, I was in attendance at almost as many Masses as she. It seems to me now that I always understood that the Catholic religion was Miss Annie's whole world, while it was only part of mine.

I never questioned this state of affairs. If this was Miss Annie's choice, it was not for me to dispute it, however much I might want to inquire into it later for purely personal reasons. I don't suppose that Miss Annie ever questioned her life, either. She had been one of three girls, all born in Germany and brought to this country when Miss Annie was but half a year old. Her father had sickened and died soon after reaching Sac Prairie, and her mother, being poverty-stricken, could not support the girls, and gave them away. Miss Annie was taken in by her foster-parents and given their family name; she was reared by them, sent to school for eight years, and in return devoted her life to them, caring for them because this was her responsibility as she saw it. Their only son married; Miss Annie did not. She always assumed that she was an adopted daughter—after learning when she began to go to school that she was not really the child of her foster-parents, and accepting this, after many bitter tears—and it was not until after her foster-father's death, while her foster-mother lay ill, that she learned through the waspishness of a cousin of the family which had raised her that she had not really been adopted, and might be dispossessed of the only home she had ever known when her foster-mother died. She appealed her trouble to Father Schauenberg, who promptly summoned a lawyer and saw to it that the ailing woman legally adopted Miss Annie, already then in her middle years.

When at last she inherited the considerable Maegerlein estate— her brother having died childless, after his wife's sudden death— she distributed largesse to every member of the family who had need of it, not because she had any legal obligation to do so, but because she felt and acted upon a moral obligation. She expected nothing and demanded nothing, not even loyalty, in return, and she received nothing except such satisfaction as she took in her generosity, not even when, in need of care at the end of her life, she found none of the objects of her generosity willing or able to take her in, though a nephew, John, did everything he could for her, short of leaving his widower's apartment to move into her house to care for her. She was that rare person, a Christian who lived by Christian precepts, unlike so many self-styled Christians who preach Christianity for others than themselves. Her very existence in Sac Prairie was a reproach to many of them, who retaliated in the only way the envious ever retaliate—by slander and calumny, even while they bowed their heads sancti-moniously at Mass Sunday after Sunday.

In later years I used to see her often on her way to or from Mass: a spare, short figure, usually dressed in dark clothes. Sometimes her face seemed a little grim, perhaps because she had no illusions about the years of her old age and the travail which was to come upon her. Sometimes she lectured me about not going to Mass as often as she thought I ought to go; sometimes she accused me of not wearing enough clothing—my arms or my legs were too bare; and once she said in a shocked voice, seeing me bare to the waist on my way to the beach, that I was "sinfully immodest." She said whatever she thought was true, and it never occurred to her that she need not speak. But no matter what she said, it was impossible for her to offend me, for she remained always the woman who by her kindness had led me into nature's green pastures, into the solitudes of trees and clouds and running water, of birds and beasts, which on so many occasions thereafter refreshed my spirit and restored my soul.

As the years passed, the quickness of her movements slowed, and she found herself unable to attend Mass as often as she had been accustomed to go. And by this time her world had subtly altered, its pace had increased, even at St. Aloysius—with Father Schauenberg retired and recently dead, and younger priests in the pulpit. Having no family close enough to care for her when at last she failed and could not live alone any longer—and she had persisted in her solitary life for as long as she could, she was moved into one "home" after another, fading from the familiar streets of Sac Prairie, unseen in the aisles of St. Aloysius, until at last she died and was brought back to be buried from the church she had loved, forgotten by most of those who had known her, save for that green memory of her in my heart, and the indelible picture of Miss Annie at the front door with a kind smile on her face and her spectacles glinting in the half light of evening, and a packet of Thornton Burgess nature stories in her hand for the boy from across the street, Miss Annie who, if she had been told later that it was she by her kindness who had led me to nature, would have said firmly, "Not me—it was God who wanted it to be."

❀   ❀   ❀   ❀   ❀

WALK on a spring evening along the streets of Sac Prairie and smell the night, hear the night. Its fragrances are of lilacs, of syringa, of jasmine, lilies-of-the-valley, flowering currant, of bridalwreath, English violets met now here, now there—sometimes in enduring cloud, sometimes in the most fugitive of hints—the perfume of flowers as if the very breath of earth turning over in the dark, the exhalation of the soil itself in this season of growth. And the sounds that come are the voices of time going by—the girlish laughter of the young, going about in couples or in aimless groups, restless, hungry for life, not knowing what life is, but sure that love is part of it, if not all in this season—the whispers of lovers in some dark, shadowed spot, the cries of children late at play, the dulcet conversations out of darkened porches, with the mysterious fragments—

— "I told her, but she wouldn't listen."

— "That was the year Pa died."

— "I never put on the long underwear."

—"And who should be there but Ollie!"

—"Nobody knows where he went to; he just took off one day and nobody ever heard from him again!"

—the fragments of lives forever unknown, as if lived in that darkness by persons belonging forever to the merciful anonymity of night.

Walk on any street, pause at any door—the night is filled with the tangibles of those who, once a part of these streets, remain eternally in the darkness, the habitants of dusk and night kept alive in the voices and hearts of those who came after. The very pulse of village life beats in the anonymous voices, with their trivialities which are the whole joy or the complete sorrow of

*anonymous others. Night permits tragedy and comedy with aloof
impartiality; it invites melancholy, it invites happiness, and the
light of youth no less than the shadow of death lingers forever in
the streets of night.*

*I meet them often going by, the young lovers, arm in arm,
oblivious of everything but the night and the moon and each
other, oblivious of the hovering hawk of time biding eternally
above. And the children playing in the dark, on the very edge
of night, while the afterglow still shows saffron and orange and
lemon in the west, diminishing to mother-of-pearl, with the
newly-lit streetlights like flowers upon that sky, children shouting
and screaming in the parks, along the streets and lanes—*Run My
Good Sheep Run—Ollie Ollie Oxen, All in Free—Andy Andy
Over—Statue—*playing for the last moment, and another, and yet
another against the summoning whistle or cry.*

*Walk on any street, pause anywhere, and listen to the pulse, the
heartbeat of Sac Prairie, and a thousand Sac Prairies abroad in
the dark.*

In my very earliest years, I used to distinguish my Grandmother
Volk from my Grandmother Derleth by designating her "Choo-
Choo Grandma" because the first house in which I knew her
stood near to the spur of the Milwaukee Road coming into Sac
Prairie from Mazomanie, nine miles to the south; and it was at
this house that I made my first acquaintance with the "choo-
choo" with its great glowing "bullshine"; but this distinction soon
passed, for we ourselves moved north of our natal place to a
house adjacent to the railroad tracks, and in a little while my
Grandmother Volk built a little house north of our own and
came to live in it, our nearest neighbor.

For all her size—and she was a large woman, if not unusually
tall, despite the smallness of her bones—she gave the impression
of being a weak, indecisive woman, chary of voicing too loud

an opinion, yet she had managed to survive tragedy and hardships
which would have overcome many another woman, and at
fifty-nine ventured once more into matrimony by marrying my
Great-uncle Philip, my maternal grandfather's brother, a widower
with a large family of his own, all now well away from home, but
likely to stop in at any hour of the day or night to add to her
work. He established a tidy shoe-repair business in the east end
of a shed east of my grandmother's house and spent most of every
day in it at an occupation he loved—a quiet, friendly man,
tolerant of children, with thick curling black hair, now greying,
and an equally thick, but less curly, moustache.

Grandmother Volk took in washing. She had taken in washing
or done housekeeping all her life since the early death of her first
husband; she had seen her children leave her in their tender
adolescence, to work where they could, sometimes with relatives
who took advantage of their innocence and worked them like
peasants, sometimes with farmers in the country around Plain,
where she lived then; and with her youngest children, including
my mother, she had gone from place to place, wherever work was
to be found, in order to provide for them. I never knew her to
have much money, but she was happy without it, as long as she
had at last, in her middle age, a house of her own, and a place
for her flowers—she was devoted to heliotrope, American beauty
roses, hydrangeas, syringa or mock orange, and garden carnations.

She had soft, pale blue eyes, and when they dwelt upon me it
was plain that in me she saw the fruiting of all her ideals about
learning—for she had these ideals so strongly rooted in her, for
all that she had never had an education herself, and had not been
able to give her children such an education in her poverty, that
nothing took precedence over them. She had known a stepfather
who was steeped in the lore of books, and from him she had
learned respect for education, and to some extent she had learned
to read herself, though she gave herself over to romances like
Thelma and *St. Elmo* and *The Harvester* and *The Shepherd of the*

Hills; she loved *The Adventures of Sherlock Holmes*—she said of him he was "the greatest detective who ever lived"—and the mysteries of Fergus Hume. But for all that she respected learning, she was unmovingly stubborn in her superstitions; she believed in dreams and always had a dream book of some sort at hand, so that she could pore over its pages and ascertain the precise meaning of every dream she had—or anyone else had, too, if it came to her ears; and she had a certain fear of a curious book of cabalistic lore, *The Seventh Book of Moses,* which she believed unlocked the secrets of heaven and earth, and which was a book in the possession of every witch—she steadfastly believed in witches, too. Perhaps the fact that she had been born in Scranton, Pennsylvania in 1856—the heart of the *Hexerei* country—and of Pennsylvania Dutch stock (what else could a name like Gelhaus be but Pennsylvania Dutch?) conditioned her to acceptance of these superstitions.

I was not her only grandson, but I was her nearest, and certainly her favorite, if for nothing more than my inordinate love for books, for even as a child I clamored constantly for books—for birthdays, Christmas, and any occasion for the bestowal of gifts—games and toys were very well, but it was books I wanted; and, as I grew older, my appetite for magazines grew too, added to that for books—for anything, in short, that could be read, though I was partial to fairy tales, detective stories—I agreed with Grandmother Volk about Sherlock Holmes, Boy Scout adventures, the fare offered by *Boys' Life,* and *The Count of Monte Cristo.* In these years work at the blacksmith and wagon-making shop was fading before the coming of cars, and there was little money at home for magazines or books; so it was Grandmother Volk who gave me of her precious pennies so that I could each week buy *Secret Service* and an occasional book of Boy Scout adventures, which I loved, but not quite to the extent of joining the Boy Scouts myself.

More, when at last I began to write, this dear, good woman encouraged me at every step, even against the doubts of my parents, who foresaw no easy career in writing—in which they were certainly right—and who thought, especially in view of the declining fortunes of blacksmithing and wagon-making, that I ought to go into some field which would bring its rewards more rapidly, like teaching, and believed this so strongly that for a little while I began to doubt myself, and, even after beginning to sell stories, I did elect to go into teaching, a choice of which I was quickly cured by the dreadful rot taught by the School of Education and the fraudulent pretensions of Professor M. V. O'Shea in that same school at the University of Wisconsin.

My Grandmother Volk never had the slightest question about my career. She believed in me. She fought for me. She doled out her pennies and nickels and dimes absolutely convinced that she was making an investment in my future, and that future must be the culmination of all her ideals for learning and education. For all the meekness with which she faced the world, she had a hard acquaintance with the world at first hand. She had lived in Plain and North Freedom, in Sumter and at various farms, and had at last gravitated to Sac Prairie, from which the older of the two daughters still with her, Aunt Bertha, went to work in Madison, and the younger, Rose, my mother, soon went courting with my father, walking in the quiet village evenings up along the river—for their first house was near the river, south of the railroad bridge—to a dance, or, more rarely, riding out in Grandfather Derleth's buggy or a hired rig. But in all this wandering around, they were never very many miles from my mother's birthplace near Denzer in a quiet rural area which is still unchanged today; they had moved, as it were, west and in a half circle from that place and had come finally to stay in the river town which lay southeast of Denzer.

My Grandmother Volk might be mute when Selina Jaeger cheated her of a quarter or half a dollar, as the old woman was wont to do; my grandmother was unwilling to lose the washing

for the sake of a quarter; she might hold her tongue in the face of
Great-uncle Philip's occasional unwarranted anger; she might turn
her cheek to meet another slight; but she gave no ground in her
steadfast belief in my future, and when she saw my first
books come to hand, and learned in her last years that
I had been granted a Guggenheim Fellowship, she felt her investment well repaid indeed. "Didn't I tell you?" she said
to Mother and others, saying as plainly as she could that never had
an investment returned such dividends. This tangible proof of
such small ability as I had filled her with great happiness, and it
was as if all the hardships she and hers had had to endure had
been balanced at last.

Great-uncle Philip died eight years before her. Then for a while
her sister and brother-in-law came to live with her, but this was
an unhappy arrangement, for my Great-aunt Mary Meng was not
one given to peaceable living and made life difficult for both
Great-uncle John and my grandmother, and this household was
soon broken up. Grandmother left her little house and came to
live out her last years in the onetime summer kitchen of that first
house of childhood, moved just east of the new house on Madison
Street, from the door of which Mother could always look into
the summer kitchen and Grandmother could always look out,
contented to have us always under eye, to observe our comings
and goings within easy conversational range of the back porch.
The world had never widened very much for her, and it was not
less noticeably wide in this little summer kitchen than it had ever
been and it grew no less wide until that July morning when she
slept quietly away in her eighty-third year.

❀　❀　❀　❀　❀

OF *mornings, no matter what the season, the musk of the*
Wisconsin pervaded the village, in frosty fog or warm vapors,
the smell of thaw or in the freshness of water, strongest on summer

days, when people were accustomed to speak of it as were it an ichthyic odor, something unpleasant, instead of the diffused pungence rising from the uncovered stones and sandbars, a rich, spreading musk which moved far back from the river's edge and lent to the early hours of the day a kind of perfume which was primal on the earth before the advent of mankind, the exhalation of the river itself, sometimes invisible, sometimes caught in spectral mists, as if the very river-bed were breathing, giving off a distillation in which was inherent the smell of earth and water and air, and out of which the wild nostalgic crying of killdeers, the plaintive calls of the solitary sandpipers, the cree-ee *of wood-ducks, the phoebe's cry and pewee's song came like essential integers, all together speaking as with one voice of many tones of the same primal sentience as the river's musk, with the first sunlight slanting to the water, and the shadows along the eastern shore inviting the angler and the contemplative oarsman in the very unawareness of man and his handiwork which remains so much a part of any running stream.*

With day's advance, the musk was dissipated. The river rose, the almost soundless lowered stream gave place to another which spoke in many voices—laughing in the shallows, rushing and murmuring around the piers of the bridges, singing among the rushes and the willows along the shore, lapping at the bars, making a sibilance of whispering where it flowed among the grasses, the stream deepening, broadening, reclaiming the early uncovered bottoms, and spreading inland, exhaling a freshness, the damp, cooling fragrance of running water; and the birds of the early hours were silent before the keening of mourning doves and the screaming of gulls, the harsh triumph of bald eagles, and the pleasant threnodies of song and vesper sparrows. The Wisconsin's voices swelled and grew into the afternoon, in late winter mornings carrying abroad still the smell of thaw, and bearing southward to the Mississippi the cakes of ice broken away from winter's persisting masses along shore, in summer inviting the swimmers

and the anglers and the river-lovers, old men who came to sit
on its banks, or walk across its bridges, and dream of yesterdays
beyond some receding corner gone by out of reach, even as the
ceaselessly flowing water went past, heedless of man and all his
work, as it flowed before the advent of man, and would flow
when earth had reclaimed the very spoor of man.

It swelled and grew throughout the day, becoming a broad
impressive river, and into the evening, when the water began
once more to recede, the bars and the stones of the river bottom
came out again, and once more gave off that musk, breathing into
the dusk, where the killdeers still cried and the owls hooted, nighthawks foraged low over the water with swallows and chimney
swifts, whippoorwills cried out of the riverside groves, and the
water gave back the face of heaven, the stars, the moon, the
planetary wanderers. A sense of mystery came upon the murmuring waters, the pulsing susurrus of the stream, the exhaling musk
invading cell and bone, with the multiple sounds of water-dwellers
strange and unknown to most listeners—of muskrats, beavers,
minks, of frogs, toads, fishes leaping from the water and falling
back in an ecstasy of living, of coot and heron foraging in the
shallows, the river given over to twilight and evening star, its voices
slowly, slowly falling away, receding with the level of the water.

And all night the Wisconsin, given to darkness, moved in the
dark like a great sentient being, breathing its disturbing musk into
the night, making man to think of earth and of man's existence on
earth, the river lying in the darkness unseen save for the glint of
starlight and the mirror of heaven, giving back in their seasons
Arcturus and Antares, Orion and Aldebaran and Vega and Sirius,
and the moon in all her phases, and the planets in their courses,
while the river filled the village and covered the countryside along
its valley with its exhalation, the musk which seemed always the
very essence of earth and running water, making itself known
unseen in the darkness, the broad stream which was always in my

youth the mecca of boys, and remained for innumerable adults a halcyon country of escape from today and tomorrow, a country changeless forever.

The Schwenker harness shop was the natural magnet which drew me when I was forbidden the Derleth blacksmith shop. The Schwenkers and Derleths were among the earliest settlers in Sac Prairie, and had been friendly for generations. Once or twice a week Grandmother Derleth went to call on Paulina Schwenker, and once or twice a week Mrs. Schwenker repaid the call; and when he was down town, Grandfather Derleth stopped in at the harness shop now and then to pass the time of day with Bill Schwenker—or Willi, as Paulina called him; and it was only natural that I should find in Hugo, their only son, born to them late in their lives, when other parents of that age were thinking of becoming grandparents, an amiable companion who shared my own delight in nature and was as "handy" with his hands at one kind of work or another as I was in getting out of work.

The harness shop was an old building when I first walked into it. It stood two stories high on Water Street, Sac Prairie's Main Street, a block and a half north of the bridge, which opened out across the Wisconsin to Madison, twenty-five miles away. Its false front looked across the street to a row of worn buildings, equally as old, and beyond them to the river, and beyond the Wisconsin to the moraine along the river's east shore. Outside, it was unprepossessing, though not without a certain warmth inherent in the old siding.

I usually came to it from the rear, setting out across the railroad tracks from home, through the Freethinkers' Park, across lots to the little walk behind the shop, framed by Hugo's "office" on the one side—a little shed in which he kept his fish-poles, magazines, and the like—and the harness shop two-holer on the other. Not far away a snow apple tree leaned over the walk, and a flowering

currant bush, both aromatic in season, and a little bed of lilies-of-
the-valley. The walk went along the north wall of a storage shed,
in which we used to undress and dress again when we went to
swim off Karberg's bar, a block or so to the north. The shop itself
was framed on the south by the old Naffz office, another frame
building of one storey, and on the north, immediately adjacent
to it, by the snug little house occupied by the Burleigh Fuchs
family, to the roof of which and the flourishing grape arbor
carrying away from the corner of the building over a kind of patio
the only north wall window of the harness shop opened.

The harness shop was mellow with age; its inner walls were
literally stained with years. It had once been a general store, but
there was nothing, save for an old fountain recipe or two scrawled
on the walls, to thin the atmosphere of the harness business. A long
workbench was attached to the north wall all the way from the
northwest corner of the building to the chimney about half way
up toward the front; in evenings and dark days it was lit by two
green-shaded lamps which shed warm pools of yellow light on the
bench and the dark panes of the window looking out to the
sloping roof and vaulting elms to the north. Beyond this bench and
the chimney, the north wall was filled with hooks on which hung
hame-straps, collars, and the like; so too the east end of the south
wall. Between them were two large counters filled with more
collars, collar-pads, Neatsfoot Oil, and other paraphernalia. Along
the west end of the south wall stood an old-fashioned secretary,
reaching almost to the ceiling, a small stepladder, and another
workbench. Between the two workbenches were an oil dip,
some wooden horses on which in the season harnesses were put
together, and two stoves, one of which was kept burning, and the
other of which was used more or less as a dummy, for Bill
Schwenker's wry sense of humor was always stirred by the spec-
tacle of the farming clientele coming in and stretching their hands
over this cold stove to be warmed on winter days. In the season
the harness shop was dark on the sunniest days because harnesses

repaired and oiled and waiting to be picked up by their owners
hung from hooks in the ceiling of over half the shop. And, like as
not, the shop was filled with steam brought in from the shed out
back, where the harnesses were washed, and this moisture always
accentuated the smell of leather and oil which predominated in the
shop.

Hugo was seldom at home in that gracious house where his bird-
like mother reigned, a house of horsehair furniture, period paint-
ings, whatnots and various antiques; he preferred to be at the shop,
not alone because he helped his father, but simply because he liked
the setting better. Hugo was taciturn and tended to be uncom-
municative, which, of course, suited me very well, since I was
always very communicative and highly vocal, and I had thus
nothing much to contend with, unless it were the occasional sly
comments which Bill Schwenker, whom we had nicknamed Eli,
Alias the Night Wind, interjected into our conversation from time
to time. Mr. Schwenker was in reality of my grandfather's generation, and he was thus already a middle-aged man when first I
knew him, a thick-set, broad-shouldered man who wore spectacles
and a moustache in his rather broad face, and suffered from asthma,
to ease which he constantly sought the relief of the green smoke
of Asthmador, which he burned and inhaled from a little tin on
the north-wall workbench, a palliative to which Hugo later
resorted also, perpetuating the not unpleasant pungence of the
smoke in the old shop.

Mr. Schwenker had a highly tolerant view of young people. I
do not recall that he was ever impatient with Hugo, not nearly
so much as Hugo might be with the clientele; he was much given
to casual comments by means of which he hailed me whenever I
walked into the shop—"Look who's here—the lost Charley Ross!
Where you been?"—"Look what the wind blew in!"—"Ain't seen
you in a coon's age!"—and similar comments, always delivered
with a good-natured smile. Once in a great while he grew impatient with our arguments, which were usually about whether or

not Hugo would join me in a hike, and at such times he exploded with, "Oh, go on—get out and walk!" which customarily ended any argument.

There is no question but that the harness shop took the place of the blacksmith shop in my esteem. Blacksmithing declined a little faster than harness-making and harness-repair. The shelves above the north-wall workbench were still host to countless boxes of snaps, pins, and other appurtenances of the trade; the repaired harnesses still hung from the ceiling hooks; the farmers came in during the season—the winter months—and stood making the small talk which is the fabric of life in such an establishment for almost twenty years after the blacksmith shop had closed its doors, and thereafter it became for a time a place for Hugo to tie flies and make fly-rods, and then, finally, a woodworking establishment, once more filling the old building with life and warmth, substituting the fragrances of cedar, birch, oak, black walnut and other woods, of resin and fillers and stains for the oil and leather of the earlier days, for Hugo, like myself, had inherited one trait above all others from his father—a need and love for work, for Bill Schwenker, like my father, was devoted to work, and was not happy for very long apart from work, and even as my father was constantly at work in his garden or at some repair in the house, whistling heartily while he worked, so Bill Schwenker could be found all week long, well into the evenings—and sometimes on Sunday, clad in his Sunday best—at the north-wall workbench, sewing on the stitching-horse or simply sitting, contemplating the view from the window, smoking a cigar, or standing at the old secretary, in which he kept a little brandy for an occasional nip.

The harness shop was soon an integral part of my daily routine. If I went down town of a morning, I took the harness shop route, and returned by way of Grandfather Derleth's; if I went down for the evening paper, I always went early, so that Hugo and I could sit on the little shelves along the front windows of the shop and peer down the street toward the post office to determine the right moment to set out for the mail—the right moment being when the windows went up after the mail had been distributed to box-holders. At the harness shop—or in Hugo's "office" out in back—he and I pored over stamp approvals for possible purchase from our meagre funds for our collections. And it was from the harness shop that we set out on our hikes into the hills or the marshes, year after year, from childhood through youth into middle age.

It was an altogether enchanting place. I used to like to sit on the top of the little stepladder against the south wall, hidden by the secretary, and absorb the shop's atmosphere, listening to the small talk of the farmers and to their excuses when they were late with a harness and demanded that it be repaired forthwith, and to their complaints, which was testimony to the occupational flaws they could not escape, for the Schwenker prices were uniformly low and remained unchanged no matter what the nature of the complaint. Mr. Schwenker's personal friends soon became our personal friends, too, and for the most part they were a highly individual lot who came in to "let off steam," as it were, much to our delight.

These friends included Mr. Karberg, an amiable old man who was confused about knowledge and belief, and orated constantly on this and allied religious subjects with the same magnificent confusion which ruled his thoughts, a hearty, hale man who used to come troubled to the harness shop, and after a monologue directed at Mr. Schwenker or Hugo and me, departed happily, with a load lifted from mind and heart, and happy he would remain until the confusion gathered again and he needed the patient ears of an audience to relieve himself once more. They included Gus Naffz, a retired druggist who was spending his declining years at fishing and caring for his two spinster sisters in the proud Naffz house of red brick at one corner of the Freethinkers' Park, and liked to come in to reminisce about the golden years of

Gemüthlichkeit at the turn of the century until he began to fret about his health and gradually went into a mental decline. They included old man Pauli, who appeared at least once a year for one of the calendars which were always to be had on the counters in December and January—and Otto Gross, a short, myopic man who talked vaguely with a tittering laugh about "blowing up" somebody or something, which he never did—and John Ganzer, who roomed above the harness shop, and was always filled with slightly risqué tales to tell—and John Baer, with his glittering golden teeth, who lived next door and carried on a constant war with his car which he drove in second gear all over town and which he swore was worthless, "Damn' car, no go!"—and L. P. Bach, known as Mr. Elpy, who had a haberdashery across the street, which, like its owner, was sinking into the slough of despond.

No matter what changes came about in the life of Sac Prairie, the harness shop was never known as anything other than the harness shop. The blacksmith shop closed and was turned finally into apartments; Bill Schwenker fell on the ice one winter day and broke his hip, and mended a little, but in the end faded from the harness shop and died; nervous, bird-like Paulina Schwenker suffered a paralyzing stroke, recovered, and suffered another and died, all in the space of one year; Gus Naffz and Mr. Elky and L. P. Bach died; old Pauli defied his doctor who told him not to split wood with his cold hanging on, took pneumonia, and shuffled off this mortal coil; Grandfather Derleth, Grandmother Derleth, and all their generation passed into the shadows; Hugo sold the fine old Schwenker home and refurbished the apartment above the harness shop—and the old shop endured.

❈ ❈ ❈ ❈ ❈

HIGH over Sac Prairie every summer morning soar the purple martins, invisible to most of the villagers who go about their daily routine with a kind of resignation to its monotony,

*unaware of that world of the sky which is only another extension
of their own private worlds, theirs for the taking—so high in the
blue as to be remote from the mundane existence of the average
man, so high that only the keenest ear hears their speech above,
where they are not foraging so much as flying about in sensuous
enjoyment of the rising sun, the morning air, at a level of awareness alien to most of mankind solely because the will to know it is
lost or repressed.*

Yet the martins more than many others are village birds, whose
comings and goings are of interest to an increasing number of
people who are never at a loss to set forth the day of their arrival
—usually April ninth in Sac Prairie—or the day of their departure,
which varies a little, but is always in early September. The
villagers know their incessant chattering, their valiant but so often
ineffectual battles with the sparrows who are forever taking over
their abodes, the long rows of them on telephone or telegraph
wires; those villagers who take singular pains each spring to ready

their martin houses, and create a great hullabaloo in chasing out the sparrows, taking down the houses and pulling out the quantities of straw, string and debris the sparrows have carried there in unguarded hours; and, in autumn, putting the houses away again, as were the martins which occupy them their personal birds, and, in a sense, also, their responsibility, like any cat or dog; yet they never seem to know what the martins are about when they are not in residence, they never see them high on wing in heaven, or foraging over the Wisconsin, or congregating for journeys other than the display they make on occasion on the wires along the river.

That they return to the same nesting places year after year cannot be doubted; they have thus a certain intimate familiarity to the plainest of men, half a dozen of whom pursue their businesses in Sac Prairie diligently all day long, and seek their recreation in bowling or poker, in baseball, basketball or football games, and yet find time to announce to their customers on that one April morning of the year that the martins are in from that southern bourne which gave them shelter during the cold months when there were no insects on wing to feed them.

Of their quiet slipping away in early September, few of them seem aware. Only those who walk the more solitary paths into the marshes see the last of the martins, gathered by the hundreds along the high wires and the poles at the railroad bridges, on the superstructure of the bridges themselves, on the telegraph wires following the rails across the Wisconsin, close together always, with occasional birds dropping down to forage restlessly low over the water with nighthawks and chimney swifts and swallows, all waiting on that hour of that day when they will set off once again into the south, come down out of Sac Prairie in twos and threes, following that age-old instinct which drives them to seek warmer climes and brings them as surely back each spring.

One day they are here, one day they are gone. In a wider sense,

that is man's pattern, too; and often men are as little noticed
between the hours of arrival and departure as the martins high
aloft in the summer morning sky.

Every child who was drawn to the river in the days of my
childhood and youth in Sac Prairie knew old Joe Lippert. He was
far more commonly seen along the Wisconsin than in the streets
of the village—a tall, swarthy man, with a growth of black
whiskers which were so seldom shaved away that I often failed
to recognize him when he was clean-shaven. He had an almost
forbidding appearance, with tousled black hair and a fierce, dark-
eyed gaze which wavered for no one, and he was dressed in
clothes which were tattered and seldom clean, for it was manifest
that he cared nothing for what people might say or think of him.
Joe was a solitary by inclination. He had never married and
lived alone in an old-fashioned house covered with white-painted
siding which stood on Water Street just across from the Wisconsin
at Karberg's bar and the Karberg house, at a point where the
river's shore diverged from the street in a sequence of one-time
islands now brought together by sandbars and overgrown with
trees and bushes of all kinds, the haunt of song and vesper sparrows, warblers, wading birds, grouse and quail, of rabbits, snakes
and turtles, and, in the ponds and sloughs, carp and suckers, which
Joe was wont to catch by hand, wading into the water, clothes
and all, to pursue them with exhausting diligence.
People were patently not necessary to him. He delivered himself
of opinions about his fellowmen from time to time which disclosed
that he looked upon them for the most part as animals which, for
all man's vaunted superiority, were markedly below the level of
the wild creatures he met in the river bottoms. Whenever he
went among men, he went frankly to scavenge, for he was in the
habit of picking up paper, sticks, boxes, cans, and everything in
fact for which he could conceive a possible use, no matter how

remote, with the result that his home soon became the repository for more debris than the river could have cast up on its banks in a decade of spring floods.

He made himself a little money by raising ginseng, which he called "sang," and by gathering more from shady places along the Wisconsin. He had a sizable garden space given over entirely to ginseng, but the entire plot was carefully enclosed and covered over by slabs of wood, old screens, cardboard, and all manner of covering, so that sunlight would not injure the delicate plants. He did no other work of any kind, though presumably at one time, when he was in his youth or middle years, he had worked at something. I used to think he had no relatives, but I learned later that his sister lived just across the street from the house of my childhood, and he had several nieces and nephews, all of whom were so much his opposite that this knowledge came as a distinct shock and taxed my credulity a little.

His appearance could be truly formidable when he was come upon suddenly in the river bottoms. He was a big man, broad of shoulder, tall, and very muscular, and in his later years he never troubled to shave at all, growing a luxuriant black beard which eventually became streaked with grey, though it never wholly turned. His bushy eyebrows were black, too, and his skin, both of that part of his face which was visible above his hirsute adornment, and of his hands, was horny and brown, not alone because of exposure to the sun but for dust and grime.

Yet he was not so much unclean as he was impervious to superstitions about uncleanliness and dubious about the multiple germs reputed to lurk in grime; all of us who haunted the river knew that Joe did bathe on occasion, for he customarily inaugurated the swimming season by taking his annual spring bath, stripping his muscular body of all his clothing and wading out into the sunny shallows along a sandbar well up from town, and gravely washing himself with a kind of home-made soap which smelled strongly of disinfectant and lye. And in summer nights he often sought the cooling river, seemingly unaffected by the hordes of mosquitoes which infested the shoreline willows and moved out over the water to feed upon anyone who ventured to bathe there.

He was a river man, not in the sense of Emil Kessler, who had rafted down the Wisconsin, or in that of Sam Schroeder, who was commonly spoken of as a "river rat," but rather in that special genre of the natural man who finds that running water satisfies some primitive need, however inexplicable it may be. Morning, noon and night, Joe was at the river. I met him time and again when he came along the well-worn paths among the close-pressing willows and soft maples which abounded there, bearing huge armfuls of dry twigs and limbs for his stove, though the ceiling-high pile in his woodshed never seemed to diminish by so much as a single twig. I encountered him wading or bathing or, more rarely, fishing, for he seemed to have a preference for catching fish in his bare hands, and he was not partial, as so many fellow anglers were, to sunfish or pike or bass, but was readily satisfied to take home a catch of coarse-fleshed fish which were scorned by most local anglers. Even in winter, when we were sleighing on the large, over-sized sleigh my father had built for us, sliding down the bank of the bottomland at the little red house where the rug-weaver, Peter Ehl, lived, or skating on the ice of Ehl's Slough, or baking potatoes in the sand there, Joe was in the habit of making appearances, to stand watching us, seldom saying anything; he never came in from the street side, but always over the snow-covered lowland on the river side.

It was plain that whatever Joe might lack in life, the river compensated him for. Wife, children, lover, mistress, friend— the Wisconsin was all these and more to him. He came to know the meaning of every voice the water gave into day or night and could tell instantly whether the river was on the rise or falling, whether wind drove waves or ripples across to the shore, whether the water was placid or troubled. Sometimes I saw him drowsing at the water's edge, his habitually bare feet hanging down into the water, a worn hat half way down his face, his gnarled hands clasped on his belly, and no matter how soundlessly I passed him, he knew I went by, for he invariably called out sleepily. His voice had a curious quality of unusual strength, a resonance; it was not an old man's voice, but one that seemed to be integrally part of the river and its environs.

He was the river's own; he belonged to the willows, the water's hushing among the roots of trees, the musk of the uncovered bottom during low water, the lapping of ripples as well as the roar of the swollen stream in time of flood; he shared kinship and occupancy with the song sparrow as well as with the turtle or the clam he occasionally dug out of the sand for food; he gave of himself to the river, and the river lent him something of itself— strength, a sense of permanence and security, none could say what. He dwelt apart from his race, however much he was part of it.

He never made any attempt to alleviate his solitude, but perhaps he was unaware of loneliness as long as he could always be within hearing of the Wisconsin. What his concept of solitude might be was not apparent; he lived alone, evidently by preference, but he could hardly have been said to be lonely. Even in winter he did not often come out of his house, from the windows of which he had the river always in view. He seemed complete within himself, and in his own eyes surely he was a well-rounded man; if he were unhappy he never gave any sign of it, and he did not betray discontent, save perhaps with his fellowmen, in the oblique fashion of his references.

I used to wonder what would happen to him when he grew too old to follow the winding paths along the river, but he never did. He passed seventy, he passed eighty, and he still sought the Wisconsin in all its moods and seasons. He gave up collecting waste of various kinds, he raised ever less ginseng, but he did not give up the river, remaining faithful to his only love, and when he died at last, he left behind him a legacy so strong that I never walked into the islands along his old paths without the conviction that I might meet him at any moment, might come upon that fierce, black-bearded face with its keen eyes rising up out of the willows and the alders which fringed the ways he had traveled so often. And though I knew very well where his mortal remains had gone, I could never feel otherwise but that his spirit had gone back to the river to be renewed and refreshed forever.

The bane of my last years at St. Aloysius was the bullies. There were three of them—one a town boy, two from the country, all hulking lads who delighted in picking upon the boys who were smaller than they, in the tradition of bullies. The nuns always did their best to discourage their activities, but most often the bullies waited until the smaller boys—and often girls—were well away from the school grounds before annoying them. As a boy, I hated to fight, but, since my grades were always better than theirs, and I seemed markedly to be favored by the nuns, who quite humanly expressed satisfaction with my progress in school, I was very often the object of their unwelcome attention.

I dealt with the town bully by making a friend of him, and with one of the others by being too crafty for him, but the third, a lout of a fellow named Linus Fahner, took to waiting at the school door for me to come out, whereupon, lacking much imagination, he would snatch my cap and throw it into the nearest puddle, with a view to booting me in the nates when I stooped to pick it up. He was too clumsy ever to achieve his end, but his persistent annoyance infuriated me to such a degree that one winter noon I rolled a snowball, held it under the waterspout to harden it, and put it beside the nearest puddle, and when, after school, my cap landed in that same puddle, I ignored the cap, snatched up the ice-ball, and let him have it between the eyes with startling results. I had thrown it with such force that I put a considerable gash into his forehead, to say nothing of knocking him down. He got up, bellowing with rage and, blood streaming down his face, charged after me bent upon slaughter; shocked at what I had done, I was too paralyzed to run, and would certainly have fallen victim to his fists, had it not been for the sudden hoisting of Linus from the rear when Matt Schmidt, one of my classmates, caught the bully by the scruff of his neck, and lifted him off his feet, and then, when Linus kicked at him, flung him face down into the very puddle where my cap still lay. Matt leisurely kicked him, picked up my cap, gave it to me, and walked away.

Linus Fahner never troubled me again, and from that day forward Matt Schmidt could have had from me anything he wanted that was in my power to give. He was a broad-shouldered farm boy, with warm eyes and a broad face much spattered with freckles of all shapes and sizes. His hair was always unruly, and his hands were already calloused with hard work. He was phlegmatic, simple-hearted, and utterly incapable of any kind of dishonesty, even to the telling of a white lie. I could not understand why he had come to my rescue, but I learned quite soon that it was simply that he admired my ability to obtain good marks in my studies, when he had to struggle so hard just to pass from one grade to the next.

And I learned that Matt liked to read, that his family was too poor even to afford a daily newspaper. In those years, we did not have a newspaper either, but we subscribed to the *Chicago Ledger*, a weekly magazine, and to *Collier's*, and these magazines, as soon as Father had finished with them, I brought to school and gave to Matt, and now and then I gave him a book I had finished with —though these were not many, for I liked to collect books and to look them over from time to time, and I did not then have very many. No matter. Matt liked what he got; he read them through; he discussed the stories with me, and I discovered that our tastes were quite similar, for all the difference in our grades. A sort of new life opened for Matt through these and other magazines I brought to him, but just the same, I never escaped the conviction that I was not doing enough for him, a kind of reaction that has remained with me throughout life. What was most important to Matt was that he had found a friend. It had simply never occurred to me that this taciturn lad needed a friend. He had never been very sociable, he tended to go his own way, and, in fact, he had little time for anything but school and work. But now his recesses were events; he gave over playing, and spent the time talking about stories and articles he had read in the magazines, and we shared common ground on subjects ranging from recent inventions to the latest adventures of the insidious Dr. Fu Manchu.

I suppose it was because of our friendship that Matt decided to enter high school, though he had not intended to. I expected to help him whenever he needed help in his studies, and I resolved that later on in life I would make him a present of a library, even if I had to write all the books in it myself—but alas! for adolescent dreams—Matt did not stay long in high school, he soon dropped out and went back to the farm to stay. And soon after, the Schmidt family moved away from the Sac Prairie country. The years reeled away; Linus Fahner was swept off by tuberculosis, the curse of his family; St. Aloysius was torn down to be built anew; and when at last I had a library for that faithful friend and sought to look him up and write to him, I learned that he too had gone to ground, and I was left with that bitter awareness of an obligation, the fulfilment of which was prevented by death.

❊ ❊ ❊ ❊ ❊

THE process of renewal which is inherent in many things we do every spring is nowhere more apparent than in the long afternoons spent "over the hills"—on the moraine east of

Sac Prairie on the far side of the Wisconsin. The afternoons are long only in the sense of clocked hours, for none is ever too long, time spent there has no limits. I suspect I go there so often not alone to inspect familiar paths and corners, long-known slopes and valleys, but also to take pleasure in a renewal of acquaintance with places with which some of my earliest memories are associated. The hills are not alone a vantage point from the eminence of which I can view all Sac Prairie—the village on its paw of land, the encircling hills, the undulating prairie between, the broad, cobalt Wisconsin winding by—nor a source of nature lore—for an observant man can find something new at each walk along a familiar path—but also a wealth of memories which bind me to these slopes so firmly that I mourn the loss of every tree felled by the woodsmen, each invasion of every turn of the hillside path by the encroaching river, and the alteration of every portion of the landscape there.

Discounting that part of my attachment which rises from sentiment, for these hills are bound up inextricably with first love, it seems patent that here in this place which changes very little from year to year there is something of that illusion of permanence which we all seek so diligently in one form or another throughout life. The hills are an assurance that some aspects of individual existence are immutable, and briefly there the flaw in the crystal is not apparent—for these are the same paths walked decades ago with Margery and only yesterday with Cassandra, these are the same vistas, the same horizons, even the same trees, flowers, fruits, so that on some days it is as probable that it was Cassandra who walked here beside me decades ago and Margery who was here but yesterday. The conviction of continuity is strong in such places where physical change is as slight as on the hills. I return to them year after year to be renewed by their seeming immutability, though I know the illusion, I know the infinite erosions and decayings which go on ceaselessly from moment to moment, and to which the mind adjusts so imperceptibly as to obviate them, so that it seems that they have not taken place at all.

I exist in such places on several planes; the eyes that perceive the fox sparrow busily foraging in old leaves do not blind the mind's eye from acknowledging that this leaning tree was once a trysting place for Margery and me, that only a little way apart a hidden hollow sheltered Cassandra and me when, in communion with the sun and earth and air, we lay unclothed in that ecstasy which is at once brother to birth and death, with the wind's whisper in the sheltering leaves and the sun warm on skin, the river's murmur and the hawk's scream ringing overhead, integral. Every aspect of the hills has its significance—the pasque flowers and hepaticas, the flowering birch and wild honeysuckle, the birdfoot violets and the delicate, aromatic white violets deep in a pocket of the hills, the soaring hawk and the pensive song sparrow, the mulberry tree and the old cottonwoods, the wing dam down along the river and the slopes where once, as boys, we shouted and cried at play—all signify an act, a state of mind, an experience, a mood which, taken together, make up the texture of a life. I come to a kind of spiritual rebirth on these hills every spring, and I renew it each year despite increasing awareness of death inherent in that rebirth, an awareness which exists independent of volition or conscious act.

It is significant, I sometimes think, that the facets of nature which quicken my pulse with that awareness of both life and death are inextricably associated with the loneliness of man's mote-like existence in the cosmos—and acceptance of man's essential solitude on earth, or by love, or both together, for they are only different aspects of the same face. Hawk, whippoorwill, lilacs in bloom, the shy white violets, hepaticas starring the slopes with their pastel colors, streetlights and trees at night, new moon and evening star, the manifold aspects of familiar houses and streets —all are symbols, all occur and recur without much alteration from one year to the next, as do the hills, of my going to which it

*has often been said that I had better travel in new places, as if it
were not true that some men learn more out of one book than
others do from thousands.*

My high school years in Sac Prairie were enlivened not only
by an early romance—that brief, poignant first love affair with
Margery—but also by the presence on the faculty of Miss
Frieda Schroeder. Miss Schroeder taught English with all the
freshness of twenty-one or twenty-two years, and she was simply
too attractive to be stood up in front of a class of adolescent boys.
Miss Schroeder's appeal was almost entirely on a physical plane,
and I often wonder how significant it is that a majority of the
girls and young ladies who subsequently caught my eye wore one
or more aspects of Miss Schroeder and were, most of them, of
what would be called her "general type," save that they were,
none of them, as blonde as she. I have no doubt that more than one
of us profoundly regretted the presence in the Statutes of Wisconsin of laws about contributing to juvenile delinquency designed
to protect us, but in this case certainly frustrating a wholly
natural instinct. I did.

But Miss Schroeder's appeal was not, fortunately for me, entirely on a physical plane. I came to her class fresh from Sister
Isabelle's, and Miss Schroeder continued Sister Isabelle's encouragement of my writing. More than this, she encouraged me
to read even more than I might naturally have done by the simple
expedient of promising any of us who read more than the required number of books extra credit in our English courses. We
had thus the triple incentive of pleasing Miss Schroeder, gaining
extra credit, and adding to our store of knowledge, and some of us
forthwith plunged into the world of books with renewed energy
and dedication.

I read everything I could lay my hands on. I began with *Mosses
from an Old Manse* and *The Scarlet Letter* and went through

book after book to *Dracula* and *In the Midst of Life*. And, because
it was evident soon that Miss Schroeder was particularly pleased
when any of us read in American literature, I took up Emerson's
Essays, and what I read there and in *Walden* profoundly influenced
the course of my life. The ideas that unfolded before my youthful eyes found fertile soil in which to take root and grow. Perhaps it was that I was already then conditioned to accept without
question what I read in Emerson and Thoreau. I do not know
that I would have come upon Emerson and Thoreau had it not
been for Miss Schroeder. There is in every life the right time for
enlightenment, for exposure to the life of the mind, for a door to
be opened into that wider world that unfolds from one's own
doorstep, a moment all too soon lost in time, and I had come to it,
and the door had been opened for the light to flow in—not such
a light as would open to me all the secrets of life and death, but
only such a light as to illumine my own path through the years
ahead. Miss Schroeder was, however unwittingly, the impulse
which drove me to the door.

I was ready to believe *There is a time in every man's education
when . . . he must take himself for better or for worse as his portion; that though the wide universe is full of good, no kernel of
nourishing corn can come to him but through his toil bestowed
on that plot of ground which is given to him to till*. I knew
beyond cavil that *No law can be sacred to me but that of my
nature. Good and bad are but names very readily transferable to
that or this; the only right is what is after my constitution; the
only wrong what is against it. . . . Nothing is at last sacred but
the integrity of your own mind*. I was open to the conviction
that *Nothing can bring you peace but yourself. Nothing can
bring you peace but the triumph of principle*.

And certainly I had advanced far enough into my life to recognize that *For every thing you have missed, you have gained something else; and for every thing you gain, you lose something. . . .
You cannot do wrong, without suffering wrong. . . . There can*

be no excess to love, none to knowledge, none to beauty. . . .
*In the nature of the soul is the compensation for the inequalities
of condition.* And surely, in *Nature*, I could not do other but greet
with deep agreement such words as these—*The incommunicable
trees begin to persuade us to live with them, and quit our life of
solemn trifles. Here no history, or church, or state, is interpolated
on the divine sky and the immortal year.*

And what I found profoundly true in Emerson, I found even
more true to my nature in Thoreau's *Walden*, which became a sort
of Bible—not one to be preached from, but one to be kept in the
recesses of my mind, not so much thought of as lived. When I
read *What a man thinks of himself, that it is which determines, or
rather indicates, his fate,* I found support for confidence in myself. My ambitions were given even greater direction when I read
*I learned . . . that if one advances confidently in the direction of
his dreams and endeavours to live the life which he has imagined,
he will meet with a success unexpected in common hours.* And I
too, preferred truth to fame or money, I had already at fourteen
begun to find my occasions in myself, I was also a fisher in time,
I appreciated simplicity, and I already knew *It is life near the bone
where it is sweetest.* It was as if I found in this book justification
for my dawning belief that, without confusing the microcosm
with the macrocosm, Sac Prairie was the microcosm which reflected the macrocosm of the world.

It is not to be thought that everything in Emerson and Thoreau
took hold of me at once; it is never thus; but, little by little, the
ideas thus taken in began to trickle into my awareness and took
hold of me, with roots that grew firmer with each passing year.
Moreover, Emerson and Thoreau were shortly fortified by Walt
Whitman and the delightful and pointed irreverence of H. L.
Mencken and *The American Mercury,* and the wise counsel of
H. P. Lovecraft, a middle-aged writer, who was a correspondent,
together with the guidance of the village librarian. Nothing there-

after was to alter the course upon which these mentors had so firmly set me. Nothing was to shake these foundations.

Perhaps it is folly to put the onus of it all on Miss Frieda Schroeder. But I think not. If she had not been so attractive as to draw upon herself all our libidinous desires, it is doubtful that I would have exerted myself so much to demonstrate my admiration for her in the only way open to me at fourteen—by reading the books I thought it would please her to have her students read. Seldom have the first faint stirrings of desire been so fruitful!

In my youth I could not have conceived of the public library without Josephine Merk, who was its first librarian, and held that position for over twenty years, retiring then only because the hand of death was already upon her. She was in those years very much a part of the soft spring evenings, the fulgent summer nights, or the smoky autumn days in Sac Prairie. She was a handsome woman, in those earlier years in her middle forties—for she was but in her sixty-eighth year when she died—a woman with finely chiseled features, grey-blue eyes, dark hair beginning to grey a little, and a face informed with intelligence.

She was one of that tribe of spinsters which at one time abounded in Sac Prairie, a busy, gregarious lot, but she was never in any sense an "old maid," or even in reality old. She had been a country school teacher, and she had taught in the graded and high schools in Sac Prairie but, resigning at last, had moved up to a place on the Board of Education and to become village librarian after the local Woman's Club had at last achieved its goal of establishing a public library. Hers was peculiarly a world of books, and her country was that of the mind, for above all else she prized knowledge and skill in its use. She never sat idly at her desk, but was always occupied with something; if she were not at work among the library cards or pasting pockets into new books, she was studying catalogs or reading a book which might as readily be Dr. Johnson's *Rasselas*, from her own shelves, as a new arrival for the library shelves. Above all, she was at pains to be unobtrusively helpful to all who made application to her, whether it were old Mr. Pauli, who was devoted exclusively to western fiction, or cantankerous Mrs. Cleland, who was possessed of an unhealthy concern with religion and looked with suppressive disdain upon all other matters. She was particularly partial to young people, doing her best to help them to read informative books as well as that kind of entertaining fiction which was at that time in vogue, from fairy tales to the adventures of Tom Swift, perhaps already convinced that the adults were beyond saving, but the young were not.

In those days I read voraciously—from mystery fiction, lore and legend to Dumas, Scott, and Poe, yet I was too impatient to learn the French she offered so generously to teach me, with the characteristic blindness of adolescence. I used to go to the library thrice a week; I would have come oftener, had the library been open. I never knew her routine at the library to vary throughout those more than twenty years. Three times a week she came, unlocked the door, and waited for her clientele. In summer she threw open the windows to air out the stuffy little room that was the library in those days; in winter she went to the hall closet for paper and wood to light a fire in the small stove that was the library's only heat, and endured the chill and cold uncomplainingly until the stove's heat spread from wall to wall. As each evening drew toward its end—the hours were from seven to nine, but she was often there half an hour longer—two of her oldest friends, Helen Hahn and Amelia Pohlman, also spinsters, came to sit and talk, finally waiting upon her closing of the library to walk down the street with her, sometimes to sit a little while before Helen Hahn's home less than a block away, sometimes to part there, leaving Amelia to walk most of the way home with Josephine.

With the carefree nature of adolescence, I appreciated her without ever thinking very much about her. The long thoughts of youth are very seldom about others. Perhaps it is that people do not emerge on the horizons of the young as they do upon those who are older and wiser; perhaps it is necessary to live a little more widely before it is even possible to see the world in which others live. For Josephine had been an attractive young girl, the third daughter of a German cooper, early in life passionately devoted to education. Her family lived close to the bone in common with most middle-class families in Sac Prairie in those years. At sixteen she had been compelled to go directly from high school into teaching country school, walking out each day from the village west of town three miles in the bright, dew-fresh mornings, and back again through the wearing evenings, only a few days' study ahead of her pupils as she was but a few years older than her charges, so that night after night, when her lonely, widowed mother ached to talk to her, Josephine could not talk but must lose herself in the tiring lessons for the coming day, so that no pupil under her tutelage need want for the answer to any question he might ask.

It was only later that she could go on to the University of Wisconsin, where she took her Bachelor's degree with ease and then, within a fortnight of finals for her Master's, collapsed under the strain of her studies, and returned to teaching again without ever taking her Master's. If she had been disappointed—and surely she must have been—she betrayed that disappointment by no sign, she did not indulge in self-pity; her sisters Ida and Helen were both teaching elsewhere; this, too, was her fate, the natural goal of her devotion to learning.

Of the deprivations in her life she was not given to think until far later, when she understood something of her mother's loneliness, and remembered how her mother had waited for her evening after evening, eager for that small talk which is the very essence of life, and cheated of it by Josephine's own pressing need to work at her books for her pupils' sake; and, thinking of her then, remembering her, now long dead, she was accustomed to say, "Oh, if *only* I had talked with her!" saying *if only* with all the anguish of one who knows that error, once made, was long ago compounded by death and can never be undone. Perhaps in this lay the explanation for the intensity with which she threw herself into working for others; the habit of devotion to learning could not be changed; it had become a part of her, it had survived the ordeal of her failure before her mother's need as well as her own failure to achieve that educational goal she had sought at the university, one her sister Helen had achieved with ease. Even then, in her later years, she was not a victim of self-pity, she was only occasionally overcome with remorse in the late realization of her mother's loneliness, which thus sharpened her own; and in a sense she felt her helplessness before the circumstances of that destiny which had made it impossible for her to accede to this trivial—yet to the older woman important—desire of her mother's, even as now it made it impossible for her to communicate to the ever impatient children the fruit of her wisdom, born of her bitter-sweet experience in that same country of the mind to which she had always been devoted.

Occasionally, in spirited conversation, she revealed a bright sense of humor, a vivid ability at repartee, not unedged with a kind of wryness, which in itself was evidence that she had reached the bitter realization which comes to all her kind—that she was never to be permitted to give of her experience to those who came after, because time so rapidly and irrevocably widens the chasm of the years between the old and the young, because the Philistines multiply far faster than men of good will, and are given so readily to the glorification of the purely material, the physical and specious.

How did she live, then, in her mind's country, when she was virtually alone in the village, not incapable of joining in the small talk of her fellow-villagers but growing increasingly away from it, a woman whose knowledge and perception far exceeded that of her friends, and who had only her sister Helen, retired at last from teaching, to talk to, and the two impatient with each other, as two women in the same house always seem to be? Was hers a deeper solitude than any other's?—one that walled her forever away from the people of Sac Prairie even while she lived among them, the loneliness of the one in the crowd, the one doomed to be so confined by her fellowmen? Even as her mother had sat day after day waiting within her four walls for the daughter who could not find time to indulge her need when she came, so now she was bound in by her village, with none to hear her speak. Perhaps the library and the clerical duties of the Board of Education were but outlets for a small part of what she had so rigidly suppressed for lack of an understanding ear.

She was fortified by a whimsical resignation. She may not have been content with her way of life, but she was conditioned to accept it without struggle; perhaps she knew, as few people did without even more pain, that struggle is often hopeless, that the seeds of maturity are planted in adolescence and even before, that each of us takes his course out of uncounted impulses and experiences, unrecognized when they take place, unknown when they bear fruit, long lost in the limbo of time. Her life had been conditioned by early privations; the point at which she might have emerged from her life's conditions had not been passed when she failed to return for her Master's examinations; and, having come back into the circumscribed life of Sac Prairie, she was ever afterward given to that life.

In her last years, I used to spend time of evenings, after I too had made my choice and returned to Sac Prairie from the threshold of the wider world, sitting in the library to talk with her, and so heard her speak of her regrets, her remorse, but never a word of her dreams and ideals, heard her speak of the spectres of pain possibly inflicted upon others by some laxity or some inability of hers to avoid doing so, of the bright future which beckoned to the young of my time, of the world's technological advances, and the retrogression from learning, which had already then begun under the leadership of the crassly Philistine. She spoke of books or of people, sitting where she could look out across the Wisconsin beyond the windows, the river agleam under the moon, to the hills ghostly in moonlight on the east shore; she spoke of old friends, of old students, of the little joys and sadnesses of years gone by. And, at the last, she spoke with regret of her condition, telling me with resigned finality that she had been failing, that she had gone through the Mayo clinic, and had learned there that she would die within a year of the cancer that had begun to grow in her lungs.

She resigned her posts at last, and went home to wait for death through the final three months of that year, with that fortitude and patience which had characterized all her life, saying often, when I called on her, "I don't mind dying, if only it wouldn't take so long!"—and died at last just after the turn of the new year, leaving her shadow to linger over Sac Prairie for years after her passing. She was that one who by the calm strength of her will alone concealed most effectively how little the rich country of her mind satisfied the most primitive of her needs—to communicate to her fellowmen—a woman who chose her own course without complaint, enduring all the darts and barbs thrown at her by those far less than she, and went her way through life to death without regret for the course she had chosen, no lonelier than a tree on a desert.

From my post in Sac Prairie I fished in the wider stream that flowed past my private Walden and eddied outward to the stars. The mails brought in magazines, newspapers, letters which apprized me of what went on outside, and when one day in the summer of 1926 I sent an inquiry about Machen's *The Hill of Dreams* to a fellow-writer, H. P. Lovecraft, and received in reply a friendly, informative letter, there began a correspondence which was to have as much consequence as my first reading of *Walden*.

Lovecraft too, recognizing limitations, had found his private

Walden near rural areas of his childhood's city, Providence, Rhode Island, where, in his winter-bound study and in the summer countryside he wrote macabre tales and poems, revised manuscripts, and penned in a fine, spidery script a multitude of letters. Though I never met him in the near twelve years of our correspondence, I seldom knew a man so well. Once—sometimes twice—a week, letters came my way on every conceivable subject, ranging across all time and human experience, and it was inevitable that passages might find a receptive mind and take root there. Wisdom, tolerance, clear judgment proved casually persuasive.

Certainly I echoed him when he wrote, *A man belongs where he has roots—where the landscape and milieu have some relation to his thoughts and feelings, by virtue of having formed them. A real civilization recognizes this fact—and the circumstance that America is beginning to forget it, does far more than does the mere matter of commonplace thought and bourgeois inhibitions to convince me that the general American fabric is becoming less and less a true civilization and more and more a vast, mechanical, and emotionally immature barbarism de luxe. . . . I cannot think of any individual as existing except as part of a pattern—and the pattern's most visible and tangible areas are of course the individual's immediate environment; the soil and culture-stream from which he springs, and the milieu of ideas, impressions, traditions, landscapes, and architecture, through which he must necessarily peer in order to reach the "outside."*

Every individual, he wrote, lives in *essential solitude. It seems to me the plainest of all truths that no highly organized and freely developed mind can possibly envisage an external world having much in common with the external world envisaged by any other mind. The basic inclinations, yearnings, and ego-satisfactions of each separate individual depend wholly upon a myriad associations, hereditary predispositions, environmental accidents, and so on, which cannot possibly be duplicated in any other individual; hence it is merely foolish for anybody to expect himself to be "understood" more than vaguely, approximately, and objectively by anybody else. . . . The very naturalness and universality of this solitude remove that condition from the more or less painful state called "loneliness," in the conception of which there is implicit some suggestion of preventable ill, out-of-placeness, or resentment-meriting defeat.* So too I had come to know, moving about in the microcosm of Sac Prairie.

He guided my reading, adding his voice to Frieda Schroeder's and Josephine Merk's, and his was the most erudite and catholic background. He encouraged my writing—above all, about Sac Prairie. *I truly believe that every creative mind is the essential outgrowth of its own native soil, and that no material is quite so perfectly adapted to it as the rich color and background of that soil.* Steadily, year after year, he strengthened my resolution and gave support to my decision to remain in this western Walden and draw from it my sustenance and strength.

Often, walking the streets and lanes of Sac Prairie, I have been made to think that houses exist on an extra-terrestrial plane—not merely as structures of wood or stone, of glass and brick, but as edifices created by people and events, the people who have lived in them and the events of their existence. For no house in Sac Prairie ever stood as just a house of so many storeys, so many doors, so many windows, a house so far from the street and so far from the alley; each stood also for the lives lived there and, approaching it, I saw the house on this extra-terrestrial plane, I saw the people who had lived there and what had happened there, just as, in passing the house in which someone lies dying, one is unable to pass unaware of impending death.

This atmosphere of houses becomes in time an integral part of the night life of the mind of the village dweller; as for instance when one nears a park conscious of the deeper darkness there is in that part of town, so one nears and passes houses with cognizance of their existence in an aura or atmosphere of past time inextricably linked with the present. And in Sac Prairie this was all the more so as the years passed.

There was one summer in particular when I was in the habit of walking along what was known as "the back street" into Upper Sac Prairie, there to describe a large loop, and walk back by the "front street" along the river. I walked tree-naved streets through the oldest part of town where the atmosphere of houses was as inescapable as the very air I breathed, and indeed a part of that air.

There was the Holmes Keysar house, squat and prim in the midst of a wide lawn. It was a white house with a broad, long verandah with seven white pillars across its front, shut away from the street by a neat white picket fence along the sidewalk. The Holmes Keysars were the childless Keysars, to distinguish them from the Keysars who had children and who lived down on "the front street." Mrs. Keysar was always thought a little "queer" because she never went anywhere except to ride out in the buggy with her husband, and, more rarely, to take the train for a cottage they shared sometimes in summer over on the shore of a lake near Madison, a cottage kept quite as close and secluded as the house in Sac Prairie. A strange woman, very stout, with a habit of going about in her yard to pick up faggots which she tied into neat bundles and put into one of the woodsheds, three of which stood behind the house—one for twigs and faggots, one for kindling and fine wood, and one for chunks, one adjoining another in neat orderliness. She always sat at a back window, but in such a way that she could look through the next room and out the front window to see who might be passing in the street and not herself be seen except perhaps as a silhouette, and then only if a passerby turned at the proper angle. Except for these windows—the kitchen's and the one dining-room window which looked out front —none of the windows of the house ever emerged from behind its blinds.

Holmes was a tall man of good build, who was habitually clad in a long, fashionable coat and a broad-brimmed hat; he wore a neatly trimmed white beard and went to town quite often to buy things for his wife. He had a penchant for buying dishes, almost as if this were demanded of him, and he required that Schneller & Felix notify him in advance of the arrival of every shipment of dishes, so that he could pick them over and buy what he liked for his Scottish wife. The two of them lived a solitary, secluded life in the house which was much too large for them, and, after his death, Mrs. Keysar was even more rarely seen, keeping to the house day and night and seldom venturing out, though she did not abandon her collecting of twigs and faggots. When at last she died and the house was invaded, it was found filled with yards and yards of calico, and set upon set of dishes, some manifestly never used; and the woodshed was packed from door to far wall with bundles of twigs tied with string against some nebulous future use.

Afterwards other people lived there, the picket fence vanished, the once prim house began to show the ravages of people who stayed but a little while, and gave way to others; but at night it emerged as the dwelling place of the Holmes Keysars—it became once more the house in which that strange recluse of a woman lived, that stout, reticent woman with her passion for saving sticks and strings, the house which was home for that dignified man who was impelled by some motive beyond discovery to buy calico and dishes in quantities she was never able to use, the childless couple who rode forth together in their buggy of evenings and went for long, silent rides. One expected to see that dark silhouette in the evening, sitting at that back window; one expected to see that frock-coated gentleman walking home from town with his purchases; one would not have been surprised to see that buggy swing out of the yard into the road and vanish westward over the prairie. For somehow, on that extra-terrestrial plane, they were still there, bound inextricably to that house, given an added mortality, as it were, dependent upon the life of the house itself. Nothing is there to say whether her seclusion was in compensation for children, whether his purchase of calico and dishes was an effort to make up to that silent woman for some unknown inadequacy in their home. They were childless, but if they wished for children, no one knew; the house, empty of the voices of children, yet had the fullness of those two to inhabit it as long as it continued to stand.

The Baker house, not far away, had not been a childless home. It was high and proud, set in a spacious area a little back from the street, with many trees around it, and nearby a summer-kitchen and a handsome and elaborate coach house, adorned with a little cupola, the shuttered openings of which invited the birds. Tall, white, with green shutters, it had a quiet dignity which pervaded the atmosphere of the entire street. Its windows were arched and old-fashioned; its doors inside were arched, too, and its front door opened upon a fine hall and an attractive open stairway ornamented with a mahogany rail and an artfully twisted newel-post. Its rooms were high-ceilinged, and a handsome bay in the parlor swept up to a similar bay on the second storey. The carpets were ingrained and Brussels, the woodwork a spotless white, and the rooms in summer were always cool, just as in winter they absorbed the warmth of a great old coal stove. A square piano stood in the parlor, as aloof as the room itself.

But the warmth of this house derived from its gracious aspect rather than from those who lived there. There were four of them in the house—Mr. and Mrs. Baker, their pretty daughter, Jenny, and Mrs. Baker's sister, Mahailey McDougal. Quite close by, in bachelor quarters, lived her brother Douglas, so that the five of them made a kind of close-knit family unit. Somehow, Mrs. Baker symbolized the house—a neat, somewhat prim little gentlewoman, soberly dressed, with a lace cap, lace ruching around her neck, and a lace fichu worn over her shoulders. Mr. Baker was a typical English tyrant demanding obedience everywhere but in his home, which Mrs. Baker ruled with gentle insistence. The McDougals, not being of English descent, were less severe, though Mrs. Baker had become more so because of Mr. Baker's proximity and constant example, and thus, indirectly, his personality. Though they lived very largely with the Bakers, the McDougals were not part of them; they exercised a greater freedom, and Douglas, in particular, took occasional pleasure in a wee drap of the spirits, perhaps to sustain himself in the face of Mr. Baker's British patriarchy.

They lavished their affection on Jenny, an only child, but all their affection—save that of Douglas—was conditioned by discipline and obedience and a certain pride. Pretty and alone, Jenny grew up within the rigid confines of the house, though in time she began to help her father in the post office, she studied at the University of Wisconsin, she taught country school and ultimately taught a little while in Sac Prairie. But for all that, she evolved in a pattern; the house—her home—was a haven, the village was a world alien to those who made no concession to passing time and changing customs. She grew up as her parents grew older—her mother gentler if no less firm, her father more autocratic, sporting a short white beard around his chin, in contrast to his sombre black coat and trousers—and she fell in love, and with Harry Mills, which was monstrous, for there was a cloud on Mills's parentage.

Mills was a popular, good-looking young bachelor, fond of hunting and riding, but who was he that he dared think to pay attention to pretty Jenny Baker, the only daughter of the Bakers of Upper Sac Prairie, Wisconsin? Mr. Baker, Mrs. Baker, prim, retired school-teacher Mahailey McDougal, and the austere, white, proud Baker house in one voice said *No!*, it was impossible, Harry Mills was impossible—and after all, was he not so much older than Jenny?—and Miss Jenny must have the very best. There was to be no more of Harry Mills, no further mention of him, and night after night thereafter, the square piano tinkled where Jenny sat at enforced practise, eating her heart out.

She had never before known love, but only an affection which, however genuine, was predicated upon duty and obedience, respect and submission; and, knowing it now, she would not give it up; she crept away whenever she could and met Harry secretly, her uncle Douglas abetting. The Bakers closed her in as securely as they could, never permitting Harry Mills to call, though they could not always keep her away from him at public gatherings. Sometimes they met by prearrangement at the homes of her friends, where they were left discreetly alone, or from which they could walk out along the tree-lined streets of Sac Prairie in the concealing darkness of night. Harry, who was a man of comfortable means and lived alone with his mother, urged her to escape with him, to go away and be married, to come back and present the Bakers with a *fait accompli*, but the habits of discipline were too deeply ingrained in Jenny; she could not, and ultimately, having failed in his own eyes, Harry Mills became despondent—perhaps some fatal malaise had been rooted in him long before—and killed himself one morning.

The Bakers could sit back, though they had won but half the battle, for even if Harry had failed her, Jenny did not fail Harry. Having once known this love, she would not surrender it; she looked at no other man; she would have no one but Harry, and Harry was gone. No argument prevailed against her. If she lacked the strength to take positive action against the wishes of those guardians of her childhood, she had that kind of stubbornness which made her father the autocrat he was, and she resisted them in her own negative way. Harry she would have, and none other. Their words were to no end, their entreaties fell on deaf ears, and in time they saw what they had done. Rebellion was in Jenny forever, and just as in her childhood she had been conditioned by the dutiful submission which had been impressed upon her, now she was conditioned by this thwarted love. If Harry Mills was not good enough for Jenny Baker, then Jenny Baker was too good for any other man. Her rebellion, her thwarted bitterness infected the very walls, and it lingered after her parents died and she was left alone to sell the house and leave it forever, herself now an old woman with traces of the beauty which had once been hers there still.

The house fell into other hands—of old people, as if it denied youth and joy before its proud dignity—but behind its prim, gracious face lay forever the spirit of Jenny's belated revolt; rebellion looked out of its windows, even if the shutters and the walls held it in, concealing it as much as possible. One felt it, walking by, as if they were still inside, in the genteel light of the lamps—the autocratic head of the house, his prim, subservient wife, the teacherish Mahailey McDougal, the indulgent uncle, and the pretty girl who, having once known a love unconditioned by duty and obedience, would never, never relinquish it, but would carry it deep in her heart forever like a shield against the prison of the house and the bewildering world outside.

Not far away, the Bickford house told a similar story. There in that low house with its eight pillars on its wide porch, the oaks towering over the roof, there were many children, but of them pretty, frail Ella was her father's favorite. He was a hard man, stern, dour, and hard-working, and he expected everyone else to work as hard. The house was a good one to come home to after a hard day of work; a pleasant house that rang with the voices of children and with the complaisant voice of Mrs. Bickford, accustomed to bowing to her husband's every wish. It was set far back from the street, white and neat, with a summer kitchen off to one side, adjoining the house, and the trees around were trimmed well up, so that the house seemed closer to the street than it was because the dark trunks rose up to afford a contrast to its whiteness. A cozy house, made all the more so of winter nights by the glow of its great coal stove, which looked redly out into the village all night long and, after the lamps had been put out, gave off a red glow to lie upon the snow outside and defy the winter's cold. Children loved the house, and they came from all over town to play there, winter and summer, though as soon as they were old enough,

Mr. Bickford expected his sons and daughters to work, and because he expected it, Mrs. Bickford did, too.

But though he was severe with all the children, his heart was lost to his Ella, who was sweet and pretty, demure and obedient. Perhaps it was because he saw in her the woman who bore her, as if his indulgence toward her were motivated by some obscure conviction that he had taken away the youth of that other lovely girl who had become his wife and that this indulgence might, equally as obscurely, make it up to her. Ella might have anything she wanted, but sweet, patient Ella wanted nothing. While all the other Bickford children grew up and went to work, soon becoming inured to their father's stern precepts and following his pattern, Ella remained the old man's favorite, and his dour, austere face lit up at sight of her, his stubborn mouth broke into a smile. She was his darling, she was his pet, she was the world where his sun rose every morning and his moon rose every night. And, because it was so with him, it was so, too, with Mrs. Bickford. She was submissive and weak; whatever he said was law in that house, and it took precedence over the voice of the storm outside or the voice of conscience within, over the oak's tapping limb or the baby's cry.

One by one the children went to work, and Ella went to school, as demure and pretty as ever; people noticed her and spoke of "that pretty Ella Bickford" and "that lovely child." Harry Campbell noticed her, too, but people thought him a little wild, a ne'er-do-well, a flighty boy too handsome for his own good. Girls liked him, but Ella avoided his eyes, Ella was unspoiled, she had a lovely home to go to, and a father who adored her, and soon Harry was mad about her, wild with love for her. Soon, as the slow months reckoned time, there was something at last that Ella wanted—the demure one wanted Harry Campbell and told her father.

And then this pillar of love turned upon her, crying out against her and the man of her choice. Never! Not Harry Campbell! Not a man without prospects. He could not bear to think of his darling at the mercy of circumstances in which she might not have adequate food or clothing. And, because it was so with Mr. Bickford, it was so also with Mrs. Bickford. Perhaps his possessiveness had gone beyond his control and he could not bear the thought of losing her; perhaps it was as he said. Perhaps long ago the heart in that sturdy frame, that stern, hard-working man, had fixed the impulse to love someone so necessary to it upon the sweet, pretty daughter, and could not any longer retreat.

His violence stunned and terrified her. She had no thought of disobedience. If her father, who had always so manifestly loved her, thought she must give up Harry Campbell, then she must give him up. But she turned in upon herself, tremulous and afraid, all her gayety, all her self-assurance crushed, lost; she turned away from life and came obediently back to her place between her mother and her father in that cozy house with its rafters so often shaken by the joyous, carefree cries of the young, that neat, spotless house which children had always loved despite the austerity of Mr. Bickford.

And then suddenly, Mr. Bickford died, and life in the house, bereft of his will which had ordered it, began to decay. The children were gone, save for Ella, alone now with her mother. If she still thought of love, she thought of Harry Campbell, long since vanished from Sac Prairie, of none other, surely. But now her duty was clear; she must care for her mother, who had relied so much upon her husband's decisions that she had lost the ability to decide for herself. Now that he was gone, Ella must decide. But Ella, cut away from Harry Campbell's love and her father's adoration, was likewise bereft, and slowly, surely, an insidious decline came upon mother and daughter.

One by one, they lost the sense of time, of obligations, of duty, of order; if they were invited out to dinner, Ella might decide quixotically an hour before the time set that her mother's hair needed washing, whereupon Mrs. Bickford, with not a word of caution of admonition concerning their impending engagement, would instantly prepare herself and submit to this ministration; so that they came at last to dinner an hour or two hours late. Dinners, concerts, church suppers, parties—it was all the same, and the house which had once been so neat and trim, so joyous and cozy, so homey and pleasant to look upon, assumed an uncaring look in the uncut lawn and the no longer spotless rooms.

Left alone at last, Ella slipped still further into decay. With no one to dwell upon that sweet, pretty girl, with no father to adore her, no lover to give her affection, no mother to care for, she retreated inevitably into a country of her mind, neglecting more and more the state of the house, and at last, even, her own personal cleanliness, for what did it matter? None cared for sweet, pretty Ella Bickford any more; time had taken them all away—Harry, father, and mother; it did not matter how she looked, or how the house looked; the children whose joyous voices had rung there so many afternoons and evenings were all gone, swallowed up by age and death, and the very streets were filled with aliens who had no part in her halcyon childhood and youth. At the last, they came and took her away, and she went without protest to the home where they placed her, and even found there a measure of small happiness in caring for an older inmate whose need for attention repeated the pattern of those years which followed the death of her father.

But about the house of evenings there lingered for me an air of tragedy; it cried aloud from its walls, so trim and white once more; it huddled under the great spreading oaks; it skulked around the summer kitchen and stood spectral in the windows, like the lost girl who was Ella Bickford, the sweet, pretty girl and her lost love, the one thing in life for which she asked, she who had never asked for anything from that indulgent parent, only to have this one denied her, the lost love and the lost faith, the lost assurance in herself, the lost heart. And there were too, the stern, dour father and the doting, submissive mother—these three—and more remotely all those children who had loved this once cozy house in their early years. But all were second to the aura of loss—of beauty, love, heart —that remained of Ella Bickford, adored by her father, petted by her mother, the demure, obedient girl, papa's darling, his "honey-bunch," with her soft eyes and her tremulous mouth, with her dainty hands and her clean skin, soft to the touch as down—all the lost love, the lost youth, the lost soul of her weeping there at that house in the Sac Prairie night like something tangible in its sadness under the great old oaks, like all the lost youth and all the lost loves hidden in a thousand secret pockets in a thousand nameless villages throughout America.

The Bickford house, like the others, stood in a part of town that was accustomed to tragedy. There, too, was the Cummings house, within a block or two of the Bickford, Baker, and Keysar houses, a house which even after all its one-time owners had gone gave off an air of gracious living, the atmosphere of New England, a house that might have been transported from some New Hampshire or Vermont village and set down here in Sac Prairie. It was low and white, with handsome pillars, so low that it did not seem at first glance to have a second storey; it was Colonial in design, thick-walled, with wooden casings at its wide-silled, small-paned windows. One part of it, the newer part, was of old yellow limestone, indigenous to Wisconsin, but it belonged no less to that earlier portion of the house, the low south wing with its handsome verandah, for it had been skillfully added, with a new porch and pillars put to its front entrance, and green shutters, too, like those on the south wing.

Dr. Cummings, who had built it, was one of the village's first doctors, a Vermonter; with his slender, even-tempered wife he had come out of the east to settle in Sac Prairie and raise their daughter Ellen. They lived comfortably and well, they lived life in so even a tenor that despite all that took place within its walls thereafter, this air of gracious, pleasant living remained, the ironies and japes of life subdued and pushed back, to rise only out of the small memories tied to earlier years. Little disturbed the life of Dr. and Mrs. Cummings, and their daughter, Ellen, grew up sheltered and secure, a lovely, delicate girl with a core of good judgment and practicality. They lived in a shell, unquestionably but indefinably cut off from the world, while Ellen grew out of childhood into adolescence, and ultimately went away to school in the east, from which she came back with George—George Cooper, her husband, so that there were four of them in the house, and not long after, a fifth, young Louis, the apple of his grandfather's eye, his grandmother's "Doody." And with these newcomers, the tenor of life in the Cummings house went on its even way, undisturbed, unrippled, unchanged, for George was energetic and ambitious, with some training in pharmacy, and the cries of a baby were no new thing for the house enclosed by elms before it and oaks behind and around one side.

But something gnawed secretly at George. Perhaps the handsome young man was not content to make progress slowly; perhaps the occasional visits he made back east with his family troubled him in the contrast they afforded to his way of life in Sac Prairie; perhaps some secret difficulty too grave for words beset him, though there was never any sign of it in the drug store where he worked, there was never any public hint that the pleasant, cheerful young man harbored in his breast the cancer of self-doubt or fear. But at home he grew ever more and more quiet, he grew morose and sullen, his temper was unpredictable; there were times he had a hunger to be back at the store, to be alone there in the evenings, to come home late, long after midnight, and none knew what torments of the flesh or spirit he endured, none knew what tempests raged within him, none knew his private Gethsemane. A dark wall seemed to divide him from the happiness of his home, a chasm yawned ever wider between him and the way of life in the old Colonial house on its shaded street where he walked sometimes by night from room to room, evading the old doctor's probing, shying from questions, until one morning he woke up as gay as once he had been, kissed his wife good-bye, dandled his youngster on his knee and was off to work, from which in a few hours he made his leisurely way to a nearby corn-field and shot himself.

After that, something was changed in the house; uncertainty came into its way of life. Doody grew up and went away to school, becoming a college professor with the urge to write, coming home sometimes, tall and handsome in his frock-coated suits, and in Sac Prairie he was beloved of children, for he was always kind to them, with a wonderful sympathy and under-standing and an insight into the child mind few adults seemed to possess. For a while the three of them who had originally been there in the house were alone together, but not for long, the dark brother waited only a short time, and Doody's grandparents were gone, his mother was alone, and then he, too, recovering from a nervous breakdown, came to join her.

Time had had its way with them in that house. Now Ellen was grey-haired, tall, and slender, as fragile as her mother had been,

but with no wound upon her spirit, no loss to her sense of humor;
illness smote her and she lay for months abed, but she rose again,
undaunted, for Doody was home, and Doody was not as once he
had been, something clouded his mind, he walked forth into the
evenings from the old house, swinging his cane and talking to himself, he frightened people, though there was no harm in him, or
he sat for long hours in the recess by the window, writing, his face
half-dark, only his hands and the paper and pen under the green-
shaded lamp visible to passersby. She knew as only a mother can
know that somewhere behind his grimness, somewhere behind his
wildness, somewhere beyond that strange rasping voice which was
his, there was still that cooing baby, that lusty-voiced child, that
darling of his grandparents, her own Doody, and perhaps she
hoped that time, in its healing strides, might erase his bitterness
against those who had mistreated him in his illness, or that the
compulsion in him to put things down on paper might bring
back the boy and young man he had been. She encouraged him
and did not complain, living there with Louis, grown prematurely
white and old.

Night after night, passing by, I saw them there—the old woman
straight in her rocker, reading, Louis writing frantically against
time, writing words he could never sell, in a vain effort to write
his way back to that even tenor of life he had known as a child.
He put down stories which would have been dated a decade before,
he wrote pleasant memoirs, he kept a record of the most trivial
events—but in everything he wrote there was some note of error,
as if a malign destiny conspired against his hope, like a composi-
tion in music in which a cacophonous note constantly repeated
destroys the integrity of the whole. Something gnawed at him, too,
even as something had destroyed his father. Was it indeed, in his
father's life and death—as village rumor had it—that the depletion
of drugs in the store indicated that George had been taking them
for a long time? And was it in Louis's case, as the villagers had it,
that he had endured no crippling mistreatment at all in the sani-

tarium, but that his mind had simply given way, that he was mad because he had always carried the seed of insanity which had only now come to flower? None could say. He wrote for hours, save when he did such little tasks around the house as were his to do, and then, of evenings, he strode forth from that house, wildly swinging his cane, and walked gesticulating and talking to himself, often in a hoarse, disturbing shout, about the streets of Sac Prairie, from upper town to lower town, a tall, robust figure, with his mane of white hair, talking to himself and the wind and the birds and the heavens, a strange, lonely man whose mind was warped by the blighting of his career, the thwarting of his dreams, the throttling of his hopes.

His mother, the gentle Ellen, was resigned at last when her Doody had to be taken away, though she died soon after, and then he, too, died, and the last of them in that house was gone. But the house remained, unchanged in appearance, the air of quiet living still an integral part of it, a pleasant house on a shaded street, seldom reached by the glow of streetlights, and, going past, I could feel still that terrible, urgent striving to justify himself, to create his private world that must have driven Louis—the face half seen, the hands, the pen, the paper—all were still there in the glow of the green-shaded lamp just within that small-paned window at the recess where he always sat, a man half way between darkness and the light, living somewhere in a borderland from which he sought in anguished futility to escape in a struggle all the more desperate because of its intensely private nature, unknown to Sac Prairie, which saw only the frightening exterior of this strange man who had once been charming, blue-eyed little Doody Cooper who used to love to watch the train come up along the river. Beset by the conflicts of their own worlds, they could know nothing of his, they could not know how in his own way he strove to hold the battlements against darkness and despair, how he fought torment and disillusion, how he grappled with his spirit in a place of cosmic space, where alien winds raged and tore, far from Sac Prairie, far from the terrestrial place to which his body was bound. But, terrible as Doody's struggle had been, the long years of quiet, peaceful living were stronger, for their aura lay over what came after.

It was not so with every house in Sac Prairie. Sometimes those who came after left their impress upon the houses in which they lived, perhaps as much because of the persistence of memory in another generation as because of their essential character. The old Oertel house—a great square pile of yellow stone, thick-walled, with deep-set windows, a cold, damp house—was as much the house where Sam Weaver and his boisterous family had lived as it was that of the Oertels, and one remembered in it not so much the Oertels, who were wealthy and lived quiet, dignified lives, as the hard-working Weavers, who rented the house, the druggist and his family, which included his mischievous sons, Ralph, Ben, Fred, and Dick and his little crippled girl, who could not walk until she was five, and then for a time was not well, little Nezzie, who sat in a hayloft and heard the shot that took George Cooper's life and who, later, had a magical experience which touched upon the essential mystery of living for her, when a stranger came to stay in that house, a Frenchman who painted pictures and opened a new world to her, a taciturn, remote man, but withal kind enough to humor the big-eyed little girl who watched and worshipped him, who wept inconsolably when he left mysteriously one night, and who did not understand why next day the house was filled with strange police seeking a quarry escaped in the night. The little girl and the elusive stranger, of whom none ever knew save that he was a man of charm who came into Sac Prairie one night and left on another as mysteriously as he had come—these remained with the old house, and all the happy Weaver children, lending those stone walls a kind of liveliness and a sense of intrigue which it never had in its earlier years and which lingered far beyond the time of the Oertels and the Weavers.

It was so, too, of the Thilke house, set as far back from the street,

along the river, as the Oertel house was close upon it. The Thilke
house was also of stone, with some Vermont marble in it as well;
it too was close to being square, but was rather more rectangular,
and was crowned with a square observatory. It was the fruit of
the labors of the Reverend John Thilke, a hardy German who
had come up the Mississippi and the Wisconsin from New Orleans,
bringing with him his German wife, a young couple who left their
mark on the village through his insatiable appetite for work. He
hated idleness with a consuming hatred, and he had no sooner
come to Sac Prairie than he went out into the rich farmland and
built himself a home where he held Evangelical church services
and Sunday school, and where, in addition of evenings he taught
the English language to the fellow Germans who were his neighbors.

He dispensed another kind of wisdom, too, which some of them
forgot too readily, when he taught them to respect the race and
creed of others, to be tolerant and broad-minded, to keep their
hands occupied. He taught his three daughters to keep themselves
busy—when they were not yet four years old, they learned to
knit, the first of many home arts in which they were instructed.
His energy flowed over the village and the prairie; he bought
land and gave it to the congregation for a church; he organized the
building of the church, taking his income not from preaching but
from his farm, from which at last he retired to build the old
stone house on the river bank for himself and his wife and their
daughters, building it well back from the street with a long, tree-
lined walk sweeping up to it where it stood on a little mound
overlooking the Wisconsin and the hills to the east. He crowned it
with his own observatory because he loved the view, and he
spent what little leisure he had gazing out over the wooded
country, and at night, he looked up at the stars. The house spoke
of rich and fruitful living; it was pleasant to contemplate that
energetic man in his middle years retiring to his observatory atop
the house, escaping wife and daughters, now young ladies, escaping

their suitors, escaping all the wilfully assumed cares to look out upon the stars and the earth around him, which certainly he found good; and I often thought of him there, when I passed that house —as well as of him who came after.

When he died in his prime—"He worked himself to death," his friends said—and his wife followed him soon after, his daughters, all now married, sold the house to Erhardt Kindschi, another retired farmer, a jolly, garrulous man who had made enough money and meant to enjoy himself. He found his chief pleasure in the amber depths of various bottles, jugs, and kegs, for he spent night after night down town and then came home, mounted to the observatory on top of his house, and from that vantage point serenaded Sac Prairie, giving vent to his joy in life in song, bellowed drunkenly forth from the observatory which had once afforded a different kind of solace to its builder. A lusty man, he knew a great variety of songs, most of which were not hymns, and he sang them unrestrainedly into the night, winter or summer. He scandalized his neighbors, he scandalized his church, he helped, indeed, to bring prohibition to his town long before it became a national statute. But he enjoyed life, and something of his joy in life remained with the house, equally as much as Pastor Thilke's love of work and hatred of idleness lingered.

Each in his own way enjoyed life, and the house held tenaciously to that joy of living; it seemed entirely fitting that later it should be inhabited by an Irishman with a large family of active, full-throated children, whose ceaseless activity seemed to belong somehow to the same appreciation of life which moved Pastor Thilke in his works and in his contemplation of earth and heaven, and which sent lusty old Erhardt Kindschi up into his observatory to sing his songs into the night. Children flowed over the house, out into the yard, down into the river, up into the observatory and out over the roof until they grew up and went away and left the house richer still in its joy of life, a kind of demonstrative joy which somehow passed by the Holmes Keysar and Baker houses and so many others in the village.

In those early years the houses of Sac Prairie made a kind of invasion of the village with their atmosphere of time past. I never passed them without feeling something of the lives which went by there within their walls; I always thought of the people who once lived there, of the joy and sadness, the tragedies and lost lives, the days of their years, the gracious living gone now, giving way to another way of life and other lives remote from those who brought the houses into being and who first lived within their walls. The Sac Prairie night was filled with spectres for me—with the strange, childless Keysars, the autocratic Bakers and their too late rebellious Jenny, whom I knew as an old woman, with pathetic Ella Bickford and her lost love, with the Cummings family and the Coopers and frustrated Doody struggling in vain to escape, with the French stranger and crippled Nezzie Weaver, with Pastor Thilke and garrulous old Erhardt Kindschi—all these and many more along every street and lane of Sac Prairie, revenants of time past.

❅   ❅   ❅   ❅   ❅

SOMETIMES spring rode into the village on the wings of bronzed grackles—known only as "blackbirds" to the villagers—announced by their reedy cries and songs come pleasantly to ear on March or April days. Their voices usually rode on the wind on those days of early spring, before robins' caroling and the keening of mourning doves rose commonly along the streets and byways of Sac Prairie. Sometimes a great throng of them occupied the spruce trees in the church park north of the house of childhood, hundreds of them gathered together making small talk, like a conclave of old friends comparing their past days.

Once come back into town, the grackles flocked together for weeks, and then dispersed—not immediately in pairs, but in little *groups of a dozen or a score—and went around examining possible nesting sites, discussing each one with an abandon that echoed along the streets and made villagers aware of the grackles' presence. Many of them fell victim to boys and men with guns, but there was never any dearth of them, and their small talk had such a quality of neighborliness that they would have been much missed if they had gone.*

Their reedy dialogues were primary in the April sunlight, a kind of plainsong that attended the opening of crocuses and squills and, in the hills, trailing arbutus and pasque flowers and hepaticas. Their talk pulsed with the life of Sac Prairie; it was one with back-fence gossip and Water Street banter; it mingled with the cries of children at play and paced the rising tide of events along the streets, swelling in this season.

I always heard it with pleasure, whether it was the commanding hullabaloo of hundreds of grackles in the church park pines, or whether the more intimate notes of nesting birds, and I enjoyed the bold confidence of the birds stalking the lawns in search of food for their young, the sun in a bronze glow off their necks and backs, and their beady eyes equally attentive to forage and to human activity within their range. This familiar talk rang out to the flapping of wash on the lines in March and accompanied the clatter of children on roller-skates; it fell to ear with the assurance of a ticking clock, marking the season as the clock marked the hour, signifying the time being spring, calling forth blade and blossom, announcing the bursting bud-sheath and the pollinating catkin, and always quickening the pulse of those who heard, and filling the too-long wintered heart with the knowledge of spring again, and the promise of April once more abroad in the lanes of Sac Prairie.

Just east of the house of my childhood, by a block, stood the Freethinkers' Park. It occupied an entire village block. It was bordered on the north by three very large clumps of lilacs, which flourished for years until a doltish caretaker let a leaf fire escape him and burn them down, and one of the stands—"the lemonade stand"—used for picnics; another of these stands, known as "the ice-cream stand," stood along the west line facing Lachmund's auxiliary lumber yard long the railroad tracks there. A trim round bandstand stood at the approximate center of the park, and along the sidewalk on the south line rose the great, barn-like structure of the *Freie Gemeinde* Hall, in which the congregation held meetings, funerals, and the like.

It rose from a cozy basement room, used primarily for dinners, and soared upwards for more than two storeys, so that the main floor was a rather cavernous chamber, an acoustic marvel. Park and building were used for many years for the annual school picnic, the major event of the ending of each school year; they were host to all the children from both public and parochial schools, the mecca of a parade, of scores of aging people who came to sit on the benches in the June sunlight and reminisce of the old days, of the onetime *Gemüthlichkeit* which had made for such a mellow, casual way of life in Sac Prairie; and for one day therefore the park was colorful and gay with children and was then again deserted for another year.

The Hall, however, was far more in use. Though, with the inexorable thinning of the congregation with the passage of time because so many members were unmarried, the Freethinkers were declining in numbers and prestige, the Hall itself was used in the years of my childhood and youth for a variety of "doings" from visits of Casperle and his puppet shows—an event of huge importance for the children—to the annual Masquerade Ball. Yet it was not so much the special events which lent meaning to the cavernous old building as it was the regular meetings of the congregation, for, lacking a regular speaker after the initial speakers had passed on, the congregation was in the habit of asking speakers in. The Freethinkers had, in fact, set the cultural tone for Sac Prairie

over many decades; they were an offshoot of the Humanist movement at the University of Prague, and were composed of dissident
aristocrats or upperclass tradesmen from the German countries
for the most part, most of them well educated, and they were not
satisfied with the customary pap to be heard from the lecture
platform.

I grew into the habit of attending their meetings—not regularly,
not as regularly as in those years I went to Mass—but often enough
to be enabled to reach out beyond the boundaries of Sac Prairie.
Many times visiting members came from Milwaukee and Chicago
—men like Leo Weissenborn, who was later to build a house for me
and call it Place of Hawks, an architect who had studied in Paris
and Rome, and had come back to Chicago only after years spent
in the nation's capital, who could speak intimately of the *Little
Review* and the Dill Pickle Club, of *Poetry* and the literary as-
cendance of Chicago during the days of Floyd Dell, Sherwood
Anderson, Edgar Lee Masters, and others, and who supplemented
at first hand the news of the creative arts I had in print through
the mail.

Perhaps of all the pleasant people I met at the Park Hall none
had the presence of Professor Max C. Otto of the University of
Wisconsin, who, as speaker, as teacher, as philosopher reinforced
my directions. *The supreme fact in a biography is ...the story
of how desires channel their way through the natural and social
environment and thus set the current of life....In all hamlets and
towns and cities men and women make terms with desires.* Even
as I, I knew, and the men and women of Sac Prairie whose lives
I had always in view. *The deepest source of a man's philosophy,
the one that shapes and nourishes it, is faith or lack of faith in
mankind.* In quotation after quotation he echoed many of my
innermost convictions—or I adopted his without cavil.

Yet it was no one person, no one meeting of significance that
mattered as much as the general atmosphere of the Park Hall and
the Freethinkers' congregation and the ideals put into practise

there. The very air in that great old building seemed to stand positively for freedom of thought, as were the Park Hall a repository for freedom itself, and the old building stood in the days of my youth as a tangible encouragement to think and act with complete freedom, respecting the rights and happiness of others. Years before, its darkness by night had given shelter to Margery and me, physical shelter, even as now it spread its unseen influence over the wider reaches of the mind.

I used to ask myself whether a man who sat each evening to watch the train come in might not be as much lonely as possessed by the romance of railroading. Surely, I once thought, Mike Weinzierl led a life of quiet desperation. He was a bent old man who shuffled along habitually with both hands in his pockets, a battered and torn felt hat on his head, and clothing which was never very neat or even very clean. His face was seamed and wrinkled; he wore a moustache, which on occasion was tobacco-stained, and was usually grizzled with greying whiskers which were not removed more than once in a fortnight, if that often. His eyes were deep-set and curiously lacklustre; sometimes, in sunlight, they were bland and blue as a baby's; sometimes, in the smoky glow of the firebox of the locomotive in the station, they were black and gleaming beneath his bushy eyebrows.

He lived alone in a little house on the western edge of the village. Yet he had company of a sort, for his neighbors were for the most part spinsters, bachelors, or widows, most of whom lived alone, too. But Mike was more isolated than they; he alone came down to watch the train come in; every evening but Sunday, on which day no trains came into Sac Prairie, he walked out of the afterglow down the tree-naved streets approaching the station, and there he sat down unobtrusively on the loading platform, ignoring as much as possible the tormenting jibes and tricks of the youngsters who were drawn to the depot at train-time from the neighborhood.

I used to see him sitting there; since the station was but a block south of the house of my childhood I went down quite often to watch the train come in. I was in the habit of speaking to Mike even as a boy, haunting the station in those felicitous years of early adolescence when, like as not, the evening train might bring in a letter from Margery, off visiting in the city, or a new copy of *Secret Service*, with a hitherto unrecorded adventure of Old and Young King Brady. He sometimes sat half asleep, or seemed so, with his rheumy eyes closed, his mouth hanging open. He sat thus until the whistle of the train at the bridges across the Wisconsin in the south end of town rose into the evening air; then he gathered into awareness, he grew alert, his eyes flashed open, his mouth closed, and he sat in anticipation, waiting on the train to thunder into the depot, spreading its acrid smoke and the flickering light from the firebox, orange and yellow and red in the evening, briefly dimming the lemon-colored depot-lights.

He never came expecting anyone or anything; the train never brought him relative or friend, letter or parcel; but he sat nevertheless in silent watching, and he sat in this manner until the train went on its way. Then he went home again, or rarely, down town, where he sat in one of the saloons and drank a little, seldom enough to make him tipsy, after which he went home. He had few friends; he had few companions he so much as greeted; he existed in a cocoon of his own, living within himself, as a snail within its shell.

What occupied his hands and thoughts? Day after day in his little house, evening upon evening to watch the lone train come into Sac Prairie, once in a while in a saloon for an hour or two. He seldom played cards, he did not fish, he did not hunt, he did nothing; sometimes he tended a garden, but this was secondary. Once he had been salesman—not a drummer, by any means—but a solitary trudger of the byways, for he sold a palliative named

Alpenkreuter, which made a rich man out of Peter Fahrney and kept Mike Weinzierl as proportionately poor, a palliative which was supposedly good for all aches and pains, from migraine to stomach-ache, and was concocted of sugar and herbs and colored water, and tasted of prune juice slightly watered down and made a little bitter. He walked all over the countryside, as far as Plain, twenty miles west of Sac Prairie, carrying his bottles of *Alpenkreuter* in a gunnysack on his back, an occupation presumably responsible for his bent posture in his last years. This patent-medicine sold well enough to make all this drudgery pay modestly enough to satisfy Mike, and he pursued this end for many years until a retired farmer with a worn Ford got the agency away from him, and Mike was forced to relinquish its sale.

He did not complain, for he was already so well along in years that he could not have walked the country roads much longer. He retired to his little house in Sac Prairie, and thereafter seldom worked except at odd jobs—cleaning up somewhere, or on occasion tending bar for a hunchback in the Astor House, a bartender who evidently felt a certain kinship for this bent-backed old fellow who came to sit now and then in his saloon. The sole feature of his day in his last years was the arrival—and sometimes the departure, which took place not long after, for the train went to Upper Sac Prairie and turned around to go back down the Milwaukee Road spur to Mazomanie—of the evening train.

What could it have meant to him? Romance, perhaps? Or did it stand for everything Mike Weinzierl had never had—the world outside Sac Prairie, the glamor of travel, freedom from drudgery and responsibility?—all those myths so dearly cherished by many men who may never have the opportunity to discover how empty they are. He walked so unsteadily that it was manifest he had some trouble with his feet, shuffling bent-backed, awkwardly, his feet bent inward, actually rocking a little on his feet as he walked, but nothing kept him from meeting the evening train, nothing kept him from his accustomed place on the loading platform and the magic wrought upon him by sight of the powerful black locomotive and the small excitement of the train's arrival—the bustle of the station-master, one-armed Beau Wardler unloading the evening mail, the discharge of freight and express, the descent of passengers. Assuredly he saw more than these aspects of the train's arrival; he read something into this event which no one could ever know because no one else had precisely his pattern of childhood and youth and age to draw upon, and no one can ever correctly discover the motives of the acts of any other human being, since each of us is locked in a web spun of threads which often each of us does not know though we assess their value past the surmises of others.

The evening train carried with it some magic which no doubt assuaged such loneliness as he knew. For many years he was a major part of the evening in Sac Prairie, together with the train, the evening station, the lemon streetlights against the afterglow, the hushing wind in the trees dark against the twilight sky, the voices of children at play—a hunched, almost nondescript old man, shuffling in silence along the streets of a country town which must have faded and altered a little more every day of his declining years, even as it grew upon the awareness of the young springing up about him and all the other aging men and women. He led a life of quiet, uncomplaining solitude, but as long as the evening train came to Sac Prairie, there was a single note of consolation, the effect of which was never evident to any of us who saw him drowsing upon the platform where he waited with the faithfulness of an old dog for the impersonal train which came and went without ever offering passage to that solitary old man who drew from it so much to temper his loneliness.

In my earlier years the Wisconsin was forbidden to me—as it was to most smaller children in Sac Prairie—unless some responsible adult went along, but the fascination of water which is common to all men was not denied me—I was allowed to go fishing at Ehl's Slough, which to the generation before mine was known as Tausend's Slough. In my time, however, Peter Ehl and his small, swift-moving wife lived in the old house of yellow stone and red brick which rose on the east side of Water Street north of the business section of the village, and a short four blocks due east of the house of childhood, from the back porch of which I could be kept in view by my anxious mother almost to the threshold of the Ehl house, for the way led through open field, across the railroad tracks, along the north edge of the Freethinkers' Park, along a little used road to Water Street. The slough lay down the slope immediately behind the house, east of the street, and comfortably west of the river.

Once over the slope I might have been miles from the village, for the slough and the areas adjacent to it were almost wilderness country, penetrated by the sounds of Sac Prairie as from a great distance. The slough was spring-fed. At its upper end it was surrounded by willows, soft maple trees, poplars, alders, and its shallows were given over to reeds and, in hot weather, to sphagnum. A great old elm rose on its west shore, not far north of the Ehl house, and older trees grew between it and the river, though only a row of soft maples stood between the east side of the house and the slough, separating the bank of the slough from lawn and flower gardens and the open doors of the ground floor of that lovely old house, opening into the quarters where the Ehls kept their loom, for they wove rugs and carpets and took well justified pride in their craft. The slough was widest just behind the house; it tapered off at either end. It was not a long slough as sloughs go along the Wisconsin; I suppose it extended less than a quarter of a mile, even counting adjoining ponds.

The slough was all that remained of what had once been a channel of the Wisconsin. All the land from Water Street to the Wisconsin's edge had once been part of the river, but now it was known simply to all of us who haunted it as "the Islands"—First Island was that land from the slough east to where in high water a channel cut through the shoreland there, marking the boundary of Second Island, which was more or less permanently cut off from Third Island, farther north and immediately adjacent to the river, by a deeper channel which did not depend on the spring or summer rise for its existence. At one time deep channels had divided the islands, but sand had filled them, and the shoreland was now virtually but an extension of the land upon which the village stood.

To this secluded haven I was permitted to go fishing. The slough abounded in sunfish, rock bass, and bullheads, and I sought it whenever Father found it impossible to take me to Second Island and the fallen linden where the bluegills were to be caught, or whenever Grandfather Derleth had no time to hitch up old Ben and go out to Lodde's Millpond to fish above the falls— the halcyon occupation of many a summer afternoon. I quickly learned that the sunfish haunted the shallows of the slough's north end, and there I spent many an hour alone, my overalls rolled up, standing in the shallow water catching sunfish—while leeches fastened themselves to my ankles and an occasional lizard rose up to give my imagination the conviction that I had witnessed the coming upriver of young alligators. Here I fished until I had my fill of fish, or until I tired, standing in the willow-sweet air, in the musk of the slough—and no body of water ever approximates the pungent musk of a river-bottom's slough drowsing in the summer sun, with dragon-flies dancing above it, and the shimmering heat bands flickering with the colors of the rainbow just over the water's surface—dreaming the long dreams of boyhood.

And usually, after I had finished, I was thirsty, and I went around to Ehl's for a drink. Most of the time they were at the loom, he and she, and I walked in to their weaving. They were always happy with company, and especially that of children. Peter Ehl was a robust man, with strong eyes, a thick moustache,

and stout muscles; she was small and dark, with gold ear orna-
ments. Both of them had roses in their cheeks. He was a martinet
in his domestic relations, but she seemed not only to bear up
under this cross very well, but actually to invite it; indeed, happy
as she always was when I knew her in those years, she frequently
wept in her last years after Peter's death, which I never knew her
to do before. When first I knew her, I used to think, from the
cast of her features, and the way she carried herself, that she had
some Indian blood in her. Winnebago were still to be seen in Sac
Prairie in those years, come down from Portage and Kilbourn
and points north to camp at the Flats southwest of town, and I
thought it not unlikely that this was possible, though it was not so.

At my entrance, work ceased, and both these amiable old people
pushed forward to wait upon me—and both did, for Mrs. Ehl
brought me the cooling drink of water I asked for, and he, with
a foxy expression on his ruddy face, came forth with a bottle of
wine of his own making, insisting that I try it. I always did, not
alone because I knew he would have been grievously disappointed
if I did not, but because wine and beer were staples of our household, and I learned the use of these potables in moderation long
before I was ten. I often suspected that the old man was hoping
that the wine would go to my head and I might make a fool of
myself, but it never did for I never drank more than one wine-
glass of it; all his blandishments proved unavailing beyond that
measure.

The weaving room was a cool place even on the hottest day,
perhaps because it was a storey below the street level, and thus
grew out of the earth; and between it and the sun to the south was
the entire structure of the older building of yellow limestone,
so that it never had more than the morning sun. It was a place
of seeming great age, for its rafters were very old; they had been
brought down by the great rafts from the lumbering country
in upper Wisconsin decades ago. It was filled with the smell of
cloth, of various fabrics, of rags—all pleasant odors, *warm* odors in

this cool room, and I enjoyed drinking them in while I sat making small talk with Peter Ehl and his dark-eyed wife.

We talked about wine, rug-making, fishing and the merits of various fish; I do not recall that we ever talked about people, except in the customary courtesies of inquiry about families; we talked about the weather, that staple of village conversation, and, inevitably, of the river, for upon the Wisconsin depended the height of the slough—if the river fell, the level of the slough went down, and if the river rose, it went up, and if the river got to flood stage, water flowed, rushing, through the slough, carrying out most of the fish, and perhaps bringing more and other fish in, perhaps not.

And, this pleasant interlude concluded, I took myself off home again, proud of my catch, and secure in the conviction that I would be able to come back to Ehl's Slough at any time to fish, never thinking that in the sure processes of change some day the slough would be no more and even the old house would come down, and the trees be cut unfeelingly away.

The area of the slough, however, was not limited to my summer pleasure. Hugo Schwenker and I haunted the islands; we walked the path that led from Karberg's all the way up into Third Island in all seasons; and we examined all the ponds in the shoreland after every rise in the river, in search of trapped fish—of which we found a great many, including one large carp which I caught by dint of stripping off my clothes and entering the pond to grapple with it. But there was no pleasure, next to fishing the somnolent waters of the slough, greater than sliding over it in winter days on the sleigh Father made for me at the blacksmith shop.

This sleigh was in reality a miniature of a full-sized sleigh, with two sets of runners and a box—the same box that rode the large wheels of the miniature wagon he also made—which held as many as four of us at a time to slide down the slope south of the Ehl house, across the slough, into the snow-clad woods beyond, where, as often as not, some of us had a slow fire going to bake potatoes in the sand beneath. It had not been built for our pleasure —my sister's and mine—alone, but also as a convenient carryall my parents could use to transport children and anything else through the village whenever they went visiting. I never brought this sleigh to the Ehl house in winter but that there were not a goodly number of village youngsters waiting for me—I should say, for *it*, for I was only the instrument of its coming—most of them older boys, who took greater pleasure in it than I did, for, after a few slides, I was perfectly ready to relinquish it to other hands and repair to the ice to slide or to the baked potatoes, for which most of us always carried a little salt.

There were always more young people at Ehl's Slough in winter than in summer. Not many children were so limited in their movements as I at that age, and there was thus a greater area in which the boys could move; Ehl's Slough suited me, and it continued to suit me long after I was permitted to fish from the boulders at the river's edge behind the Electric Theatre, or to go alone to Second and Third Island to fish along the sandy banks for pike and bass, though, if the truth must be told, I suppose this was so because I never was very much of a fisherman—the dry fly was not for me, I was too impatient for it, despite Hugo's scorn, and I was too lazy to cast lures into the water; I enjoyed fishing as a contemplative sport, so I was devoted to a worm on a hook and a corked line and the long, pleasant hours I could while away with my eyes fixed upon the cork on the water and my inner eye fixed upon some dream impossible of attainment, contemplating an enchanted country which had its beginning and its end in that limitless region of my imagination, a country in which, unlike so many of my friends, I was not up and about doing some great and noble deed, but only existing as someone for whom things were done because I existed, a proliferation, no doubt, of the same innate lassitude which prevented me from spending my energies casting for fish.

Ehl's Slough, so easy of access, was exactly right for this kind of dreaming. The sunfish were always easy to catch, and the setting was in its way idyllic in its solitude. Perhaps none of the dreams in which I indulged at Ehl's Slough ever bore fruit—they flocked to me in such numbers that I could no longer recall any one of them—but how pleasant it was to while away those youthful hours in such an enchanted place! Even though the years took me away from its environs, I never failed to recall those happy days whenever I passed the house in later times, and it was always as if I need but step down over the bank, and walk past the great old elm to the northern reaches of the slough to be transported at once into those early years of childhood and youth.

It was no intentional irony that one-armed Beau Wardler was called "Beau"; life had made it so. He had once been a handsome young man, a great sport among the girls, as much pursued as pursuing, though none of my generation would have thought so, seeing him as I was accustomed to see him in my adolescent years. He was then an aging man of indeterminate years, with sharp dark eyes, a deep brown moustache, and hair of the same color. He dressed drably but never shabbily, and in the years that I knew him, he was a man who kept his own counsel.

Beau Wardler was an integral part of those spring and summer evenings, so many of which I spent with Margery, in vain pursuit of that phantasmal ideal of first love. Beau met the evening train and trundled the mail down to the post office in his little cart, a low, capacious box set between high wheels, easy to push even for a one-armed man who seemed old to someone too young to understand the meaning of age, though he could not have been sixty at that time. He always seemed to be a man much given to introspection, though he seldom betrayed any sign of inner turmoil.

He used to stand patiently beside his cart, on rare occasions taking part in the trivial small talk of the platform loafers at the depot, and he seemed even then a solitary figure, though I knew he had sons, I knew them, and to a lesser extent I knew his olive-skinned wife with her ebony eyes and black hair, for all that she did not go out much, carrying on virtually no social life whatever. I remember him as vividly as if it were but an hour ago that I last saw him: that dark figure with the empty sleeve standing against the afterglow, his coat as black as oncoming night, his broad-brimmed hat a relic of past years.

Children and young people are inevitably too taken up with external faces, with making the acquaintance of the world around them, the façades which become manifest to their senses, to see behind these façades. It never occurred to me, I know, that Beau might be unhappy or sadly troubled, that he was anything but content in his role as mail-carrier. At one time, not long before, he had also been the village lamplighter; he had gone about from corner to corner to light the old-fashioned kerosene lamps then used in Sac Prairie, but within the years just past, electricity had come to the village, and the kerosene lamps were relegated to oblivion, together with Beau Wardler's role in their maintenance. Other children before my time had known him on his rounds with his ladder and the long taper he used; now a new generation came to know an older man who made his daily trips to and from the depot bearing the mail and was as much an aspect of life in Sac Prairie as any other.

Perhaps it was because he was so regular in his duties that he could so easily be taken for granted. His taciturnity and solitude in reality concealed a growing confusion and despair within. Perhaps he was one of those incredible people who have such an inclination toward misfortune that they are thought to attract it because some flaw in their characters opens them to disaster. All the brightness in Beau's life came early; perhaps from the day he lost his arm in an accident and suffered the concomitant blow to his ego he began a slow but unhalted decline in mental outlook which made him an easy prey to the events of his later years.

The young girl he had married soon turned into a termagant; with each child that came to them, she arrogated unto herself more and more authority, and slowly Beau began to be superfluous in his own household. The once garrulous young man became increasingly silent and bitter; he had no one with whom to share his troubles; his wife, having helped create them, could not be consulted; his growing children were impatient; his old friends had thinned in ranks and were scattered.

But his wife was not alone Beau Wardler's trouble, nor the rankling wound of the loss of his arm and the blow to his self-esteem and the pride of any healthy animal in his appearance. The little money he had managed to save out of a life of industry which had driven him to work whenever work offered itself to him was unwisely invested. When Kuoni & Son, a local store and quasi-bank, went into bankruptcy, a large part of his savings was lost. After this blow, he strove more vigorously than ever to recoup his losses, but he never could, no matter how earnestly he tried. Yet, despite the unbroken succession of misfortune which was his lot, he continued to hope, and this sustained him; he hoped against odds which became increasingly insurmountable, against the shrill invective of his wife, against the children's lack of awareness, and he carried on as best he knew how.

He bore his burdens in silence for years. How many years, no one could guess. All the while he hauled the mail to and from the depot, all the while he made his quiet responses to the greetings of the young lovers he sometimes passed, and the children running for home in twilight's last hour, all the while he went his solitary way, discharging his obligations in dignified silence, Beau Wardler walked in the shadow of a loneliness all the more intense because those he loved were incapable of understanding the grief within him.

He too had his hopes, his ambitions, his ideals; like everyone else, he had come to one disillusionment after another but, unlike many other men and women around him, he lacked other dreams and ideals with which to replace those lost, and the compromises he was forced to make were demeaning. Either because he was stoic or because he was proud, nothing of the terrible struggle for spiritual survival which went on inside him was ever allowed to show. He continued to do what work he could, he went on his way with the fixity of purpose commonly associated with men of the highest integrity. He was not much given to laughter, but he was always sympathetic with children.

Perhaps the absence of laughter ought to have given away his inner conflict—this and the distance in his eyes. There was still one solace left to Beau Wardler: the last of his savings invested in a bond company in nearby Madison. When this bond company, too, failed, and swept away the remainder of the little money he had worked so hard to earn, Beau hauled the mail for the last time one evening, then went home and hanged himself in the cellar beneath his little house out on the edge of town.

More than most other men and women in Sac Prairie, he could see the world once he had enjoyed and loved growing away from him without compensation for its loss, he could witness the spreading darkness of his circumstances, he could see how he was slowly, inevitably becoming an alien in the years of his age, as so many men and women become with each increasing year. None knew how great were the burdens he had not shared; yet most people suspected how terrible they must have been to him, to have driven him to this dark destiny. Once he had accomplished the task of destroying himself, it was borne in upon people who missed him that this deed had lurked in his thoughts for a long time, that he had had recourse to it only after his last island of security had vanished.

Dead, he became even more a part of the Sac Prairie night than he had been alive; the children who had known him, the young people who had grown accustomed to meeting him, met him still in minds and hearts—that taciturn, one-armed old man, with the direct dark eyes framed in crow's-feet, and the ruddy face—trundling the mail down the nocturnal streets, a man who had been as solitary in life as he now was in death.

❋ ❋ ❋ ❋ ❋

QUITE *early in life I fell into the habit of making a daily excursion each evening into the bottoms of the Wisconsin—"the marshes"—walking along the tracks of the Milwaukee Road toward Mazomanie for a distance of two miles or so and back, sometimes by way of the bridges over the west channel and the back river or dwindling east channel of the Wisconsin, sometimes by way of the highway nearby, sometimes following the east shore of the Wisconsin to the railroad embankment at the east end of the back river bridge. The tracks led through lowland areas for some miles, east of the Wisconsin, lowland that was a rewarding diversity of woods, sloughs, meadows, and marshland, where great fields of Joe-Pye weed shone lavender in late summer and autumn, meadows flamed green in spring, oak groves vied with willows and osiers, and the whole was framed by a low moraine just east of the rounding trestle which bent from the area of the woods at the bridges toward the south, to the higher range of the Wisconsin Heights to the southeast, the heights and slopes once held by Black Hawk in the Sauk War of 1832. The tracks led past places which had long had names or which were given new ones by Hugo Schwenker and myself—past Dead Dog Hole in the back river, past the Ice Slough, the Spring Slough, over which curved the long trestle, the brook and the Brook Trestle, the second brook with its accompanying trestle, the Mid-Meadow Trestle, the Triangle Lane Crossing, and finally Heiney's Crossing, which was usually the turning place.*

It was a country teeming with wild life. When first I walked there, I had little conception of the vast diversity of nature. I went at first to get a little away from myself and the occupations of the day; but soon a normal curiosity got the better of me, and I went quite frankly to learn, a slow process by the method of trial and error.

There were errors, many of them. The first time I heard spring peepers (then called hyla pickeringii, *now known as* hyla crucifer), *I thought birds made that fluted choir. By all the marks of identification afforded in the best guides for ornithologists, I gravely and certainly identified the song sparrow as the vesper sparrow; it was not until years later that I learned how similar the songs might sometimes be. For an even longer time I made the absurd error—for lack of seeing them and of any other method of identification—of thinking the trilling of the toad the voice of the tree frog,* hyla versicolor. *And for a little while after sight of the first beaver to invade the Sac Prairie country in over six decades, I thought it an overgrown muskrat; its tail, however, was not visible during that time, and the hour was dusk.*

A slow process, but infinitely more pleasurable than any other method could have been. It led to a yearly calendar of spring voices, arrivals, autumn and late summer departures, which I soon began to keep. It spaced the year, measuring time, as it were, on a different clock, dividing the calendar into seasons of birds and frogs. Every winter was made endurable by anticipation of that hour in March in which the kildee *of killdeer or the* conqueree *of redwings first rose to the ear, of the first peeper's wavering fluting, of the first woodcock's aerial dance, sight of which remains far more satisfying than any mere personal achievement, for there is something about the launching forth of the woodcock in its aerial dance that is ineffably stirring— seeing that small, almost grotesque figure, soaring ecstatically aloft in an immemorial rite, twittering and chirping, flying in dizzying circles ever up and up, faster and faster, only to drop at last to call again and repeat its dance. There is something divine about this rite, something which beggars all description and transcends any picture—the dark body hurtling up against the afterglow among the budded, leafing trees in an ancient pattern which is an ecstasy of nature before which a man must stand in humility and wonder, and the knowledge that here is a thing of pure, unalloyed beauty which is vouchsafed only to those who learn, however slowly and ineptly, to use eyes and ears. Nor is it*

necessary to know that this is part of the bird's mating ritual, which becomes manifest soon—it is only necessary to see and hear, to appreciate, and to recognize that somewhere within there is a pulse, remote and no less wild, that beats in harmony with that wild heart above.

In this haven of birds and frogs and lesser beasts I walked the evenings away, year on year, except when mosquitoes plagued me too much or the cold became too intense. I walked the cinder-pungent railbed through the evensong of birds and the primitive cries of the batrachian population of this lowland and found there

not only surcease from the day's tribulations but often also resolu-
tion of creative problems and balm for the oppressing irritations of
existence common to all men.

That the placid, pink-cheeked face, so markedly Teutonic,
which Father Aloysius Schauenberg presented to the world might
conceal the most poignant kind of spiritual isolation, the isolation
of the informed, intelligent human being among the Philistines,
very probably never occurred to the people who met him on the
streets of Sac Prairie. His strong blue eyes looked out upon the
world from under a clear brow crowned by white hair; he had a
broad Roman nose, a firm, fine-lipped mouth, and his skin had
the texture of a child's. There was never a cloud to mar the
serenity of his features. In build he inclined a little toward portli-
ness, but he was not a large man, of less than average height,
dignified in his manner, as befitted a man of the cloth, and he
maintained that dignity whether he was at reading the Mass or
whether he sat in a restaurant booth over a cup of his favorite
coffee royale.

Father Schauenberg had come to Sac Prairie soon after the turn
of the century, still a comparatively young man. He had behind
him an excellent secular education at the Universities of Bonn and
Heidelberg; as a graduate, he had come to America to take a
position as secretary to the Bishop of Chicago, and this amiable
old man had presently convinced the younger to join the priesthood. He had therefore the benefit and advantages of both secular
and clerical training, and was the more balanced man in all he did
because of it, since he did not suffer, as some of the clergy did,
from training which began with youth in its most formative
years and shut away everything secular, thus warping the ability
to make balanced decisions and predisposing clergymen to blind,
unthinking obedience to hierarchical authority.

For a while he continued to serve the Bishop, but soon he was ready to assume the duties of a parish and went into northern Wisconsin as a young pastor. Whenever he recalled his first parish, in his last years, he spoke of it as an idyllic place. "It was a wilderness parish, literally," he would say. "A paradise filled with game. I could go out before breakfast and shoot a grouse—just enough for a meal. I never shot more. There were Indians there, too—fine people." He moved to another parish nearby, stayed there a little while, then came to Sac Prairie, where he faced a formidable parish debt and other obligations, all of which he met and retired in the fifteen years he served the parish as its pastor, after which, developing angina pectoris, he relinquished the active life of a priest, made a trip to Germany, and settled down to spend his remaining years in the village to which he had become attached, reading his daily Mass, occasionally substituting for an ailing priest or helping out on special holy days in his own former parish or in others of the vicinity.

Save for an impatience with children and arrogantly stupid people, he was an admirably balanced man. He frightened most of the children in the parochial school by the brusqueness of his manner, but, though he was firm in administering justice, he was a stern and fair man who could be kind, and often was. His impatience stemmed from a sensible appreciation of the value of time, which few others seemed to have, and I cannot recall that his treatment of children ever resulted in anything traumatic. He had no theory-born ideas about sparing the rod; the erratic and often witless dabblers in child psychology were casually brushed aside, as was fitting, for he adhered to a strict code of punishing misdeeds and inculcating the young with a healthy respect for reasonable authority and intelligence.

He was seldom anything but understanding. I often came to think in later years that he understood people too well, for he came to a greater tolerance in his last decade, though it was very probably not the result of any compromise with his ideals, rather the amused resignation of a man wise enough to know that, though the degree of illiteracy might diminish, the essential nature of the human animal did not alter very much. He could understand the ignorance of the common man and would not pass judgment upon him; he could not abide the arrogance of the semi-literate and made short shrift of them, brushing them off with decisive bluntness. He had doubtless undergone many a catharsis, he had surely been seared more than once by the corrosive fires of his engagements with the Philistines, whose numbers were ever increasing, and he had realized long ago that even the attempt to meet them on common ground was folly.

In his prime, he spent a good deal of his time fishing and hunting; his companions—testifying to his lack of any of that picayune prejudice which infects so many of the presumably elect—were most generally agnostics or Freethinkers, who were among his best friends throughout his life in Sac Prairie, much to the bewilderment of a considerable portion of the Catholic laity who had been given the childhood impression that all non-Catholics were by the will of God doomed for eternity either to hellfire or Limbo. By the standards of his parish, Father Schauenberg was destined to be lonely in heaven; what his flock did not know and never suspected was that he could not have been any lonelier in a theoretical afterworld from which his friends of this life were excluded than he was in Sac Prairie, where his friends died, one after another, and he was left largely alone among the Philistines, save for an occasional younger man who had the benefits of a wider education and could carry on a discussion on a plane Father Schauenberg chose without recourse to the superstitious and archaic conventions to which the Philistines paid homage.

I used to encounter him in the barber-shop, in the post office, or in the restaurant where he ate dinner, and lent both an ear and support to his credos, as he did to mine, for they were not very dissimilar. He was unalterably opposed to any form of dictatorship, and devoted to that of the truth alone; he had pronounced and positive beliefs about man's relation to his world and to his afterlife; he scored the Church in political action, the hypocrisy of bishops and priests, the petty simony practised by priests within reach of Sac Prairie, and laughed at the bishops' plaintive ranting against secularism, laying the blame, if there must be blame for such trends in thought, squarely at the door of the Church's own secular materialism. "When I was studying for the priesthood," he was wont to say, "we were taught to think. Nowaday, they're just taught to obey—like sheep." I asked him on one occasion whether he had ever regretted taking orders. "If I had to do it over again," he answered thoughtfully, "I'd become a surgeon. You can cure the body."

So he had come to this kind of bitter disillusionment; he had learned that the body might be cured, but the soul needed more than a priest to lead it to paths of righteousness and honor. A discerning, intelligent man, a man of sound judgment made with caution and consideration could not have helped learning that the flesh and spirit of his fellowmen, the sheep in his flock, were sadly weak, and that any alteration for the better in the pattern depended on something within. Perhaps at one time justice and honor had motivated the acts of the mass of men; but in his own years it was often painfully apparent that envy and greed, accompanied by its concomitant lust for power, ran like a cancer through the fabric of human society. "The atomic bomb has aroused fears that mankind may be destroyed," he observed in the last year of his life. "No one has demonstrated why it should be saved."

He was not cynical; the flame of hope still burned deep within him. He had lived to see the ladies of his parish vie with one another for the favor of his presence at their dinners, and cover one another with vituperation and slander if he chose someone else's table; he had survived being lionized by an Amazonian woman whose past life had been colorfully checkered; he endured the pulpit attacks of one of his successors, a narrow, materialistic man who was not worthy to clean Father Schauenberg's shoes. He went about in his last years as if he had weathered every storm, and the buffets of wind and weather, no matter of what magnitude, could no more trouble him.

But he was troubled, nevertheless; he was as profoundly troubled as any sensitive and intelligent man must be in the face of the decline in public and private morality which is always symptomatic of the beginning of a society's decay; he was disturbed by the increasing lack of responsibility, both personal and social, in the rising generations; and he was dismayed by the thinning and fading of personal dignity and Christian honor in the priesthood of which he was himself a member. More than this, he was deeply lonely; he corresponded with relatives in Germany who had survived the second World War, and to whom he sent countless packages of food; he visited a few friends in orders here and there in Wisconsin and as far away as Kentucky, but their ranks were steadily thinned by death; he read his papers and his letters; and he strove to live without thinking overmuch of the vast seas of ignorance which swirled all around him.

He was cordial if met on the streets, but he was not given to talking much, perhaps because he had so often been reminded that few of the people he was likely to meet in Sac Prairie could have anything to say that he might want to hear. For thirty years he had given himself to the trivial affairs of little people to whom these affairs were of vital importance, and he had treated them with the same importance; he had discharged his obligations to the cloth faithfully and honorably; he could no longer endure the concern of his fellowmen about the superficialities of good and evil which troubled them so futilely, and he made little attempt to do so unless forced by the laxity of their pastor to heed the helpless and give them what spiritual comfort and physical assistance he could, for, not only did he still serve as their confessor, but, despite his living on a very small pension, he was generous with what little he had, in obedience to the Lord's adjuration to the priesthood to be not afraid of poverty.

His appearance alone inspired respect and confidence. The unwavering eyes, the firm, steady gaze, the expressive mouth, even the cigar he habitually smoked, combined with the conventional black suit and topcoat he usually wore to lend him substance and dignity. He was in the habit of coming down town once or twice a day from the place where he stayed, pausing here and there, and going back home again, seldom having found a kindred spirit in this brief peregrination. His poise was seldom publicly ruffled, though on one memorable occasion he berated a woman at the polls for saying she had voted against Roosevelt because she had found it hard to buy as much butter and sugar as she wanted, by shouting in a loud and embarrassingly carrying voice, "Woman, you're too stupid to vote!"

His temper was historic in its occurrences. He held it in quite well, but whenever he encountered one of the Philistines holding forth with bumptious arrogance and in abysmal ignorance on a subject of which he knew considerably less than a South Sea aborigine, he was certain to explode volcanically if exposed to such vociferous ignorance for any length of time, as he was on occasion in the barber-shop while he waited to be shaved. On such occasions, even as he had done with the slow-wittedness of pupils in the parochial school during my own childhood, his thick neck slowly turned pink, then a wave of red washed up from his collar to his cheeks and temples, and finally a mottled, almost purple color made its appearance—after that the deluge of his scorn and wrath. "*Dummkopf! Lümmel! Kalbmoses!*" he was in the habit of shouting in a deafening voice. He would launch into a bitter denunciation of loose-tongued ignorance which usually served to cure any street-corner or bench authority for weeks thereafter, much to the edification of his listeners. "*Esel! Rindvieh! Schafskopf!*" His outbursts, far from encouraging resentment, were of such magnitude that they only increased the respect in which he was held by all save those unfortunate victims of the wrath they had brought upon themselves.

But he did not much indulge his temper; he did so only when the pressure of arrogance and stupidity became unbearable. For the most part he was content to pursue his course without troubling himself about the affairs of his fellowmen. Having learned long ago that his ideals, however sound they were, were no longer applicable to the human race in its present stage of development, he retired into himself and lived out his years without seeking to reform a society, the average member of which was too hopelessly a Philistine to be inculcated with anything which did not have an immediate or foreseeable reward in coin of the realm.

I knew what solitudes lay behind his bemused eyes when he spoke to me and shook his head over the state of the world. He understood that the ranks of the Philistines had grown and were swelling with each moment; he knew that men of good will were lessening in numbers; and he knew too well, with the poignance inherent in the inevitability of death, that his life had gone by, that there was nothing he could any longer do to stem the tide of Philistinism, and that, looking back now, there was so very little he had been able to do despite the high hopes and ideals with which he had ventured into an increasingly materialistic world from the Bishop of Chicago's haven. It was understandable that he should look back to his first parish as an earthly paradise; he had not yet then seen the world as it was, the grossly material quest of the Philistines had not yet found its way into that remote village in Wisconsin's north woods.

He was a leader of men, but there was no one left who could understand his leadership, who held to the same principles; and even the professing Catholics of his later years seemed to him to subscribe to an altered Christianity, changed by vacillating perspectives among the bishops and priests themselves. He was almost the last of the little group of men he had associated with, and when at last he died and was given a pompous and meaningless funeral in the tradition of the Church, his passing left a vacancy in Sac Prairie no one could fill.

❋　❋　❋　❋　❋

A GREAT part of the delight of the song sparrow's threnody, of the lark's lyricism, of the redwings and the hyla choir, is that the enjoyment of each is purely a fortuitous circumstance. None can be ordered to taste, as it were; no man in this north temperate zone can go out any time he pleases and hear what he likes of these wild voices. To be sure, there are days and evenings in spring when all can be heard almost without end, but these do not take place nearly as often as a man would like; he must seize the moment, he must take every opportunity to present himself at the place and in the time when the likelihood of hearing these voices is greatest.

It is in just this element of chance that so much of the pleasure of hearing each spring the first killdeer or the first woodcock lies; it is something that rises out of the spring evening day after day in the area of residence, and a man pursues it day in, day out, walking by and hearing nothing, until one unknown moment of one unknown hour the familiar voice, lost since the spring gone by a year ago, rises once more to announce the new vernal season, and the pattern comes full circle to begin anew. There is something in a man's blood that springs up just as the sap rises each spring, as the birds give forth song once again, as the creatures stir themselves at the end of winter—something that marks man's kinship to all earth.

Until the moments and the hours have all been gathered in, until all the voices of spring have sounded, the element of magic lingers—and even afterwards there remains always the sense of expectancy, for every evening in the country offers some potential

*new or strange pleasure, which, like all that have gone before, is
kin to the pulse which beats as one among birds and men and trees
and earth itself.*

In later years, Carrie Patchen was remembered as "the one who
met the trains." Her older sister, Elva, taught school, but Carrie
never seemed to do much but walk down into town from the
Patchen house and meet the trains. She was a pretty girl, dark
and with flowing hair, vivacious, and in her eyes a kind of
distance, as if she were forever looking beyond the mundane
circumstances of today into some future filled with promise
of adventure or romance, of love of drama transcending the
prosaic events of life in Sac Prairie.

She never wore the same dress twice in a day, and changed
as much as three times—each time she came down town, whether
to shop, or to meet the trains, though, as the years wore away,
she began to show a partiality for a dress of purple and lavender,
with which she invariably carried a sunshade of the same colors,
in which she went, flamboyant, to meet the trains—that brought
to Sac Prairie in those days the drummers who fanned out into the
countryside, to Witwen, Black Hawk, Leland, Denzer, to Harris-
burg, Cassell Prairie, even to Plain—to sell their employers' wares.
It was the drummers Carrie went to meet, and it was with them
she was often seen later in the day, in the balmy evenings in Sac
Prairie and late at night at Lodde's millpond and the Flats, at the
Ferry Bluff and Sugar Loaf, along the river roads, spooning in the
hired buggies from the livery stable.

Once Carrie was a fresh, clear-eyed girl who used to go with
her father, a boatman on the *Ellen Hardy*, up and down the
Wisconsin when the boat made its run. She belonged, people said,
to "a good family"; her uncle was superintendent of the schools,
and the Patchens lived in a fine old house down a little way
from Water Street and not far back from the river, two blocks or

so, on a little rise from which the hills rising east of the Wisconsin were clearly visible in all their green beauty. The doors of the best houses were open to her, and she stood on the doorstep of the world, enchanted by its invitation but hesitant to take it, as if she were reluctant to leave Sac Prairie for that unknown country beyond the limits of the community.

She was a modest, soft-spoken girl, shy and easily embarrassed. She fled from school at every occurrence that upset her—a sudden coughing spell, a feeling of faintness, a misspelled word—fled with cheeks flaming on the edge of tears. She was eager for life; she reached out to it, perhaps, with increasingly frenetic anxiety, so that something of her fear that she might miss what life had to offer communicated itself to those near her, and the pattern of her life became one of casual dalliance which held no meaning beyond the immediate afternoon or evening of its occurrence. The picnics at the millpond, the ice-skating on the frozen Wisconsin of a winter afternoon, the long moonlight rides along the country lanes west of town—with the harness salesman or the man from Butler Brothers or the drummer who sold shoes to the Sac Prairie merchants—had only a present and led to no future; the beaux of those years bought her trinkets, candy, flowers, but none offered what she most wanted—a ring.

Her impatience shocked the staid. One by one, the doors long open to her were closed, and after her father died, Carrie lived in a village which had become one of closed doors where once there were pleasant openings into sunny rooms reaching back to childhood. Whispers about Carrie rippled along the shady streets, fanned out from the depot, where every villager who traveled by train—and many who took the *Ellen Hardy*, which docked not far away—saw Carrie walking slowly along the station platform under her purple sunshade, gazing downriver in the direction from which the train must come. Carrie was "fly," people said, or she was "not nice" or a "man-chaser" which "no lady" ever was, perpetuating a myth which gave the lie to reality.

But within her heart Carrie Patchen was still that eager young girl, shy, easily-embarrassed, soft-voiced and gentle, who was anxious for the taste of life, both the bitter and the sweet, before she must look into the face of death. And life for Carrie Patchen came in on the train twice daily from Mazomanie and presently rode out on it again.

She spoke to no one of her hopes and dreams, but pursued her solitary way with undivided persistence. It did not seem to her that life and romance could exist in such a little town as Sac Prairie; love, passion, heroism, tragedy, comedy, courage, eternal hope, faith, hatred, jealousy, violence, murder, perversion, irony —all burned and shone and smouldered all about her, but she saw them not, she saw only the train that brought up from Mazomanie the promise of romance and adventure, the train—old 1040 and the orange coaches of the Milwaukee Road—that held out to her twice every day save Sunday an invitation to some new experience, some untouched emotion, the fulfilment of a dream.

Her teens went past, her twenties washed away, her thirties came and went—and always Carrie made an attractive figure on the streets and lanes of Sac Prairie, a taller than average woman with thick dark hair, small-breasted, with a wasp waist "nipped in" above her wide, feminine hips. She flowed along, always beautifully dressed, looking as fresh as a violet with morning's dew still trembling upon it, and many an eye turned upon her from behind a blind, from over a shoulder, disapproving though it might be, concealed a smouldering envy which betrayed itself only in the anger of condemnation visited upon her.

For a long time she seemed ageless; she seemed the very spirit of the youth which haunted the countryside and the river of moonlit nights, gay, charming, beautiful to look upon with her flawless skin and her dark eyes and her fine teeth, but defiant of convention, daring to do what it was not considered genteel to do, seemingly unaware of the formidable doors closed against her since she had never sought to enter those austere houses in which, she was sure, life pulsed at its lowest ebb, bound to conformity by the narrowest of laws—but as Carrie slipped into her forties, age began to touch her in scarcely visible lines in her smooth face, in fugitive grey in her hair. Now, with Father and Elva both gone, Carrie and her mother lived alone, each living life on its own terms —the old lady, as a member of one of the founding families, still welcome in every house in town, Carrie a stranger within those same walls, an outcast among her own, an exile in her own country who never shed a tear or knew a qualm of envy or a twinge of pain at the doors closed to her, valuing her freedom more, her compulsion to seek life where she believed it must hide, to tempt romance and adventure to come to her from the trains that rolled into town. Her eager eyes scanned each strange face as it came within the range of her vision off the train, as if this might be the one through whom the way to excitement and glamor, thrills and high romance were open to her.

But the drummers who took Carrie out were somehow not unlike her classmates or the young men about town, the young men who loitered at the drug store or the post office and sometimes whistled at girls going by; they spoke the same lines, they set the same scenes, they acted out the same comedy as had they come to Sac Prairie only to show how very much alike they were. Undaunted, Carrie never gave up hope. She lived in this dream year after year, decade upon decade—through her forties and her fifties.

And then, one day, her mother died quietly, and Carrie, who had never known life, who had always seen romance and adventure eluding her eager fingers, understood suddenly that the last barrier between her and death had been taken away. She buried her mother and met the trains no more, locked herself into her house from which she could see only the stack of the locomotive and its smoke on its way into and out of Sac Prairie, her dreams dissipating like the black smoke that poured so thickly from the stack and was thinned to nothingness by the slightest wind even as she watched. And was this not, too, her life?

Carrie was not long satisfied with mourning. If she had followed a will-o-the-wisp, it was never too late to turn her back upon it. Even at sixty, Carrie was a handsome woman, her figure more ample now, but her face still serene and attractive. She turned from the drummers of her dreams, searched the village and met the eyes of a widower her own age—and smiled. They were married at once, and Carrie turned her back on Sac Prairie and the doors for so long closed against her, slipping away with her husband, never to come back, leaving only the vivid memory of that beautiful girl who met the trains, a ghost in lavender and purple forever under her sunshade in a place as changeless as the fading photographs in an old album.

❋ ❋ ❋ ❋ ❋

NOT long after I had made the decision to remain in Sac Prairie to establish a post from which I could look out upon the world, I took to celebrating each vernal equinox that was cloudless by going into the marshes to watch the rising of Arcturus, the bringer of spring, the ploughman's star, going in over the bridges or coming up the tracks from Heiney's Crossing in the pregnant March twilight, walking into the deepening dark through a night usually soundless save for the first quavering cry of a peeper or the low cooing hoots of a long-eared swamp owl or the challenge of barred owls from the deep woods not far away, nights of fragrant thaw smell in the nostrils, crisp with frost in the darkness, of water and the wet earth, of cinders and railroad ties, and sometimes the medicinal pungence of pussy willows, always with my eyes fixed upon the northeast rim, under the Big Dipper's handle, watching for the amber eye of Arcturus to rise above that black line of hill or tree.

*Whether the weather was cold or warm made no difference;
if it were warm I dawdled and listened to the sounds of the night;
if it were cold I kept moving, up and down, forward and back.
Sometimes I reached the Spring Slough Trestle, sometimes I
turned at the Triangle Lane Crossing to look toward the line of
dark hills above which the star would rise, never deserting this
rite, but waiting upon the rising of Arcturus as were its amber
glow the announcement of the season of growth itself.*

*To this pagan rite I gave myself every March, and felt a primi-
tive harmony with the opening earth and the night and the
stars, marking each rustling in the grass of the open embankment
where a mouse or vole moved about, taking note of that early
peeper sending forth his fluting song into the chill, uncertain air,
lending an ear to the colloquy of owls—the bell-like sounds of
screech owls, the ringing hoots of barred owls or great horned
owls, the persuasive, ventriloquial calls of the swamp owls—marking the swing to westward of Orion and Taurus and Leo, the
turning up of the Dipper, the declining glow of Sirius, and
knowing myself integral in this setting, knowing that I, too,
waited, as the least bud, the least root, upon the rising of that
amber star over the northeast hill, its first gleaming quickening
the pulse as the morning's sun would start anew in every root the
flowing of the sap.*

On rare occasions in the last year of her life, I encountered on
the streets of Sac Prairie of a summer afternoon Miss Poosey
Lachmund, a frail, almost wraith-like woman in her sixties, with
greying hair and a kind of birdlike appearance. She walked
slowly because her heart was bad, she had had a "stroke" and had
come back from New York to die in her native village, and,
seeing her, you could not readily believe her in any way a woman
of some mystery—yet so she was, for she had been gone from
Sac Prairie almost forty years, lost in the anonymity of the city,

without a word of her activity in the metropolis of New York.

Once, long ago, she had been the baby of the Lachmund family, the youngest of seven, and her autocratic old father had gazed upon her with an unaccustomed fondness. The last child to come into that family, she was his "little papoose," she was his darling, the old man showed her that irrational, withal sentimental attachment which so commonly stems from an aging parent, flowing forth to the last child of his loins, regardless of the possible animosities and tensions, the division of loyalties and affections within the family circle. In the effulgence of his favoritism she basked until his death; she was already then a young lady, petite, thin-faced, not attractive, nor yet unattractive, but curiously bland of appearance, compelling neither admiration nor repulsion, fastidious in manner, quiet and somewhat reserved, though capable of enjoying herself in the various ways in which young women of the century's first decade took their pleasure. She made some effort to support herself, and failed—she attempted to sell bonds, and soon involved her friends in losses; the antagonism of her older sister, Irma, whom she had displaced in her father's affection, flowered at the same time, and she departed unobtrusively from Sac Prairie and made her way to New York.

There she was lost for almost two-score years. If on occasion a Christmas greeting was received from her, there was no word of her occupation, her address—nothing to tell what she was doing. Visitors to New York sometimes accidentally encountered her; she passed the time of day with them, no more. Once she was seen in the company of a man, and again; so the legend grew in Sac Prairie that there was "a man in her life," and people talked about "Poosey's beau" in that knowing way which is but the indication of a lack of knowledge, creating a nebulous man according to their own fancies and endowing Poosey's mysterious existence in an almost equally mysterious milieu with this creature of their imagination. Once, too, she was met in bitter weather

walking the streets of New York, cold and shivering, by a fellow
native, somewhat older than herself, who stopped and inquired
of her health and was told that the "place" where Poosey stayed
was having furnace trouble, it was as cold inside as out, and
so asked Poosey to come and stay with her until the repairs had
been made; and, though Poosey was noncommittal, as usual, yet
she did show up one day, dressed as if for a visit, and there she
stayed for thirty days, leaving the house every morning after
breakfast, and returning every evening for thirty days, at the
end of which time she did not return. But in all that time she
uttered no word of her occupation, of her daily destination, of
the place where she lived; she was capable of taking her breakfast
and supper with her hostess every day for a month and never
saying anything at all about the most prosaic events of her days.

She lived in this remote, inscrutable fashion, secretively, until
ill health overtook her, and, a diagnosis disclosing a heart condition,
she wrote to her older sister, asking her to come to New York
to get her. Thus she returned to Sac Prairie, as unobtrusively as she
had left, came back to take up her abode with the sister whose
once great animosity had served to give her reason for departure
years before. And with Irma she lived in the same withdrawn
secrecy, saying never a word of her years in New York, expressing
no curiosity about the affairs of her family or of the village
during her absence.

What had she done in the vastness of the city? What role had
been hers? Kept woman, secretary, clerk, Madam, bookkeeper,
procuress, seamstress, hostess, saleswoman, buyer? She might have
been any one of them; there were no telltale stigmata. She
looked the same on her return, save for having aged, as on the
day she had left: thin, frail, bird-like, quiet, her bland features
neither attracting nor repelling; so that you thought of her as
just existing, hardly more. She rode about in Irma's car, unper-
turbed at her sister's neurotic recklessness as a driver; or she

walked with Irma, or alone, keeping herself to herself, answering every greeting, but never saying anything about her life away from Sac Prairie.

She existed perhaps in the world she had left behind her; and perhaps in that world she had lived in before she went to New York, the world of her childhood which was Sac Prairie at the turn of the century, a tree-bowered Wisconsin town, a lovely village on the bank of the Wisconsin, where she had been her father's "little papoose," the center of her world, the focus of its affection, little Poosey Lachmund, the baby of the family. Perhaps no other world had ever really existed for her. None could say, and never by so much as a misspoken word did Poosey betray herself.

Of what her life with Irma in that house on the shore of the Wisconsin was like, no one knew. The old antagonism was not dead, for all that it was overlaid now by the need to care for Poosey; it smouldered always in the background, manifesting itself in autocracy, impatience, irritability, all of which Poosey could endure wordlessly, knowing her sister's understandable curiosity, but secure in that knowledge which was hers alone, that knowledge which, if it were but a memory of a dreary round of unalleviated labor day after day for almost forty years was yet, in its very strangeness to all others, a treasure which existed as long as she herself existed to testify to the inviolability of her life, sacrosanct, as it were, immune to the prying of everyone else.

She lived less than a year after coming home. If she had meant to speak, she was given no opportunity, for her lips were sealed by a paralytic stroke that kept her silent until her death days afterwards. But there was that in her eyes that said she would not have spoken if she could; what secrets lay locked in the breast of that frail little woman taking the sun on days of warmth along the streets of Sac Prairie, principally on Water Street, from which she could see as she had always seen in her childhood and youth the cobalt waters of the river, lay there forever, never to be put into her words, never to be shared, never to be known by anyone but Poosey Lachmund.

❋   ❋   ❋   ❋   ❋

THE voices of the wind are endless in their variety. Not so much the winter's keening wind or the rush and roar of storm as the vagrant fugitive winds of spring and autumn, which come into the village and over the prairie from the hills on all sides, rustling in the poplars and cottonwoods, making a dry sibilance in the oaks, a joyous bubbling in birch and aspens, a whispering murmur in the willows, and a long hush-hush in the grasses, winds that animate the trees with separate life and pass invisibly along the cheek and the hand like cool fingers and memory made green anew.

Many nights I walked out into it, into the fierce tearing, into the gentle drifting, into rain-washed air and dust-laden air, walking against it or with it, as the mood took me, and taking pleasure in its wild freedom, for the illusion of which so many men sacrifice heart and soul. But the wind's freedom is no illusion; a wanderer from far places, it brings to Sac Prairie the smells of a distant country—the smell of the Dakotas and Nebraska in the hot summer night, the fertile fragrance of corn, the pungence of the cranberry marshes burning in upstate Wisconsin, the smell of pine woods in a forest fire; it brings down the fresh, clean fragrance of pines, it catches up the pollen of red cedars from the hills and brings it down into the low land along the river.

And who does not know the strange, unaccountable rustling of cornleaves? You feel no wind, no movement of the still summer air; nevertheless, the cornleaves quiver and rustle, setting up an incredible and mysterious sound in the dark as if the endless rows had trapped the wind for their own, an eerie but wonderful sound, the corn speaking for earth itself and all the creatures who walked upon it in that place from the beginning of time, the wind unseen, unfelt, but heard in this ceaseless rustling, like the spectre of winds audible there in the infinitesimal movement of the cornleaves, so different from the long hushing of wind in the wheatfields. One moment the silence is profound; then suddenly rises the furtive whisper, the susurrus intensified and growing, and soon the field trembles and rustles with the voices of this wind in the cornrows.

I am alive to it, to the wind wherever it lists, however it makes itself manifest, like a movement of time itself among the vast spaces of the universes.

In the years of my childhood and youth the only holiday we celebrated at home was Christmas. Holidays followed a set pattern, which called for Thanksgiving at Grandmother Volk's, and New Year's at the home of my Great-uncle Joe and Great-aunt Lou Gelhaus, who, after their retirement from the home place above the White Mound Valley, lived in various places in Sac Prairie. All of us gathered at each occasion in this unvarying pattern year after year. The fare was almost as unvarying as the arrangement—we always had chicken; indeed, I never tasted turkey until my first Thanksgiving away from home, when I was invited to dinner by Donald Wandrei in Minneapolis; the pies were always pumpkin and mince, and, while vegetables allowed of some variation, the range was never very wide. But the food was always excellent in quality, and, always being so, it was not the distinguishing element of these gatherings.

Rather it was the character of each occasion which kept it warm in memory—the playing of the Victrola, an old-fashioned instrument, at Grandmother Volk's, where we heard everything from *Listen to the Mocking Bird* to *Cohen on the Telephone*— the rollicking memories of life in years gone by that were always stirred at Great-uncle Joe's house—and at home my father's determined attempt to ply Great-uncle Joe with home-made wine in an effort to "pifflicate" him, as Mother put it. Essentially, I suppose, Great-uncle Joe and Great-aunt Lou were the catalytic agents which made each holiday an occasion.

They were two people constantly at gentle odds. My great-uncle was a bluff, hearty man, heavy-set, with a florid face and merry eyes that shone from above fat cheeks. He wore a moustache most of his life, more or less to balance the thinning hair of his head, and he had a deep, booming voice. My great-aunt was slighter in build, shorter than her husband, with a laughter-lined face. She wore spectacles at such an angle that she could look over them with ease; the light always seemed to glint off them and to conceal the fact that her blue eyes were sharp and observing when her manner suggested inattention. She always seemed to be keeping one eye on Great-uncle Joe, as if she wanted to be sure what was going to happen next, being certain that wherever he was, something was bound to happen, and very probably something she would have to stop, once begun. She had a rather musical voice, a quality which was accentuated by the quaintness of her expressions; she was accustomed to saying "Heavens to Betsy!" and "I declare to goodness," and "My conscience!"; she would say "I knew plegged well" and "Therefore I say" and "My soul and body!" as naturally as if she had been born to such expressions, and perhaps she had been.

Wherever they were, there was a great deal of noisy merriment. Once the meal was over—and everyone pitched in to help set and clear the table—an afternoon of card-playing began. My parents and the family generally were addicted to euchre; they all played this with a heartiness I have seldom encountered anywhere else, talking constantly, slapping their cards on the table to a loud rapping of knuckles, praising their game, shouting and laughing, and sometimes calling down a partner for a poor play, and the like, all this to the accompaniment of my father's insidious attempts upon Great-uncle's sobriety, Father from time to time getting up to go down into the basement for wine to press upon Great-uncle Joe—dandelion wine, elderberry wine, grape wine—and very often a deliberate mixture of the three with some linden blossom or elderberry blossom wine thrown in for good measure; but, though Great-uncle's face got redder and redder and his voice louder, I never saw him really intoxicated, which I have no doubt Father took as an inexcusable affront to his wine. It must have been frustrating for Father, but Great-uncle never turned down a glass of wine, especially in the face of Great-aunt Lou's admonitory, "Now, Joe, now Joe, you've had enough!" and her laughingly embarrassed aside to the rest of us, "That man of mine don't know when to stop!" whereupon Mother would flash Father an angry glance and Father would get up and try it again.

This went on all afternoon and continued after supper, for dinner was always a meal eaten at noon, and the evening meal was supper in our home. It made for a wonderfully warm harmony; it gave a sense of unity to the family, and a kind of continuity to existence, and it seemed to me that it went on a long time, though it could not have been for more than fifteen years or so, all told, for Great-uncle Joe had not left the farm until after we had occupied the house of childhood. Yet these family gatherings continued until his death in 1930, after which Great-aunt Lou gave up their house in town and went elsewhere to live, at first with one of their two sons, then with a niece closer to Sac Prairie, and the little holiday gatherings were events of the past.

Long before this, I had deserted the household of such afternoons, to go to the harness shop or to find Hugo Schwenker and take a hike down along the back river or down the Railroad Bridge Island south of town, to return only in time for supper, except on such occasions as the talk at home turned on relatives, of which I had an uncounted number still living in the area of Plain west of Sac Prairie. Then I stayed, to absorb as much of this lore as possible and store it in my own memory against the time when I would hear these voices no more—a time which came, as always, too soon. It is never given to anyone to assess properly the significance of a word, an act, an event at the time of its occurrence, and it was so, too, of me, for I never saw these pleasant holidays in their proper perspective until the central characters were gone beyond recall, though Great-aunt Lou lived for twenty years past the last of those pleasant family gatherings, long enough to reminisce about them herself as part of her own past as well as of mine, and to enjoy a kind of secondary existence she had been given in stories I had begun to write about her and Great-uncle Joe.

❋ ❋ ❋ ❋ ❋

OF winter nights the voices of the trains came into Sac Prairie with special intimacy, particularly on nights of snow, coming through the moist air from Merrimac and Baraboo north of town, from Mazomanie, Black Earth, Arena, Spring Green, and Lone Rock on the south—the endlessly varied voices of steam locomotive whistles, not yet given way to the flat notes of Diesel engines. I used to stand on the park path late at night where the sound fell to ear and listen to the mellow whistling, trying to determine where the 11:05 was—first at Black Earth— hills shut off the whistling at Cross Plains, before Black Earth— then at Mazomanie, then, diminishing, toward Arena, after which I could follow the locomotive's voice all the way to Lone Rock, beyond which it was lost.

On such nights Sac Prairie was asleep; there was little movement in village streets on winter nights; there was only the sibilance of snowflakes among the barren branches overhead, and darkness all around, save for a few distant windows still lit— Mae Bowman's at the far corner, where she sat reading the morning paper still, and the light that burned nightlong in Kate

Fleeson's little house and a light in the upper window of the proud Naffz house, where one of the sisters read deep into the night—and, facing me, the deeper darkness of the old house of yellow stone just across the street from the park, a house where once a woman had taken her own life and another had gone mad; and I listened as to tangible bonds to the vast world outside the microcosm of Sac Prairie, listened to sounds as mysterious and far away as that world was mysterious and far away, stood

with snow forming a layer on my uncovered head and my shoulders, listening as to some voice speaking to me, while the dark shadow of the Park Hall loomed behind me, with all its memories of that tenuous first love for Margery, so often met here in the shadows when we dared not meet elsewhere.

The whistling rose and fell, infinite in its variety. How much a part of life in Sac Prairie it was then! It seemed on such nights that the village was the center of a vast network of railroads; sometimes the whistling was augmented by the ringing of bells, the rushing of long freight trains through the night, the hollow roaring of many cars crossing the bridges over the Wisconsin, making it to seem that Sac Prairie itself was a railroad junction town, instead of but an isolated station at the end of a spur nine miles away from the main line, making it seem as if I, too, were at the world's center of life, instead of but my own.

The whistling of a locomotive always arrested me. I stood and listened for different reasons—an old nostalgia, the mood for poetry—and sometimes, in that snowy darkness, I put down lines for a poem—a kind of spiritual isolation briefly assuaged by these voices out of the night, testifying to the presence not far away of other lives, equally solitary—as if there were not such in every house within the range of eye or ear. I stood listening until the voices faded and were gone, and the night returned to the village and I to myself.

Even as a very small boy I was aware of Billy Ynand as an individual who stood apart from the mass of adults; only a dullard could have been unaware of that energetic, fast-talking man with his bright eyes and his loquacious tongue, a man bent a little, but neither by age nor by adversity, a man whose greying hair belied the sparkle in his eyes and the lilt of his voice. "Why, say," he would say, "I knew your grandfather, by golly, I did, I knew your daddy when he was just so high, just knee-high to a grasshopper. By golly, I did!" You could not help recognizing him, warming to him, even if people thought him more than a little mad.

He was not mad at all. He had a pixy-like sanity one might have envied, save that the concept of God troubled him endlessly, invading him and stirring him to word and deed, to flights of wild fancy in which he wove the image of God into the texture of his life. He worked hard, but somehow he had no gift for hanging on to money. He had a wife, a patient, long-suffering woman, and three children—a daughter who had grown up and married not once, but twice; and two sons, one of whom was not well and grew progressively less well until Billy went around saying with a positive air, "George is going to die!" even though George was on his feet and working hard. But George died.

He worked at everything. He dug dry-wells, ditches, cesspools; he put up buildings, he painted barns and sheds; he was ever willing to lend a hand to anything by which he might earn "an honest dollar." He had no use for any other kind, and if he were improvident, it was not for his own sake, save for such rare moments when he was moved by some inner compulsion to have one of his tracts printed in leaflet form so that he might distribute it more widely and satisfy his need to communicate. He was abstemious to the point of abhorring liquor. "Once when I was a boy I drank some beer and then I called my mother names and I swore," he was wont to explain. "It wasn't me that did that, by golly, no!; it was the devil in the glass of beer. So I swore I'd never drink another drop, and from that day to this, by golly, I haven't!"

Some people thought little of him, but, curiously, a great many others thought of him with affection, little people, as he was accustomed to put it, "like you and me." People who thought well of themselves were in the habit of dismissing Billy as a "loafer," which he was not, as a little "touched," which he did not deserve, or as a "nuisance," because he was insistent about his beliefs and demanded their attention so that he could impart them. Few people were willing to listen to him, and therein lay the reason for his loneliness.

For Billy was lonely; he was dreadfully lonely, because he had so much to say and so little time in which to say it, and no one would listen to him. Small wonder that he talked at length to children, whom he delighted, and to whom he must have seemed very much like a grown-up elf or a pixy grown old. "Why, say, I knew your grandfather," he would begin, and soon he was telling them about the days when he was a boy and the rafts came down the river, unimaginably big rafts built of cribs of lumber, and "Say, we'd be swimming, we boys, and we'd holler at them fellers, and they'd throw things at us—wood and such stuff—and we always carried it home; there was a use for it!" And he would tell them about Billy Hopinka, the Sky Pilot, the Racing Wonder, the ice-skating champion of 1890 because Billy Hopinka was Billy Ynand, and he had pictures of himself, all clad in tight-fitting white, to prove it, and not so long ago he had been in the habit of skating up the Wisconsin all the way to Portage and back to Sac Prairie before the dams were put in along the river nearby. He held something of fascination and everlasting wonder for children.

He held less for adults whose sense of wonder had been dulled or lost. To them he was tiresome or troublesome, which he did not notice or, if he did, affected not to recognize. He sought them nonetheless; he meant to speak; he would not be denied, whether he spoke of his early years in town or whether he related an incident designed to prove God's beneficence. With every year of his age, he was inclined to commend God for everything that had happened to him, and his insistence began to trouble people. Perhaps it stirred dormant consciences and made people uneasy; perhaps his very insistence seemed to them proof of his irrationality.

I used to see him often, unpredictably, at any time of day, in any corner of Sac Prairie; he was as likely to be encountered on the riverbank as in the high school, where he usually undertook to lecture the principal on the proper instruction of religion in the schools, and to point to himself as living proof of the benefit of God's friendship; he was on the streets as much as he was in the stores, on the outskirts of Sac Prairie as much as at its heart. He was neurotically restless; in his own words, he was "always on the go," and he meant to keep "on the go as long as the good Lord allows it." He sought some indefinable surcease which he could not name; it was not alone a listening ear, for many a time I listened to Billy and saw that there was something more he sought, something just beyond his reach—it was not the Catholicism he had given up long ago, it was not simply happiness or contentment, it was not any rational thing.

Something lurked behind his bright eyes, something remained unheard in his loquacity, something stirred within him like the worm and gave him no rest. Sometimes when he spoke, it seemed almost as if what he sought were the key to being, the explanation of life itself, or perhaps a personal reason for existence which eluded his grasp. Something just out of reach drove him, made him restless in his striving for goals which had much to do with life and death, with God and eternity, and yet lent themselves neither to clear vision nor to articulate presentation.

He never changed throughout his life. He seemed always carefree and happy; though I never saw him worried or troubled, he was not without his burdens. His wife died, and he grew older; as he aged, there was less and less work he could do. No matter; he went about as before, challenging his fellowmen, provoking discussion, doing things as impulsively as a boy of ten, which, in a man of seventy, startled and disturbed people who had long ago forgotten what it was to be a child of ten. "I'm an optimist," he would say. "Other people see the doughnut—I see the hole." And what was beyond the hole but the whole wide world? And what was in the doughnut but a soporific for the stomach?

"Why, say! I knew your grandfather, by golly, I did!" he would begin, and spin his yarns about the old days gone by, not with that nostalgic sadness assumed by so many old people, but with gusto and relish, with the air of informing his listeners of their misfortune at not having lived then, without, however, deprecating the present. He could recreate the youth of the town, the rafting days, when the chief artery of traffic was the lordly Wisconsin rolling by; he could bring back to momentary life the people of his youth—not only one's grandfather, but the associates of that progenitor. He had never ceased to be a boy of five or ten or fifteen; he had never stopped being that uncertain young man who did not know whether he ought to marry his Anna or not—"How could you treat me this way, going off so cruelly without a word?" she wrote to him in letters which I found thrown away long after her death and his own passing from the village scene; he steadfastly refused to grow old or to admit that for him, as for all of us, death waited at some rendezvous in time to come.

He was a man who needed affection and understanding, and did not have them; in the press of living, people were too busy to understand him; he needed some outlet for his restless spirit, to abate the compulsions within, and he found it too seldom to do him any good; he needed a root in the future as he had a root in the past, which none could have; and he needed, above all, kindness and gayety and some assurance that what could not make its mark on time forever nevertheless left a little sign in the hearts of men. He sought to mitigate his loneliness by his loquacity, by pouring out what lay in his thoughts, by printing and giving away his leaflets testifying at one and the same time to his delight in his past years and his firm conviction of a future in heaven.

As he grew older, his talkativity increased, and there was evident in it, to many people, an edge of irrationality. This was something I had never observed, yet it was possible that it existed. Billy himself became a burden and, with that cruelty grown from the rigorous restrictions of an increasingly complex living, he was presently carted away to the county poor farm, where he had taken from him the freedom he had always so loved, the familiar streets and faces of Sac Prairie, the beloved scenes of his childhood and youth. He escaped from time to time; he made his way back to Sac Prairie and resumed his old habits before he was taken away again; he even on one historic occasion made a journey to the state prison and talked to the inmates on his experiences as Billy Ynand and Billy Hopinka, the Sky Pilot, to the

accompaniment of a fanfare in the newspapers. But invariably he
went back to the poor farm.

He was not happy there. His restlessness and his loneliness had
no assuagement whatever, and the unfortunate habitants of the
buildings in which he was confined were too concerned with
themselves and their own plights to listen to him. He could not
long endure this virtual imprisonment. One dark day he mounted
to the attic of the central building housing the county's un-
fortunates, and there quietly hanged himself. He had enriched the
byways of Sac Prairie by his living; he left them desolate at his
passing, dark still with the restlessness that drove him, the blind
seeking which gave him no peace, and which now haunted the
places he had known like a question forever unanswered.

❋ ❋ ❋ ❋ ❋

*THE Spring Slough was the magnet which drew me
afternoons and evenings in the spring, and early in the morning
hours of many summer days. It was a long body of water, ranging
in depth from a few inches to eight feet, begun with a large, relatively shallow lake or pond north of the trestle, carrying through
a narrower neck to a wider portion which stretched away between
tree-girt banks almost to the brook in the south. Blue flags lined
its shores, with cat-tails, Joe-Pye weed, buttonball bushes, osiers,
willows, soft maples, birches, elms; yellow pond lilies grew on its
surface, and in its shallows arrowleaf flourished, and at all times,
in hot weather, great masses of sphagnum dotted its water. Like
all the other sloughs along the Wisconsin, it was spring fed,
though, before the level of the Wisconsin fell as a result of water-
shed controls at its headwaters, the slough was refreshed by a torrent of water from the swollen river every April and June.*

*The Spring Slough teemed with wild life. I used to sit on the
trestle absorbed in the movement of muskrats, which went about
their lives up and down the slough, foraging, mating, fighting; in*

the less obtrusive lives of bluewinged teal and mallards and wood ducks and their fledglings learning to swim and take care of themselves; in the circumspect caution of beavers, come from the colony house to cross the slough to where young willows and poplar growth offered them food, watching them climb out on the banks, cut a sapling, section it, and gnaw away the bark. Painted turtles occupied the logs which were always to be found in the slough, splashing off as I came along, climbing back out of the water after making sure that I meant them no harm. And occasionally otters invaded the slough, coming up from the brook, spending their infectious joy in diving and playing and hunting the slough for an hour before returning the way they had come, their joyous cries falling away behind them.

The water was never still. Muskrats and turtles broke it; now and then a brown water snake slithered by; flies danced over its surface; sunfish rose, and great northerns came to surface and swirled away; the summer cricket frogs climbed out on the lily-pads and ballooned their throats in song, as in the spring months the hylidae crowded the shallows along the shore and filled the day and night alike with their primal music. On rare occasions a mink or weasel made its way along the shores, in silent, relentless hunting.

Phoebes and pewees nested in the vicinity; warblers—particularly, in season, prothonotaries and blackburnians, and all summer long, redstarts, myrtle and other nesting warblers fed upon the flies and mosquitoes and gnats which were always present above the water. Redwings sang out of the Upper Meadow, which spread away east of the slough and the railroad tracks to the Mazomanie road and, beyond it, the low hills where the moraine tapered off from the north before coming up against the more formidable Wisconsin Heights in the southeast, the setting of the only near battle of the Black Hawk War. Crows always cried from all horizons, and very often majestic hawks—redtails, red-shoulders, ospreys—soared, screaming, out of the woods and high above the slough and the meadows and the hills, up against the wind, into the air currents, there to float in lonely serenity, sometimes with their mates to engage in an inspiring show of love play, high, high over, almost invisible, commanding all the woods and the river bottoms and the hills, while great blue herons came gliding into the slough to stand motionless in the sun-dappled shallows fishing. Now and then harriers quartered the meadow for the mice which were in the deep grasses by the thousands, adding their small rustlings to the symphony of nature's voices always to be heard in this place throughout the green seasons.

As the afternoon waned and the long shadows crossed the slough, some voices were stilled, and others rose—mourning doves, cardinals, field sparrows, and, as darkness came on, the nostalgic song of the whippoorwills, and, above all, the crying of the frogs—the peepers in a great choir out of the Upper Meadow, the cricket frogs from nearer the slough, the pond frogs conversing across the water, the woods frogs uttering their hoarse croaking out of the tree-grown bottomland to the west—all pulsing and throbbing as in the very rhythm of earth itself. I never tired of listening to the frogs' primal music, which seemed to me to convey implicitly a continuity that carried back to the beginning of time and would carry on to its end. This was true, too, of the hot stridulation of cicadas on summer days. Sometimes, when I stayed late of April and May nights, the east banks of the slough were invaded by boys from the village, come down to fish for bullheads. They sat just south of the trestle, or up along the shore of the pond, near a bonfire, which made its orange glow warmly in the darkness; very often I joined them for a little while, taking a pole, or sitting at the fire making the kind of small talk which is essential to village life—of weather, local politics, the trivial events which seem so important in the life of such a social unit as a small town—come inside, as it were, for a little while, and returning again to the cosmos outside where the sustaining voices were not the hum of life in Sac Prairie but the

*voices of the winds, the talking leaves, the siren music of inter-
planetary spaces.*

*I used to sit on the Spring Slough Trestle to read and write
and dream, spending time as wisely as I knew, watching the
years pass, at first slowly, and then with increasing swiftness,
and never counted a moment there ill spent.*

Now and then, in my nocturnal wandering about Sac Prairie,
I paused here and there, drawn by the old houses; and I stopped in
—now to visit briefly with Millie Pohlmann or Helen Hahn, now
to stop by to say a few words to Helen Merk or Minna Schwenker,
spinsters all.

Millie Pohlmann lived in a little house set back a distance from
the street-corner, small in the manner of early houses in Sac
Prairie, and darkened by the closepressing lilacs and the trees—
two sentinel spruces, a butternut, a border of fine elms, which
all but concealed her house from the exploratory rays of the arc-
light over the corner crossing. She lived there alone: a tall,
gaunt-looking woman, whose face was much wrinkled and had a
forbidding appearance, though it belied her good nature. She
dressed habitually in a fashion just gone by—not precisely old-
fashioned, and always in good taste, but leaving one continually
with the conviction that she had made these dresses herself out of
excellent and most durable material and could not in conscience
discard them until they were more worn. The atmosphere of her
house was contained in her handiwork—the crochetings, the
samplers, the knitted pieces and hooked rugs. These things were
everywhere, and her samplers hung even on the walls, so that her
rooms had a kind of individuality to be met nowhere else, and the
very walls seemed to communicate intimately the patterns and
designs over which she had labored with such assiduous care.
Even the humming of the wasps which lived under the eaves of
her back porch, and the twittering of the swallows habiting her

chimney invaded as from an outside world far away, and the rest
of the village was lost to this haven.

I had known her for years, and she had never changed. She
worked in the canning factory, where in late June and early
July she sorted peas, and where in August and September she
sorted ears of corn. This was evidently her only source of income,
but she made it last throughout the year. She spent every Saturday
evening in the library, sitting with Helen Hahn and Josephine
Merk, ending their day together in that sort of casual small talk
which warms with its intimacy and confers upon those taking
part a certainty of the rightness and worth of living. In her late
years, she came to my own home to celebrate New Year's Eve
with scores of others. But she belonged to that little house just
west of St. Aloysius, bounded on the west by the Milwaukee
Road's spur into the village, and on the east by the rectory and
the church.

I wondered about her often in relation to others, and once I
even wrote a short story about her—or rather, about a projection
of her as a younger woman, perhaps one tritely disappointed in
love, for she had always been a spinster. One night long after,
seeing the yellow lamplight escaping a chink in the shutters,
I walked up the board walk to the porch and knocked. She
was there and alone; she had been reading in a book from the
library and complained of its small print, which tired her old eyes.
As we sat talking, I caught sight of a cabinet photograph standing
just out of range of the brightest light and, looking at it, saw
that it was of a tall, very handsome young woman, attractively
coiffed and dressed, posed with a baby. I could not identify her,
and at length asked who she was.

"Why, that's me!" said Millie, astonished that I could not
recognize her instantly. And so it was—handsome, attractive, with
a good figure. What had become of her? Perhaps she was all
around me, forever lost in scores of samplers and crochetings, in
dozens of hooked rugs and knitted pieces, that handsome, well-

figured young woman posed there with her nephew. I was oblivious of her telling me about the gold neck-ornament she wore—a relic of her father's forty-nining days in California—and indeed, of all else, for the conviction was all-powerful that something far more than the energy of her fingers was held in the work she had done.

And thereafter the house was haunted for me—haunted by the young woman locked away in gay samplers, crochetings, hooked rugs and other pieces—and Millie, too, whenever I met her on the street, seemed no longer one woman, but two—the young woman of the photograph and the woman she was now, separate and distinct, as if the yearning for life which must have been natural in so attractive a young woman had been suppressed and straitened and put away, slowly, bit by bit, year after year, poured out of her fingertips in those countless pieces that filled the little house on the corner. And when I went past it in the evenings, I thought of them both within those walls, the woman she was reaching into imaginative worlds of romance and adventure in books from the library, the woman she had been silent and aloof, not even reproachful, on the walls, the floors, the furniture, two women apart who were yet one.

Helen Hahn, too, had been attractive as a young woman. She lived her spinsterly existence in a little red brick house, green-shuttered, with white trim, and a neatly shingled roof, on the river side of Water Street, with a pair of ancient elms towering above it, so that on summer days her home was constantly protected from the sun's heat, and at night it lay shadow-flecked in the moonlight. And at night, Helen—if she were home, as she most often was—sat in the darkness behind the blinds looking avidly out into the street, eager for its life from this vantage-point, taking part in life in this withdrawn fashion. When I went in, she plied me with questions. We used to call her, jokingly, the "town pump," at which her friends all laughed good-naturedly, for it could not be denied that she wanted to know everything about everyone, not to decry anyone's forbidden pleasures or unashamed sin, but simply to satisfy a craving for life at second hand. Her house seemed damp, but it was not. It was neat, clean, spare of decoration, save for a tea-set in which she took great pride, and there was the ever-present river, manifest in the pungences and odors that invaded the house—of fog, of thaw-water, of high, silt-heavy water rushing by—and the sounds of the water among the stones at the abutment and the willows along the shore behind the house. The Wisconsin and the hills across it were at her back door; the constant hurry of traffic were out in front, on the west side; an old building which had once housed the Electric Theatre—the first in Sac Prairie—rose up on the south, and another even smaller house, of frame construction, on the north.

The house had an atmosphere of genteel age. Her parents had lived there before her, and before them, others, for the house was almost a century old. You came into a little vestibule and immediately ascended three steps to the main floor, after which you descended again into the ground floor, which ordinarily might have been a cellar, but which was largely taken up by a kitchen, very cool in summer, and always moist throughout the year, for it was underground save for its opening to the river's shore. In this atmosphere, somehow, she belonged; when in later years she took to living with her brother a block away, she seemed out of place, like a visitor in his big house, and not a resident.

She was short rather than medium in height, with fine features, white hair, and a slightly jutting jaw; she had a habit of looking up at one from behind her spectacles, inquiringly, but perhaps this was only natural, since she habitually inquired of this and that, of one person or another, with an eagerness which belied her mild-mannered appearance, reaching hungrily out after a vicarious kind of existence, until it came to seem to me, passing at night, as if the house itself were reaching out for a life other than it had,

crouched there with its windows darkened and Helen behind
one of them, forever peering forth into the world with the barrier
of the wall between, crouched like a sentient creature, anxious to
take part in the active life of Sac Prairie, but uncertain, hesitant,
and perhaps afraid.

This was not so of Helen Merk.

She, too, lived in a house set back from the street under the
widespread limbs of soft maple trees, but there were two storeys
in her house, and she lived in both of them, for despite her age,
she was extremely active with a kind of unquenchable energy.
Since the deaths of her sisters, Ida and Josephine, she lived alone.
Long ago, Josephine had feared for Helen's eyes; she had been
afraid that Helen was going blind, as a doctor had hinted, and she
had worried about this even while her own death was rooted in
her, destined to bring her life to an end more than a decade before
Helen's; but her pale blue eyes did not look blind behind her
spectacles, she saw well enough save when reading, at which she
required a magnifying glass, held firmly in one hand over the page
while she read.

It was thus I found her most often when I stopped of an evening
—sitting at table with the glass in her hand, reading by the light
of a green-shaded table-lamp—not only *The Capital Times*, but
*The New Republic, The Nation, The Saturday Review of Litera-
ture, The Atlantic Monthly,* and all those outlets of challenging
opinion which give her pleasure for, being active, she was intel-
lectually alert. She took delight in an animated discussion and
often stirred up discussions, frequently taking a side in which she
did not really believe for the sake of argument. She was rather
tall, with a most forthright expression heightened by a strongly
prognathous jaw, and a direct, provocative glance; her eyes were
unwavering, her greying hair never quite pat—nor would she
have wanted it so—her restless mind constantly seeking to
establish some point in conversation.

Very probably because of this the house, too, seemed alert and active; it seemed rather a port for intellectual pursuit, for scholarly enterprise, than a place in which to live. The sitting-room was seldom the parlor, until a radio came to take its place there, and even then the parlor was used only secondarily; the place for visiting was always what, in most Sac Prairie houses, would have been the dining-room, the round table in the center of which was always littered with papers, magazines, and clippings, and the magnifying glass was there, too, under the green-shaded lamp—this room was the center of the house. A case of books stood off in one corner beside a couch, and against another wall stood a little table on which there was always a natural decoration of some kind—a vase of buds, flowers, leaves, of seed-heads—never debased by silver or gold tinting, as in so many houses—always attractively arranged with that kind of artlessness which makes for the best design. In winter I often brought her cuttings of alder and willows, in catkin. In other seasons the Merk table was crowned with what were called "old-fashioned" flowers—bouquets of feverfew, painted daisies, bleeding hearts, straw-flowers, zinnias, nasturtiums, and the like, those flowers which had been grown in village gardens for many decades throughout the century of Sac Prairie's existence.

Being interested in controversial discussion did not make her argumentative. She had pronounced and positive opinions, which was good; there is no flavor about a man or woman of no convictions, no color or individuality; and Helen Merk had flavor, color and individuality. Whatever she was not, she was a *person*, and you could be sure of being set right in case you were wrong and dared to challenge her. Like all people of positive opinions, she was often impatient with stupidity, and she had no time whatever for hypocrisy; indeed, the very mention of the name of Irma Lachmund, a local paragon of self-esteem and rude snobbishness, was enough to draw forth choice and well-pointed comments, sometimes tinged with cynicism, but not often. Her personality took possession of her house; it invaded the walls and flavored them, too, with the alert awareness which was hers, so that it presented outside a falsely bland façade, and the moment you stepped inside it, you had the impression that events were beginning to move, quite as if your very presence were a challenge. She had spent most of her life teaching, but this experience—so often likely to be unfortunate and confining—did not leave her mind in a rut, but only added fuel to an insatiable desire for learning, and spurred that intellectual inquiry into the motives and deeds of man which is the mark of the cultured person who is alive on more planes than one.

Miss Minna Schwenker, however, carried on an inquiry on but one plane. She sallied forth from her little house on the western edge of town, the rim of the prairie, day and night, and went in search of gossip, bartering her own in exchange quite frankly and unashamedly; the doings of her fellow villagers were her first interest and there was no good reason why, since these doings were the very stuff of life in Sac Prairie, they should not serve as her staff of life. She was a garrulous woman who began each year with the conviction that she would not live through it, and yet prepared to the last stick of wood for the coming winter, a way of life she continued year upon year, from seventy to ninety, each year convinced that this year was her last, but not really believing that she would die, and so making sure of her winter supplies.

She had been what in Sac Prairie was called "a practical nurse" —that is, a woman without formal training in the nursing profession, begun no doubt as a midwife, and expanding into every form of nursing, at which she was notably successful, save for one little quirk—a secret devotion to brandy or whiskey, which dizzied her now and then; so that, if any patient of hers was being given brandy or whiskey, it was certain that Minna would have more than his share of each bottle. In later years, when she had stopped nursing, hard liquor proved too dear for her; and she bought beer instead and found this beverage in the end as satisfactory.

When she smiled, her face was very pleasant. Sober, she was a little austere, partly because, being quite old, her straight hair, cut at her neck, hung down grey and severe on both sides of her head, her spectacles were perched half way down her nose, and her skin had a leathery quality which was seasonally altered when, for some inexplicable reason, it reddened and peeled in patches over her nose and cheeks. In her late years she was very spare, close to being bony and angular, and her pronouncements took on an air of being heaven-sent, since she was manifestly so much closer to the grave than away from it.

For she did pronounce judgment right and left; she laid about her with spectral thunderbolts for all and sundry, irrespective of age or creed, with particular attention—as a result of her years of experience in nursing—for those hypochondriacs who, being only slightly ill, became doctor-chasers or fancied themselves dying at every alteration of pulse or temperature. She was also, being a steady church-goer, strongly interested in sin, though she had no spoken conception of genuine evil; she was aware only of certain transgressions, which were interesting—it was not Mr. Paley's drinking which aroused her wrath so much as it was his wife's constant whining and complaint about his mistreatment of her, mistreatment, Minna knew, which came about because Mrs. Paley could not leave her husband alone, but must nag and begin to beat him whenever he came home intoxicated, until the be-fuddled fellow had to defend himself as best he knew how; it was not the flagrant violations of law perpetrated by children from time to time which inspired her denunciation—it was the parents who always sought to defend children by placing blame else-where and seeking to shift it from their own shoulders, where it very properly belonged most of the time; it was never the lechery of the young men she condemned—it was the invitation of the young women which was wholly responsible in her eyes, for she had lived long enough, she said vehemently, to know that men would always be "that way," but it took women to bring it out into the open.

She spent much of her time calling on the sick, or on Miss Hester Duff, who could be equally acrimonious, and the two of them always had a wonderfully vitriolic time together; and doubtless the sick were given a new lease on life to be informed of all the goings-on, from simple laxity about church-attendance to suspected adultery, in Sac Prairie. When she was not out calling, she sat at home reading the weekly papers in her kitchen, her light burning bright for all to see, and she hoping that someone might come to call. Being at the edge of town, there were only two houses in her block; her barn, filled with the wood hoarded against the winter to follow her "last year," bordered the alley on the north; her house occupied the center of the block, and to the south along the sidewalk was the usually dark house where the widow Buchenau lived with her daughter.

The house was low, close to the ground, with a gable-room upstairs. It was very old, having housed her parents before her; she spoke of it as "the homestead" and was proud of the handiwork of her cabinet-maker father whenever she took time to think about it, though she gave samples of it away lavishly to anyone who flattered her with attention, and was particularly the victim of Mrs. Prangle, a feral-faced and acquisitive woman who went about with the tenacity of a pack-rat gulling all the lonely old women in the village just sufficiently long to separate them from some antique of value for her collection, which she prized above all else. Miss Minna, for all her perspicacity in worming out the details of sin and error in Sac Prairie, never seemed to catch on to the activities of Mrs. Prangle, and thus missed a splendid opportunity to pass a well-merited judgment in which heaven might have concurred.

The house brooded under a broken old maple on one side of its front, and a row of younger elms on the other, as well as a hackberry out in back, while blossoms, from tulips to sunflowers, stood in season along the south wall. Approaching the house at night, you saw in all that block only the light in the kitchen window, where Minna sat reading or dozing; she was loath to go to bed until the last hope for company had vanished, then only she took herself off to her high bed. But the slightest sound at her doors, front or back, brought her with startling rapidity, as if she feared the knocker at her door would be gone before she could open to him, and you were hardly seated before there came the inevitable query, "Any news?"—which did not mean of war or peace, of occurrences in Washington or London or Rome, but of the far more important events in the life of Sac Prairie.

The house lay almost somnolently there on the edge of town; the light in the kitchen window was its single, sleepless eye, turning on the village for any sign of life, nefarious or otherwise; it shone forth for blocks; I saw it often for many years when I walked by two or three streets away, and from time to time I stopped by to impart such news as she might be interested in hearing, only to learn a great deal of unexpected information from her in return.

Even in her late eighties, she could be encountered almost at any hour of the night, carrying a little basket in which she had brought food to someone, now on her way home after spending as long a time as she could at the bedside or with the family of some ailing villager. And at even such meetings she was ready and eager to pause and talk, anxious to pass on such news as she had learned that day, with all the interest of a pioneer woman who had no access to radio or newspaper, whose only contact was with her fellow-pioneers. Miss Minna in a sense was still a pioneer, and the house was a pioneer's—no longer of logs, though part of it was as old as any log house in the region, but one of those neat, "second" houses built after the first dwelling was outgrown. The Schwenkers were a large family but, apart from nieces and nephews, Minna outlived them all, and her low little house had an air of watchful waiting, prepared equally for life or death, but preferably for more of life.

❄ ❄ ❄ ❄ ❄

FOR *a long time, Thursday was stock day in Sac Prairie. Farmers hauled cows and pigs and calves into the stockyards along the tracks just south of the depot, and there they were loaded into stock cars sometimes brought up by the incoming train to be taken out that same day, which meant that the train had to stay late in town to load the stock into the cars. On such nights I had to stand offside somewhere along the line while the train went by.*

Two short blasts of the whistle invariably announced its approach to the railroad bridges, so there was always time to leave the rail bed. I used to like to watch it most particularly from the south shore of the Spring Slough—or from the neck of the Lower Meadow, where I could see it winding its sinuous way toward Mazomanie along the east rim of the meadow like a toy train, never moving very fast, for the cars often numbered beyond thirty or forty, a hard pull for old 1040. Its rumbling across the bridges announced its coming while I waited. It came hurrying through the dusk of the lowland, rumbling through the woods and waking echoes where it passed, momentarily stilling birds and frogs until the trembling of the earth and the echoes died away. Though it always came as an intrusion, it was a familiar one, for the same ritual was part of the Milwaukee Road's program for more than half a century, and the chuffing locomotive, the line of stock cars, the orange caboose all passed by with a proprietary air, and for a long time the acrid smoke lingered, the earth's trembling subsided, while the red and green lights behind the caboose dwindled to far stars down the tracks and at last winked out around the hills two miles to the south.

The train had gone by so often that it was an integral part of evening in the marshes, just as the night mail's motor sounding far overhead, or the woodcock's aerial dance, or the killdeer's nostalgic crying. The whistling for the bridges, the glowing fire-box, the engineer's wave, the trailing smoke, the clicking of the drivers, the sighs and groans of the Spring Slough Trestle when it crossed, all were part of every Thursday evening in the marshes. The train never silenced birds or frogs for very long, as if they too were accustomed to its passing.

But somehow that country train on its single track line embodied in the evening air all the romance of the epic of railroading in America, all the blood and tears, all the silver and gold, the profit and loss of one human venture, and it was always symbolic to me that on this little spur, the railroad's fight against nature is endless, for at the slightest relaxation of vigilance, the willows, alders, the vetches, osiers, wild roses, horsetails and bouncing Bet soon worked away the trestles, and the wild grape and woodbine could conceivably pull down the telegraph poles with their humming wires, which, on winter days, echoed Thoreau's telegraph harp. To me this struggle always stood for the fate of all human endeavor against the vast, unlimited force of nature, and I faced this thought inherently in the passing of the stock train, in the way the hylidae resumed their halted choir, the redwings renewed their songs, the toads began again to trill even while the train dwindled down the tracks into evening and the night.

John Kleinlein lived in a pair of houseboats on the Wisconsin, moored above the bridge and just over the bank from the railroad station in Upper Sac Prairie—a big man, gross with fat, with a thick moustache and wild, tousled hair crowned with a kind of captain's cap, which he had worn so long that it seemed moulded to his great body. Sometimes at night his voice rose from the water where he sat on the railing of that boat in which he lived —the other he used for storage—as he talked to the darkness, or hummed a little German tune. The river was his home, and he was not often abroad in the streets, save when he sold fish.

He was a solitary by choice, reflecting something of that same character which had distinguished his father, who had broken with a titled family and flung himself off to distant America from Germany, spurning the title when it came down to him at last after the leavening of death. John grew up apart from his sisters and brothers; he was always by himself, in the woods or along the Wisconsin, and when the Civil War broke out, he enlisted and left Sac Prairie as part of a company collected by a local captain of the militia. Of his adventures in the war he said little, but admitted when he was charged with it, that he was one of thirteen men who had taken Jefferson Davis prisoner, a deed for which he had been paid three hundred dollars, like every other man of the thirteen; but as time went by, and John grew more queer, people came to doubt his story.

He became a stone mason, married a German woman, new to America, and settled down. Not very long afterwards, his wife began to act strangely. She was finally taken away and institutionalized, and later on, after she had improved, she left John summarily and returned to Germany. It was then that John moved into the river boats and told people who asked that he liked to live along the river because his wife was lonesome where she was across the river in the hills, out of which she called to him from time to time, especially by night.

He alarmed people with the extravagance of his fictions—by speaking of his wife as if she were still with him, or hidden away in the hills around the Sugar Loaf and Black Hawk Lookout; by telling people he had gone lobster fishing on the Mississippi, and had stopped along the way at Berlin and Heidelberg; by constructing elaborately fantastic explanations of the simplest events, a course he pursued so effectively that alarmists succeeded in having him taken away to the county home, and having a guardian appointed to look after his interests. Some time later, when his guardian discovered that the keepers of the county home were renting John out as a stone mason and keeping his earnings, steps were taken to free him. It took a while to accomplish this, but at last John came back to the houseboats on the river.

There he went on as before. He lived on a meager Civil War pension, which he supplemented by selling fish in season, and in autumn gathering wild grapes to sell to housewives who found them necessary to making jelly, and to their husbands, who fermented them for other, equally felicitous purposes. He salvaged wood from the Wisconsin, as well as many other things that came drifting down. Each day was an adventure for him; he never knew what the Wisconsin might bring to him; his boats lay three hundred miles from the river's headwaters, and every rainfall might send freshets into the river far to the north, bearing some new trophy for his houseboats, one of which was already filled with all manner of debris he had rescued from the water churning past.

He lived on fish, and there was always about him a vaguely unpleasant smell of cooked or decayed fish, not quite vanquished by that of whiskey, for John was never without that amber comfort. Often, in his cups, he serenaded his wife, shouting across the river toward the hills dark under the stars. Sometimes he went out to work in Sac Prairie, for age did not diminish his skill as a mason, but in general he avoided work; he preferred his lazy life on the river; he enjoyed the voices of the water, and he had an adolescent fascination for the locomotive which went by once or twice a day, chuffing along on the embankment above him, as well as for the traffic which moved back and forth across the bridge not far below his mooring. Though he had not been born to it, he was essentially a river man; the Wisconsin fulfilled almost all his needs, and whiskey satisfied the rest.

But he was lonely. Sometimes, of spring nights, when the old man was maudlin with drink, his voice rose in wheedling accents, directed toward that long lost wife, begging her to come back, a voice filled with pathos, thrust into the night like a tired sword. What differences had lain between them none knew, but more than one of the townsmen suspected that John had proved too hard to live with, so hard, indeed, as to have driven her almost out of her mind, so that, on her recovery, she fled to her native land, never to return. His sober statements, especially to the young, that his wife had hidden herself away in the hills and was lonely there were a reflection of his own life—it was he who had hidden himself away here beside the river, he who was lonely.

Like so many people who lived alone, he often talked to himself. Startled passersby frequently heard a round of nonsense—aimless talk and meaningless words—directed at the fish he was frying, or the fishing tackle he was in the act of cleaning, or a box in which he kept cooked fish against the time he wished to eat them, or simply at the night and the stars—a farrago of small talk, of weather, of fishing, of the day's events, the tissue of his life; his voice came drifting up out of the night, mingling with the soft sounds of the water, lapping against his boat, rushing around the bridge piers not far away, hushing among the willows along shore, one with the *krark* of a night-fishing heron, blending into the sounds of dancing woodcocks from the opposite bank.

Where he lived was always attractive to children because it represented a youthful ideal of privacy and freedom; they came and fished from his houseboats; they sat and listened to the grotesque fantasies he created, unknowing whether they were meant for them or for himself; and they were careful not to carry home too much of what he said, lest their parents, those inexplicable aliens, forbid them to go near the river. His place on the broad surface of the Wisconsin at Sac Prairie—which was not far above the wider Mississippi—was a port in a wider world; all the river was open to him, hundreds of miles of water, countless bends around each of which lay a vividly beautiful new country, against which Sac Prairie at his back was but a mote in the sun. The whole valley of the Wisconsin was his domain, though he seldom chose to visit any of it; here he stayed, on the river next to the shore, with the majesty of the locomotives behind him, and the open river before.

He was like a symbol left by passing time, a man held over from years of *voyageurs* and *engagés,* of fur-traders and Indians, of Frenchmen passing down the stream on their way from Quebec, of raftsmen and steamboaters, of dugouts and showboats—one man left to remind those who were growing up in new generations of all time past, all time lost. Yet he had none but a tenuous psychic bond to that past; he did not belong to it except by a thin extension, though his very presence in his houseboat on the river seemed to suggest all that teeming life which had once moved up and down the Wisconsin many decades before. Often by night the smoke of his pipe or cigar drifted up through the darkness, and it stood for a tangible man, the great, fat old man who lived out his years closer to running water, the night and the stars than to anyone in Sac Prairie, one not bowed by misanthrophy, but encased in a shell of protective solitude none could pierce.

What passed through his thoughts he never said. He spoke with reluctance and only when pressed of the time he had helped to capture Jefferson Davis, as if this belonged to so remote a past he no longer wished to remember it, and indeed, it may have been so, for he lived well past his time, though he looked no different in his eighties from the way he had looked in his sixties. He never spoke of his wife—save only when he was too drunk to know what he said, and then he spoke rather to her than of her, as if she were within hearing, only hidden from his sight, within his reach if only he knew where to turn to find her. He never spoke of his family, though three sisters and a brother still lived in Sac Prairie; they seldom saw one another, but there was no animosity among them, only indifference—the others were close together; they visited one another daily, and gathered together; but not John—he remained isolated in his chosen retreat, and when he spoke at all it was either to pass the time of day or to say meaningless things, so that more than half the village thought him mildly deranged, an impression he did nothing to alter.

His very roughness—his unshaven face, his rude manners, his ill-kept clothing—all suggested a kind of immortality. He resisted the onslaught of illness; his whiskey was his strength, and the river, when he chose to enter its waters, his only cleanliness—he did not otherwise wash, and, on one occasion when a doctor sent him to a hospital, he was outraged when he was bathed.

Yet at the end, he confounded his detractors, for, taken ill, he voluntarily elected to return to the hospital, bathed every week, kept his single room scrupulously clean, and every day dressed well and walked down town for his meals. It was as if he meant to deliberately turn his back upon his beloved river, but, perhaps more fundamentally, he grew to enjoy being troubled about, the care he received at the hospital satisfied an unfulfilled longing he had nursed all through the years for his lost wife. There he stayed until he died. Even after death he amazed the village: out of his meager income, he had managed to save almost two thousand dollars.

But this hiatus at the hospital was not an integral part of the man who lived in his houseboats on the river; with his passing, with the disappearance of his boats, something of past time went, too, a last link to a romantic time gone by was cut. Sometimes of spring nights the echo of his cajoling voice crying to his lost wife hidden in the hills of his mind fades across the inner ear, and the smoke of his pipe seems faintly still to haunt the dusk.

✳ ✳ ✳ ✳ ✳

THE most gracious singer of all in the river bottoms is the song sparrow. He is joyous or pensive, gay or melancholy, nostalgic and hopeful—and all these at once. I have heard him sing since the earliest days when I went fishing off the Second Island with my father, when that melodious threnody rose and fell all along the river. He accompanied the peregrinations of Hugo Schwenker and myself up among the islands and into the marshes, of Karl Ganzlin and me down along Dickerson's Slough, of Grandfather Derleth and Raymie Geier and me out at the mill-pond, where we went to catch sunfish—not a water bird, but one always to be found in the vicinity of water—at the brookside, the river's bank, the edge of pond or slough.

I have never heard that threnody without a lifting of spirits, the heart leaping up, no matter what the season or the hour of the day; the song is as appropriate at the edge of evening or in the depth of night as it is at dawn or in the heat of afternoon. The song sparrow's melody starts something up in me, something that does not seem to end—a thought, a theme, an idea, intangible—that is half its charm—so that each time I hear it I am persuaded into a familiar dream, for it is a dream, one of those dreams about which, on waking, you remember nothing save that it was a thing of beauty.

It is a song that fills the heart with the sound and musk of running water, the sweet pungence of willows, the whisper of wind in leaves, the very essence of peace. Perhaps, indeed, it is this conscious suggestion which makes the song seem so ineffably beautiful—the beauty of seeming peace to someone in constant turmoil within, someone bereft of inner peace. I am not sure enough, or glib enough, to say. But cause is of no moment; effect alone has meaning.

Often, early in the day, I used to meet the bent figure of old Mrs. Block on her way into town from her timeworn house, the last house on the western edge of the village. She always pulled along behind her a little wagon into which she could put such

groceries as she bought, a wagon which creaked when empty
and creaked when full. She was a woman of greatly advanced
years, short, still somewhat stout, with as wrinkled a face as were
it of the texture of dried apples, the skin dark with that bronzing
associated with old age, her pursed mouth all but toothless, her
dark little eyes sunk into hollows, and her hands clawed and
bony. She was partly deaf, and could not hear unless she were
shouted at; in turn, she did not speak without raising her voice,
too, a voice that was harsh and strident for her inability to hear
its tones, and was besides, heavily accented, for she spoke more
surely in German than in English, and customarily lapsed into her
native tongue.

She lived alone save for a grandson, a great tub of a fellow,
good-natured company for her, and such domestic animals as she
tended—a pig or two, some cats and a flock of chickens, all of
which had the run of the house and could be found in the
parlor as readily as in the kitchen. "They don't do me any harm,"
she would say in explanation, and her inference was clear—these
creatures were more surely her friends than most of her own
kind in Sac Prairie. Yet she bore no one any enmity; she asked
only to live in peace, and offered no tribulation to anyone, either
by word or deed.

I do not recall any alteration in her appearance in the decades
I knew her. When first I was aware of her, she was in her middle
seventies, and she lived to be almost a hundred. During all that
time she was usually clad in voluminous skirts, dun or brown or
black in color, an outer skirt and two or three underskirts, a waist
of some similar sober shade, and a black shawl over her head. She
walked with a peculiarly erratic gait, doubtless because her joints
were stiff, and she seemed always to be lurching from one side of
the walk to the other. Yet her pace was steady, if slow, but not any
slower than it had to be; she had a house and garden to tend,
and a grandson to cook for, and she went about these tasks with
a regularity which permitted no delay.

"*Wer bist du?*" she would ask, peering myopically at anyone who halted to talk to her. She had to hear a name three or four times before she caught it, but once she knew, she placed you immediately in the roster of your family. Sometimes she would tell the story of her life—how her father had brought her sister and herself across the sea in a big ship, how she had been a pretty child, so pretty that a wealthy fellow-traveler had offered to buy her, an offer her father had indignantly spurned. But to this now she looked back with ineffable regret; her life had been very hard; she had raised a large family, and the grandson she now had with her was there only because he was the unwanted son of one of her daughters. "If only—if *only* he had sold me!" she used to cry out, sure beyond question that nothing could have been more difficult than her way of life, as if only the sheer necessity of remaining alive to take care of her family and at the last of her grandson had kept her alive.

She was used to doing her shopping in the morning, on two or three days a week, coming down town sometimes even before the stores were open, for she had been up for hours then, and making her way home directly, save on rare occasions when she took the opportunity to call on people who had been kind to her, and sat taking a cup of coffee with them and telling them how things went with her. "*Es musz gehen. Es musz gehen,*" she would say, shaking her head as if to say that all the woes of life as well as its joys were the inevitable way of the world, and no human being could do anything about it.

On summer afternoons she and her little wagon sometimes went from door to door selling the product of her gardens—carrots, onions, rutabagas—of these she seemed to have an inexhaustible supply, as well as the eggs her chickens laid. She trudged along the streets in the hot summer sunlight, occasionally with the aid of a crude staff, never seeming to mind the heat, though she was so amply dressed that it was doubtful she ever felt it. By this means she supplemented her grandson's income and thus her own, so that when next she went shopping she could indulge herself in a piece of candy or some other small luxury.

She would go into the stores, sure of what she wanted, and call out for it in her harsh, raucous voice, fumbling with her money, but eventually handing out the correct amount, and then take her departure, without undue haste, all in her own good time. The storekeepers were invariably considerate of her, however otherwise they might have borne themselves toward less troublesome but perhaps more arrogant customers, and saw her on her way from one store to another, or finally to the side street leading away from the business section out past the Catholic church, the high school, the depot and the grain elevator, block after block to the western edge of town, where her house sat all alone on the rim of the prairie, with a soft maple tree at one corner of it, and a cluster of lilac bushes before the front door, an old house, long weather-worn, for its paint had peeled away years before, and with a garden on the town side of the house looking very small against the vast expanse of fields which stretched westward toward the ridge of hills diminishing bluely into the horizon.

She had known very little in her life but work and care, pain and sorrow. "If only—if *only* he had sold me!" How despairing was that cry! How difficult her life must have been that she should have come to look back upon that shipboard incident as the most important event in her existence, that event which might have altered the course of her life! Her eyes, when she spoke so, were distant, looking back into that halcyon past as to a dream forever surrendered but still existing somewhere untouched by time and circumstances. And if her life had been so hard, yet she had survived it, and one could doubt that she would have survived any other existence as readily. It was a tribute to her indomitable will to live that she was to be seen week after week on the streets of Sac Prairie, wheeling her squeaky wagon to and from town, when many another, far younger woman, had someone else to wait upon her declining years.

What went on behind those ruminative eyes? I often wondered. She never spoke of the present at all, except to say that her grandson was a comfort to her in her last thirty years, that he was "a good boy," and showed her more consideration than some of her children had done. She always spoke of the years gone by, of the years of her youth in this new country, of her marriage to a farmer, a rude, uncouth man, who had made her work from dawn to dark and often by night, and had bestowed upon her one child after another, until her youth and her beauty were alike faded and gone, and she was old without ever having known the joy and pleasure of freedom and the young years which, for her, had meant an early marriage and the premature responsibilities of motherhood. She used to say sometimes she had been "born old," for the only youth she remembered was the attention she had won on the crossing from Germany so many years ago, and to her the man who had offered to buy her shone in memory like a shining knight; he might have been an adventurer, an elderly roué, even a man in the white slave traffic—anything but a philanthropist—no matter; he had seen her beauty and her youth, he had wanted her, and now, in retrospect, whatever life he might have offered her must surely have been happier than the one she had lived, so that she could cry out against her father with absolute, unquestioning sincerity, "If only—if *only* he had sold me!"

She had a quality of agelessness which was perhaps the single compensation for the misery of her life; if she had aged early in life, she had lived for so long unchanged that one never thought of her as growing older; she seemed to be as old as she could grow —wrinkled, wizened, with skeletal hands, her progress along the streets snail-slow compared to that of the village children; she was the epitome of age. Yet she was not decrepit; she moved about under her own power, and she spurned all offers of assistance with genuine indignation, save on such occasions as she did not feel well, and then only would she allow some old friend to take her home in his car.

Time and again she cheated death. She took sick and her life was despaired of, but she invariably recovered to be seen down town time and again, buying her groceries and hauling them home, independent and stubborn, for this obligation had become not only a rite, but one of her sole reasons for leaving her house, and afforded her a kind of holiday. She went nowhere else in public; the "doings" of Sac Prairie saw her not—she never attended shows, card parties, school functions, plays, dances—though once in a great while she showed up at school picnics held in the Free-thinkers' Park, wandering like a lost soul through the grounds, renewing for a little while perhaps memories of happier days when her own children had taken part in just such gatherings. But those picnics were abandoned in later years, and she was seen no more save with her wagon on her round.

Sometimes she merely muttered in reply to a greeting; sometimes she paused and stared after someone who had greeted her, trying in vain with her failing sight to identify the one who had spoken to her. If she needed direction or any kind of information, she hailed the first person she met. *"Du!"* she could call out, *"Du!"*, ask her questions, and be gone. Despite her grandson's staying with her, she was much alone, for he was gone most of the time, working somewhere, or idling with a fishing rod along the river, for he was much given to this pastime and took great delight in exhibiting his catch before he took it home for his grandmother to prepare. Her deafness, her fading sight, her solitude in a world from which all the companions of her youth and maturity were gone in death all combined to isolate her; she lived in a world not of faces, for she did not often see her children, but rather of lesser creatures—her pigs, her cats, her chickens; and her occu-pation in her house and in her garden, where she could not see well enough to distinguish clearly between vegetables and weeds, might have been a sensible alternative to solitary brooding.

She came down into town without fail past her ninetieth birth-day and well on toward her hundredth, which she failed to reach.

Despite all the sickness which had come upon her and failed to vanquish her, at the end she took to her bed and rested quietly for a while and then died, not so much because she was ill, but simply because, after so many decades beyond that dream of the life that might have been if only her father had sold her, she had grown tired.

❀   ❀   ❀   ❀   ❀

NOTHING more arresting comes out of the woods of a summer night than the song of the pewee. Be it in two notes or three, or perhaps one long drawn-out keening note, the song's nostalgia makes its instant appeal to ear and heart. It comes drifting out of the woods darkening with dusk and twilight, a voice belonging to that world of half dark, though it is no less to be heard at mid-day, when it is but one among a score of others. It arrests, it challenges, it seduces with its invitation to anyone outside that perimeter of darkness, drawing him in, in spirit, certainly, if the flesh but stand to pay its tribute to that invisible singer.

The song of the pewee seems to stand for all that is unknown about a woods. Why this should be so, I do not know, but I understand that one comes to listen for the pewee's voice year after year, as I do. Anyone heeding that invitation to come into the darkening woods would seldom see its source, for the woods at night is a place in which to come face to face with one's self, to acknowledge the mote-like insignificance of man in this cosmos. I think of the pewee sometimes as the essential voice of the woods, though the song is often little more than a breath, a whisper, a small keening which drifts out upon the evening air like a melody from time gone by, yet it commands the ear, it challenges the heart, it demands awareness that here in these notes the woods speaks to every listening ear.

Too, it is the summer's one unfailing voice, raised in every kind *of weather, dry or hot, wet, humid or windy, cloying or cool, the one unwavering voice which speaks for the depths of the woods in which by night there are so many fugitive movements and sounds, rustlings, snapping twigs, strange muted voices, which symbolize that vast, intimate life being lived without cognizance almost side by side with the humming mills of the human beings who are still so far from any integration with the land. In its own way, this dulcet song is as beguiling as any aspect of the woods at night, and as unknown; dusk and darkness are its proper conditions; the enclosing woods its most fitting milieu. It speaks for the woods, it speaks for all the wild earth, asking over and over for man to come in, to come back to that primitive intimacy with the earth and the sky, with brooks and trees and hills and all mankind's wild brothers.*

Pe-wee, pe-wee, *it says.* Pe-a-wee . . .

Come in, come in, *it says.* Be not afraid . . .

—making its invitation throughout dusk and darkness, speaking for the forever mysterious woods, where the very trees in their windy susurration seem to hush and respire, respire and hush with the pulse of unknown night and the rhythm of the planet on its way through eternity.

When I was a boy, there was, apart from the lavish offerings of river, marshes, hills, only one place of entertainment for young people. True, there were occasional medicine shows and carnivals come to town, and once a year the manufacturers of Buster Brown shoes sponsored a gala parade in Sac Prairie, which vied with the annual school picnic, but only the Electric Theatre could be depended upon for regular entertainment, week after week. When my sister and I were children, we went with our parents on the "family night" to see Pearl White, William S. Hart, Sessue Hayakawa, Charlie Chaplin, Fatty Arbuckle, and a galaxy of others, though we were on tenterhooks all week between movies in our devotion to the melodramatic serial which was always a part of such programs, designed to lure the customers back week after week. But inevitably, as I began to explore the village on my own, I preferred to go to the movies with Hugo or Karl or Mark, and on such occasions I grew less aware of the screen and more conscious of the audience and the setting.

The Electric Theatre rose on the riverbank half a block north of the harness shop; it was a great rectangular building of yellow brick, with a store on the ground floor, and the theatre upstairs, reached by two enclosed stairways along the south and north walls, though, because the ticket office was at the end of a little hall at the head of the south stairway, the north stairs were used only as an exit. In the years of my adolescence the ticket office was occupied by the manager, Bill Henning, a house painter by trade, and the projection booth inside by a variety of young fellows, among whom I remember best Elzy Huerth, very probably because we were all more familiar with Elzy since he and his widowed mother lived up the street only a few doors from the theatre, and he was the owner of a rowboat, which, presumably, gave him a leg up the social scale over the rest of the river-haunters who were not boat-owners.

The obligations of the manager did not stop at selling tickets; it was his duty also to keep the player piano going, which he did by punching a button in the office whenever the spirit moved him, which was usually when he became excited at some scene he watched from the opening through which he leaned into the theatre from the office, as a result of which there came about some of the most hilarious combinations of screen action and accompanying music conceivable by man—scenes of desperate tragedy were accompanied by bucolic ditties like *Won't You Wait Till the Cows Come Home?*, violent screen battles came on to the tune of a lullaby, wedding marches set the background for murder, and so on. It was also part of his responsibility to keep the patrons happy, which meant primarily Mrs. William Dresen, who never missed a movie and was thus an asset to the business. Bill was constantly scuttling in and out of the office before each program began, and sometimes during the program in an effort to quiet riotous children down front, particularly Si Tarnutzer, who participated vociferously in all the action on the screen, groaning aloud at every blunder made by the hero, shouting warnings to the cowboys of impending Indian attacks, and leaping out of his seat to jump up and down in excitement, all of which added considerably to the charm of an evening at the Electric Theatre. In between time, Bill found occasion to entertain us with praise of his son, Charlie, the oldest of three sons; Charlie was in the Navy, and to hear Bill, the sun rose and set in Charlie, a not uncommon phenomenon associated with first-born children.

The boys—and to some extent the girls—always carried on a kind of war with Bill—and with Regina Dresen, as well. For all that she had had a very colorful past, Regina was determinedly self-important; as the most faithful patron of the movies, she arrogated to herself all kinds of privileges. She fixed upon "her" seat, and she meant to sit in that seat whenever she came to the Electric Theatre; Bill Henning saw to it that she did. In the course of achieving her purpose, Regina affronted many of us. There were two kinds of seats in the Electric Theatre—the folding chairs and the "good" seats, which were, truth to tell, little better than the folding chairs. Regina sat to the right of the center section, at the aisle, for she was a big, buxom woman who liked to stretch her fat legs into the aisle. We sat, the dividing aisle between us, directly in front of Regina and her husband.

And because, in front of me, sat Margery and Norma Kahn, my head kept ducking forward and back through most of the picture. This bothered Regina on two counts—first, because it distracted her a little, second because Margery was her niece, and not Catholic, and Regina had set herself against any romance between her niece and a Catholic boy, for Regina, having sowed many a field of wild oats, had now settled down and was the organist at St. Aloysius, pious in her devotions, as is so often true of many once hot-blooded women come to old age. We too sat in the "good" seats along that north wall, and Regina thought to solve the initial problem of distraction by having the management move the seats and substitute folding chairs for them.

From the time that the management acceded to her wishes in this, we subjected both Regina and Bill Henning to all kinds of harassments, from sending other people to sit in Regina's seat to the loud pretense of seeing rats in the aisles, creating frequent diversions to add to the general din and disorder of the evenings at the old Electric, all to make sure that Regina's enjoyment of the movies was diminished by a good deal more than a boy's head bobbing back and forth a distance of eight rows in front of her.

Eventually the seats were moved back, and the harassments came to an end, which was just as well, for by that time I was in the throes of first love, and the evening at the Electric was fulfilled if Margery was there, no matter what was on the screen, and it was hollow and interminable if she was not, and I no longer cared about Regina, or listened to Bill, or watched to see whether old Mr. Frank came, treating himself to a bag of peanuts and leaving his wife at home, as usual, or whether Si Tarnutzer threw himself into the spirit of the picture, or whether a chair would collapse under Christ Fuchs, whom we all thought a very fat man, judged by the standards of youth, or looked to see which girls the more sporting blades were bringing to the theatre....

It seemed to me in those days that the Electric Theatre was there for a long time, but it was not, and everything seemed to come to an end at one time—that first romance faded and died, high school days came to a close and we scattered to walk different paths, and one day the Electric Theatre quietly closed and another theatre opened in Upper Sac Prairie, after which the evenings at the old Electric fell back into the past with remarkable swiftness, soon belonging irrevocably to time gone by.

❅ ❅ ❅ ❅ ❅

EARLY in the summer mornings the veery's harp vies with the lyricism of wood thrushes in the region of the Spring Slough—wood thrushes nearby, all along the slough and the embankment of the railroad, the veerys calling from deep in the woods, out of reach, almost out of hearing, like the acme of something unattainable, their songs rising in the hours before the dew has begun to evaporate, before the day's heat reaches in along the railroad tracks, when the inhabitants of the bottoms have been about their business only a little while and the creatures of the night have repaired to nest or burrow a scant hour before.

The veery never sings very long; as the day burgeons, he becomes silent and is not heard again until dusk enfolds the woods, and sometimes not until another morning. I used to hear him especially on days of July and August, when I went for a short walk along the tracks, no farther than the brook or the east end of the Spring Slough Trestle, and back again; and I paused here and there, arrested each time I heard that harp-like threnody. I never saw the singer, but I knew him for all that. I heard him so rarely—as if he dared come no closer to mankind's boundaries in Sac Prairie—that I could count his songs every morning and never have counted very many, and finally I went only to hear him.

I suppose this is always nature's challenge—the seldom heard, the seldom seen—these become the goal of the walker, all else seeming commonplace, despite its beauty, for the frequency of its occurrence. So it was when once I saw a great black gyr-falcon, and another time a great grey owl; I kept on looking for them, and saw the gyr-falcon once more, but the owl never again. On some days the veery did not sing, and was doubly attractive to ear and

heart on those days when he did, and all the choir of the birds,
all the matins rising at every hand took second place to the veery's
harp, which became for me the spirit and voice of the summer
morning in the woods.

You could meet Rich Monn sometimes late at night, woefully under the influence, shouting his defiance of the universe, bewailing his lot—not an old man, indeed, hardly into his middle years, not ill-favored in looks, but a lost soul. In his sober moments he cared tenderly for his aging mother; in his cups he abused her. Some deep inner dissatisfaction gnawed at him; some frustration embittered his life. Rich had been a sailor, a factory worker, a village employee; he had once wanted to be an artist, but he worked little at it, and it could not have been this failure which compelled him to drink, for he never seemed to have taken it seriously enough, and he mentioned it amiably in his sober moments as a man talks about something he once wanted vaguely to do, but had voluntarily given up long since. What it was that ate at him no one knew, for he never said. The grievances to which he gave voice in his drunkenness were generalizations against government or petty personalities. He was best left alone, for in bibulous conversation he inevitably wanted to fight, as if in his befuddled state he conceived of every adversary as the embodiment of his woes.

In my childhood there were more like him—old man Quimby, for instance, who staggered his way homeward and seldom reached there; I used to see him lying drunkenly in a ditch or in one of the parks, sleeping; or Barney Jaggers, who had a shrew for a wife, though he himself was a pleasant, easy-going fellow— no sooner did he come into his house than she ranted at him like a virago, though he sat quietly listening, which enraged her so that she attacked his submissive silence by striking him, and, when he had raised a hand to defend himself, she ran from the house screaming to the neighbors that he was beating her; or corpulent Flem Baltes, who was afraid of the dark and of the invisible beings inhabiting it, and ultimately put a wire around his neck and hanged himself. In later years, however, Rich was almost alone in his determined intemperance, for no one wanted to drink with him beyond an initial glass or two, his quarrelsomeness being well known, and few wished to dare it.

Sometimes I listened to his ranting, when I came upon him in the night. There was something about him where he stood all by himself under the trees and the stars, on the edge of the streetlight's glow in the darkness, that was symbolic of many men and women, not alone in this Sac Prairie, but in all the Sac Prairies of the world, something which spoke, out of that pathetic, ludicrous figure, of the spiritual isolation of so many people, something which made the thoughtful onlooker to wonder what thin line divided him from that other, knowing perhaps that the distance of chance or Providence was less great than the few steps separating one from the other in that darkness. And where in such moments was the pleasant-spoken fellow one knew when he was sober? And, on the other hand, where was this raging torment of the drunkard hidden in those sober moments?

There was never any doubt as to which was the real man—it was this haunted, lonely creature, who was truly a nocturnal wanderer, this angry, raging man whose fury against the intangibles of government was surely nothing more than despair at the emptiness and meaninglessness of his own life. He never said anything memorable in his cups, nor did I expect him to. He existed on a different plane, somewhere out of reach, where no one could touch him, no word could impress him, where he walked blindly in his own private darkness, sharing with no one. But his solitude, his despair, his unseeing rage were tangible things in the Sac Prairie night, and you thought of him as lost to himself, as if somewhere he had hidden himself, the boy and young man he had been, and was forever making his futile search to recover something he never knew he had had.

They said he did not want to face reality. But which reality? Was it that of his sobriety or of his intoxication? Or was the one unreal and the other real? As he grew older, he sought the solace of the bottle all the more; there was something there which was real to him beyond the mundane trappings of his sober existence, and perhaps his abuse of himself was the rage of a man who longs for death but is too cowardly to seek it himself.

But, as sometimes happens, because of circumstances and events which touched upon his life, he changed almost imperceptibly as he passed fifty. Perhaps it was that at this time his mother became gravely ill and had to suffer an amputation, so that thereafter the responsibilities of his little family—there were but he and his mother—fell upon him, and he gave over liquor. He went about to those places where he was most frequently seen —the harness shop, the hardware store—and said, "I'm on the wagon," and then, later, "I'm off that stuff."

No one believed his reformation would last. Yet, strangely, it did. When his mother died soon after, the villagers looked for him to return to the bars he had frequented for so long. He did not. Instead, he spent all one winter yielding once more to the wanderlust he had known as a young man; he went to California, but was more than ever satisfied with Wisconsin when he came back.

His reformation had wrought yet another change. Whereas before he had spent his grievances against persons and government in his enraged words, now he took to lecturing all who paused to talk with him and were known to indulge in liquor, about the evils of drink, the effect of alcohol on the body, all to such an extent that his former companions—of whom there had never been many—tended to avoid him, for his glowering gloom about drinking spoiled their pleasure in a glass or two now and then, for few of them had ever been so given over to alcohol that they were accustomed to intoxication.

Perhaps he had some intimation of the damage liquor had wrought upon him. In his last year he complained frequently of dizziness and lack of breath. Yet he would not cease working, driving himself beyond his endurance. Perhaps his reformation was as great a shock to his system as his excesses had been before. His time of reformation did not last long, through no voluntary act of his; he worked too hard one day, came down off the roof of the house he was dismantling, and fell dead in his little summer kitchen, less than three years after his mother's death. He lay for a day before he was found. It was an irony that he was borne to his grave by some of his nocturnal companions of earlier years.

His death disclosed what never crossed his lips, revealing a secret he had never shared. A sister, going through his things in the summer kitchen where he kept them, came upon a bundle of letters and found them to be love letters written to him by a young woman, a teacher who had taught in a country school west of Sac Prairie. His sister was astonished to learn that Rich had been in love, so clandestine had he kept his romance. What had happened to that romance? Had it been so fragile that it had not survived? Or had it faded and died after she had taken a position elsewhere? His sister had not the heart to read the letters, and destroyed them.

Rich had also left poems he had written to the object of his affection. Labored verses, true, but his own, put down in pencilled drafts, with many erasures and deletions, poems singing the glory of their "meeting place"—

> "Where two rivulets unite
> To babble over a rustic dam,
> Laughingly both day and night . . .
> Is there a place on all this earth

More close to paradise?
Does it not seem as sacred
As any other earthly sod?
Has it not all the beauty
And grace adorned from God? . . ."

written long after they had parted. There had never been any
other love affair in his life and, soon after, he had begun, with his
enlistment in the Navy, that restless wandering which was to become so much a part of his existence for two decades.

Perhaps it was the failure of his only romance which had embittered him so against the world; perhaps he had so idealized
that one young woman that none other could take her place, an
idealization of love itself, for he could not have known his school
teacher as well as he might have; his love had existed on so delicate
and tenuous a plane that it had never known any disillusionment
save the hour of parting, so that it may have been that she remained forever enshrined in his memory as the very personifica-
tion of ideal love, without blemish. Small wonder then that he
could turn to no other, but looked ever inward to that one
memory which must have seemed to him forever a singularly
perfect thing.

These letters, his poor poems, a few books, some faded
photographs, a few clippings from newspapers—these were his
most cherished possessions. It was to these that he always returned,
these and the memories to which they belonged, even as he belonged to them. These were the world he shared with no one,
so that when he came back of nights to his whitewashed little
house, he retreated into a past that was forever warm and made
pleasant by the mementoes of the one perfect thing he had known
—that unalloyed love, untouched by the disillusionment that is the
inevitable portion of all love, the dream from which he never
awakened, and to which he sought always to return—as much in
the solitude of his little house as in that terrible, drunken isolation

when, in the dark hours, he roamed the streets, blind in his own
night, venting his rage and despair upon the stars and the wind in
the elms, knowing beyond hope that he could never go back into
the brief reality of that one unforgettable dream.

❋ ❋ ❋ ❋ ❋

NO *nocturnal voice seems lonelier than the whippoorwill's. Perhaps it is that somewhere in the past it represented
something unattainable to me, as it still does, something only a
little way ahead, something in the dark, out of sight but never
quite out of hearing, to be reached for but never to be found,
something lonely, desirable, apart and lost, belonging to me but
not to be touched, like childhood or youth, accounting for the
nostalgia I read into the song.*

*I know that the psychiatrists tell us that the urge to go home
again, back to irresponsible childhood, to the womb, might ac-
count for this kind of reaction, but this to me is a concept related
not to the self nearly so much as to the desire of the self to be
merged with the universe, not as in the psychiatrists' death-wish,
but in a spiritual oneness which is akin to the eternal quest for
unity with God or with that omnipotence which is represented
in the concept of God.*

*Long ago, when I was still a child, I used to go visiting every
summer at the hilltop farm of my Aunt Annie Ring, west of Sac
Prairie, between Plain and Spring Green, a setting which afforded
a magnificent view of the prairie south of Spring Green, which
opened upon the wooded slopes and valleys all around, which
ought to have satisfied my need for the outdoors. For two or
three weeks I remained with my mother, grandmother and sister
among my cousins there at the farm. The boys who were my
cousins were either too young or too old to be companionable,
and the girls kept to themselves. The days were spent in visits to*

other relatives in nearby pockets of the hills, in hunting for wild strawberries in the woods back of the farm, in hikes. By the end of the first week, the novelty of the farm had worn off, and I grew progressively more homesick for the Wisconsin and its islands, for the sloughs and the familiar hills, and on some days I would climb into an apple tree at the corner of the orchard and spend hours just sitting there alone, looking into the distance where Sac Prairie was. And in those nights, early to bed, I was awakened by the crying of the whippoorwills, numerous in the darkness of the hills and valleys. Perhaps somehow the whippoorwills came to represent the unattainable desire of that youthful heart, the longing for home, but home as more than a refuge for the body among familiar places.

However it may be, the song of the whippoorwill surpasses all other nocturnal sounds in mind and heart. This is the last migrant to call in the spring, late in April usually, and it can be heard all summer long, sometimes until October. All other nocturnal voices are second to it. Quite early after my return to Sac Prairie from that one venture into city living, I took to going out at night to listen to the whippoorwills, in a conscious effort to exceed the 1,088 consecutive calls once clocked by John Burroughs; I went out many times every season, stopping the car to listen west of town and east and south of Sac Prairie, but it was a quarter of a century before I achieved that objective—1,507 consecutive whippoorwill calls in an unbroken succession, and then knew the irony of hearing them from my own doorstep.

I can understand how the whistling of a locomotive at night may sound lonely, how it may symbolize flight, escape, but I cannot say how the crying of a whippoorwill brings a tenuous mixture of joy and sadness out of the dark hills, nor how it represents all the lost hopes and dreams, how it stirs the visions and longing of boy and man, as if it were not a bird but the disembodied voice of night itself, of the very earth brooding in the

darkness, the changed and the changeless, the living and the dead,
time past and coming time, the boy who was and the man who is,
forever one.

Long ago, when I was a child, I used to see the Trautmann
sisters of evenings about the lilac-haunted grounds of their little
earth-hugging house on Water Street, north of the business section of Sac Prairie. They seemed to me then creatures of the
dark, like the moths that appeared after sundown and fluttered
briefly about in the dusk before darkness shrouded them. I existed
in awe of them, perhaps so many children had so frequently repeated the delusions and gossip of their elders, who thought the
sisters mad because an autocratic old man of Sac Prairie had once
had them committed for a short time as insane when they had
attempted to cure a fever by sweating it out on the porch of their
little house, though village gossip also insisted that old Paul
Bauman had gone to these lengths only to secure certain valuable
property the sisters would not sell him, and, having got hold
of it, put no further obstacle in the way of their freedom. Certainly
on their return from their ordeal, their property was no longer
intact.

They were manifestly nonconformists. They were well-
educated, they had taught school, they had a great respect for
education. As a little girl, Miss Rose had been so eager to learn
that she had often walked all the way from her home near Roxbury
east of Sac Prairie and crossed the Wisconsin on the ice in the
dead of winter's coldest weather to attend school, at one time
daring the ice floes of an early break-up to take her examinations,
in which she placed first. They subscribed to all kinds of papers,
among them one called *The American Nonconformist*, published
in Iowa by a gentleman with whom Miss Barbara was accustomed
to correspond, giving her opinions with great clarity and striking
intelligence, if positiveness, which so impressed him that he, for

one, could not believe in the insanity of the sisters, and ultimately set in motion a chain of events which resulted in their release. They kept to themselves most of the time, being self-sufficient. They had always been that in a kind of nonconformist way which no doubt irritated their more conventional friends and neighbors, who were quite ready to believe the worst of them, as small-minded conventional sheep always are of those who scorn or defy conventions. Their home was one of those old-fashioned little houses, built low, of one storey, with trees towering above it—oak, mulberry, maple and others—and great bushes of lilacs pressing close upon the house on almost every side. Something there was almost always in bloom or in fruit, attracting many birds, and sunlight and moonlight lay with equal felicity in patterns of light and shade on house and grounds. Usually of an evening a single window shone with yellow lamplight, for they were too old to trouble much with electricity, and they had no wish to hem themselves in with change, preferring the familiar, as so many aging people prefer to cling to something long known and forego the psychic readjustment necessary for acceptance of the new.

They habitually wore very long full dresses, usually grey or brown, the colors of decades before. Despite their existence in an aura of the strange and sinister, they were invariably gentle and kind, they answered when spoken to, they were unobtrusive, and went their way without troubling anyone. When first I knew them, they were in the habit of wearing sunbonnets, which were at one time a familiar sight in Sac Prairie but have since almost passed out of use; from deep within these capacious articles of head-wear, their round-cheeked faces looked out, brown of skin, wrinkled as russets kept too long in a dry place. Their eyes were grave, contemplative, pleasant; they peered from their faces as from a place much farther away, from a greater depth then was immediately apparent.

After their rescue from the asylum, they had vented their indignation upon old Paul Bauman and the village by writing a booklet—*Wisconsin's Shame*—in which they told the story of their cruel treatment; but since this was "before my time," as one is wont to say in Sac Prairie, I was not aware of it until years later, after they were gone, and then I read it, interested in knowing what they had written, curiously moved by their forthright title and its three sub-headings, one of which proclaimed that they had been kidnapped and "run into an Insane Asylum."

"During the latter part of August, 1888, my sister Barbara and myself made a short stay on our farm, situated about two and a half miles from Sac Prairie, for the purpose of looking after our crops, which were then being harvested. On returning home . . . my sister remarked that she had again contracted malaria, to which she was especially subject while on the farm, it being located near a swamp. The next morning . . . she had a fever chill, and proceeded at once to take a sweat for relief. Wrapping up in a blanket, she seated herself on the porch to take a sun bath. She also put the bedding out of her chamber window, on the roof of the porch, for an airing and sunning. It was a warm day, and our neighbors, seeing her thus wrapped up, must have thought it singular, and made remarks about it. It was also reported that we slept on the roof of the house.

"Saturday afternoon, Martin Leim, one of the most loathsome, debauched, and debased creatures of Sac Prairie, was sent to tell father, who was then on the farm, that both his daughters were insane. Father said he did not believe it, for we had been there the day before. Whoever employed a man of Leim's stamp, had nothing good in view. Why not send for a physician, if something unusual was noticed to be the matter with us? . . . About two o'clock Sunday afternoon, the sheriff and two constables came to take us away. . . . No one uttered a syllable relative to insanity, but to all our inquiries as to whither we were going, no definite answers were given; some said to take a ride, others, to visit friends in Baraboo.

"Mr. Bauman did not show himself that afternoon, though, as

I found out later, he made an application to the court to cause our removal. Were we so dangerous Saturday morning, that he found it necessary to employ a special messenger to Baraboo? Mr. Bauman had not conversed with us two minutes. He came to me Saturday, about ten o'clock, and asked me to come to his office at two o'clock in the afternoon, for the purpose of drawing up a school program.... At the same time the hypocrite had made an application for a judicial inquiry. Upon a second application he became our guardian! After performing these friendly (?) acts he kept himself aloof, but had his tools to attend to the rest....

"Can Mr. Bauman explain what hurry there was? We molested no one. If he noticed that all was not right, why not perform the friendly act of calling competent counsel in our case? Why delay and call for a judicial action first, unknown to us? Why not prevent the mean act of having us examined by doctors, at an unusual time of day, secretly and without calling relatives and friends to see that our personal feelings were respected, and that the whole proceeding was conducted with impartiality? Why assume guardianship without our consent and knowledge? We had a right to choose our guardian, if we needed one.... I doubt if Mr. Bauman has any conscience; for how could he do as he did, and walk abroad under the sunlight? He ought to hide himself forever from a beneficent atmosphere. His actions show too plainly what object he had in view."

Certainly the record of their experiences, written jointly by Miss Rose and Miss Barbara, is one of horror; that they were not the hallucinations some readers attempted to brand them is patent in the evidence of other contemporary documents. They indicted attendants, superintendents, physicians with damning effect, but they reserved their special scorn for Paul Bauman and those of their neighbors who had done nothing for them, leaving it to an interested stranger, the editor of *The American Nonconformist*, to inaugurate the investigation which ultimately resulted in their freedom, after two years of their lives wantonly taken away.

Nothing remains to say why their father was intimidated into helplessness; nothing to explain why, if what they charged was untrue, old Paul Bauman did not exercise the legal prerogatives which were his and bring about the suppression of the book by injunction to restrain sale and collect damages from its publisher. It went into three editions, an orange-covered booklet selling at fifteen cents a copy, and doubtless it found many readers in and beyond Sac Prairie, though perhaps, as so often happens, no one had paid much attention to it other than to use the booklet as a topic of casual, no doubt malicious conversation, for old Paul, with his autocratic and arrogant ways, was heartily disliked in many places, and afterwards it receded into the pattern of the past and was glossed over by the endless succession of minutes and hours and days that went by. Yet none could have escaped the fact that, though he had cause for successful action, Paul Bauman did not take such action.

Of what Paul Bauman must have felt, there is no record. How he must have seethed and fulminated behind his front! But how the sisters must have thwarted him in the first place, to have excited and driven his arrogant ego to so terrible an act of vengeance as the one he carried out against them! He, supposedly a leading citizen of Sac Prairie at that time, the clerk of the Board of Education, which employed Miss Rose as a teacher in the public schools, the faculty of which knew full well that Miss Rose had never shown any sign of insanity, descending to an act so abominable that only his overweening arrogance could have prevented people from ignoring him at his exposure. A large-framed man with a bushy beard and hard, uncompromising eyes, a man who ruled his home with an iron rod and never left a doubt about the gulf that yawned between the members of his family on the one hand, and the servants and village poor on the other. After this booklet made its appearance, only a man of such incredible pride and ego as to be blind to the lightning in the hand of God could have walked the streets in serenity. But old Paul did not believe in God; he believed only in himself, in his will, his desires, and perhaps he walked in comfort at the thought of the hideous cruelty and brutality he had caused to be visited upon two helpless women who had refused to accede to his wish. But his head was held high thereafter with ever-increasing effort, and surely he was not blind to the scorn in the eyes of those he had been accustomed to scorn.

He lived with the indictment of *Wisconsin's Shame* for two decades, and then died. The sisters lived on. There are people who are said to live "beyond their time," which is to say that they have refused to conform to change and progress; but the Trautmann sisters were ever nonconformists, and no one could question that. Destiny, which had already treated them cruelly, had one last irony in store for them. Years after their bitter experience—and no doubt in very large part because of it—after their tribulation had been forgotten by the public, Miss Barbara, the elder, began to grow queer, she imagined herself pursued by someone with homicidal intentions, she believed someone had poisoned their well, she developed paranoid tendencies and was quite mad when at last she died, leaving Miss Rose alone.

Miss Rose lived on into her nineties, attended at first by a large entourage of cats, all of which had proprietary rights in her and everything in the house; they were wont to follow her wherever she went, though never beyond the boundaries of her property, where, often as not, they awaited her return, sedately secure in the knowledge that she would go no farther than the local library a few blocks away, there to have some conversation with Josephine Merk and return.

In Miss Rose's last years, a school-teacher niece came to live with her, a quiet, reclusive woman, who managed to combine her profession with whatever duty she conceived toward her old aunt. Miss Rose died at last, a decade after Miss Barbara, and both the sisters made bequests to the local library, to signify their respect for books and the learning to be had from them, a last expression, perhaps, of their awareness of the ignorance of those neighbors and acquaintances who had so carelessly permitted the indignity visited upon them to take place without challenge.

They left, too, an unmistakable atmosphere about their little house, and not even the time gone by since then or the changes wrought in Sac Prairie have altered it much, so that there is still about it a brooding sense of mystery, of the inexplicable, of haunting bitterness and sadness, a kind of passive resignation, of moonlight and two strange old women, habitants of dusk.

❋   ❋   ❋   ❋   ❋

NO winter is ever so long or so bitter but that, by mid-March, the ear is attuned to that first harsh zeep *which announces the return of the woodcock and is but a prelude to the vaulting ecstasy of the bird's aerial dance. Sometimes the bird arrives as early as the fourteenth of March; sometimes not for two weeks later; but whenever that first nasal* zeep *rises out of the chilly twilight, whenever that dark body first hurtles aloft in its wonderfully stirring dance against the evening heavens, the silence and the darkness of the winter nights are done for another year. But not until then—for the early killdeer ceases to call with the setting sun, and so too do the redwings and the bluebirds and song sparrows which might have preceded the woodcocks' return. Only the woodcocks cry and dance for some hours into the night, beginning not long after sundown.*

In this avian ecstasy there is inherent an experience which enriches all who behold it, something primal, something which went on before the arrival on the scene of man and his works, something which may last beyond man. I never tired of watching the aerial dance of the woodcocks, and on several occasions I managed, by dint of perseverance, to make my way to the place from which the bird had risen—once he was safely aloft—for the woodcock habitually returns to approximately the same spot from which it rises. On one evening, I sat on a stump while this long-billed songster stood within reach, less than two feet away, making his harsh calls, tipping his body awkwardly with each cry, and vaulting suddenly into the heavens, to circle with the wind winnowing in his wings, chirping excitedly in his mating dance.

I learned in this manner that approximately five seconds elapsed between the end of the descent after a flight aloft, and the beginning of the next round of calls, a period of time which seldom varied unless the bird were disturbed, though the number of calls before the dance took place again varied considerably. Watching that awkward body while the bird called, made that ecstatic flight seem all the more impressive with an impressiveness and a primal beauty which belong to this rite of spring as to no other.

The first promise of the spring evening, after the long, still winter nights, lies in the rapture of the woodcocks, in which instantly all the tribulations of the frozen season are dimmed and lost.

If you had met him on the streets of Sac Prairie and passed the time of day with him, you would have said of Louis Karberg that he was mild-mannered almost to old-time courtliness, a man of good will beyond doubt, a considerate old gaffer who had not forgotten that kindness and courtesy were an essential part of life as it should be led; and you would have little reason to suspect, unless you were permitted some intuitive perception enabling you to look for an instant behind his eyes and his manner, that he was a man adrift in a sea of doubt, far from any shore, a floating island, as it were, in an ocean compounded of iconoclasm and agnosticism. Though he was robust in his appearance—indeed, in his last years he looked very much like a portly Buffalo Bill, with a similar white thatch and goatee—the spirit within him was worn thin for all its futile assaults upon the increasing materialism of his time.

He was a desperately lonely man, though his appearance belied it. He was ruddy of complexion, with a glory of hair, dark when first I knew him, but later streaked with grey and whitening, a moustache, quizzical blue eyes, a fine, firm mouth, and bushy brows which were never trimmed but allowed to jut impressively forth. He was one of the few men in Sac Prairie who habitually carried a cane; he owned a variety of walking sticks and did justice to them, swinging them grandly on his good days, brandishing them or thumping them resoundingly against the floor in the heat of an argument. He was heavy rather than fat, and, while his manner was usually mild, he could be bristling with fierceness whenever he faced anyone who doubted his credos.

He was a man sorely confused in mind. Long ago, when he was a little boy, he had been brought up by a dogma of the German Lutheran community in which he then lived; day by day, month after month, year after year, it was dinned into his ears by mother, teacher, and minister that *"Glauben ist nicht Wissen!"*—to believe is not to know—and somehow it had become his unshakable conviction that *belief* in anything was wrong to being sinful, that one *knew* things, one never simply believed them. As he grew older, therefore, and became aware of the contentiousness of the race, he became more perplexed and bewildered by the beliefs of people who ought to have been informed, in his eyes, with knowledge similar to his own. And when he spoke, he always said, "I know," when he should have said, "I believe"; but he meant to say "I know" and by his own judgment, he did know.

"I know that there is an All-Knowing Spirit that is God," he would say. "I know that a thought that thinks is alive and where all these thoughts come together there is knowledge." And he would try with long-suffering patience to explain his convictions, becoming more and more confused, until his very words reflected the chaos within. "Might is Light," he would say, "and where

Light is there is God, and therefore I am God," which, to the initiate, was semantically nonsense but theologically sound, for he meant to say that insofar as the Lord God was the giver of light, as the sun and the soul are both light, then he, having a soul, was integrally part of the fount of knowledge, the omniscient and omnipresent God. But his thoughts were capable of no order; there was confusion within and chaos without; his ideas and credos were lost in a morass of meaningless verbiage, and year upon year he was subject to the deepest, most excoriating torment of the spirit in his fruitless efforts to set forth his knowledge in the face of the mounting conviction of his fellowmen that he was harmlessly but certainly mad.

Perhaps it was a tribute to his courage and to the hope he nurtured that he did not retreat into some form of insanity in the face of the unalleviated frustration which was his lot. That he might be wrong never occurred to him; it was the rest of the world which was wrong. Perhaps he had identified his aversion to change, so common to all mankind, with every aspect of his childhood, including his simple religious instruction, and it was impossible for him to relinquish it or even to question the wisdom of what his forebears had imparted to him. He went about year after year striving to explain himself; he stood on street-corners waving his arms and his cane in the heat of his frantic words, speaking rapidly lest his listener escape him; he went into stores and talked to whomever would listen; he wrote letters to newspapers, where they were printed, much to the mortification of his wife and daughter, for the letters were as confused as his spoken words.

Sometimes he had visions. In the deeps of night he would start awake and call to his wife to say, "Vi! Vi! I have seen the Lord. He came to me in a great cloud and showed me the way to go." Thereafter he would wait his chance to rise in church during a lull in Sunday gatherings and tell his visions and his dreams, his hopes and his convictions to that audience. Sometimes, in his eagerness to preach, he would slip up and take possession of the pulpit itself to tell all who sat before him of the error of their ways in believing only what they should know, as he knew, an act which convinced his audience only of his mental instability and caused him to be eyed askance at no matter which church he attended, since he did not confine his spontaneous sermons to any one denomination.

He must have been an unhappy, puzzled man for most of his life, growing more so in his later years. Whenever he found someone willing to listen, or someone who would not attempt to "confound" him or "mix up" his thoughts, as he put it, someone who would hear him out without argument, he was supremely happy. A glow as of almost supernal contentment lit up his features, his eyes sparkled with joy, a smile held to his lips, and for days this happiness lasted unalloyed by any event of his daily existence, no matter how discouraging such events might be. But he seldom found anyone to listen to him. Now and then I heard him out in the harness shop, to the accompaniment of Hugo's clattering at the workbench, or on the bridge, when I met him on my way home from the hills of an afternoon; but as often as not I was as disputatious as any villager encountered on the street.

He had come into Sac Prairie as a young man and set himself up in a little shop where he tested eyes and repaired clocks; this shop was his first pulpit, and his landlord was his most patient listener, fortunately one who responded to his less positive characteristics, which included a boundless good-heartedness. Across the front of his shop he erected a large, home-made sign, featuring a pair of spectacles; this commanding sign he later transferred to his home on the riverbank not far up the street from the harness shop, when at last he removed his tools and clocks to the house and carried on his diminishing business there.

In his shop he could hold forth without end, and often did. But he was as generous with his own time when others needed him, as he expected others to be generous with theirs whenever he called upon them to listen. He had a way with clocks; he could repair the most ancient teller of time; later in his life, as he retained his health well into his eighties, one began to suspect he had a way with time itself. He was such a congenial man that it was difficult to associate him with the man he became in the grip of his obsession; they were like two different men, but, of course, they were only the Janus-faces of the same man eternally in conflict with himself.

"What is this that is not the same to you as it is to me?" he would ask. "I know this is a bench, that is an awl, that is a chair; you know these same things, too. I know there is an All-Knowing Spirit that is God..." But upon this rock he foundered, for whenever he was asked for proof, he could adduce nothing but the words of his ancestors, the scriptural texts, and the conviction firmly imbedded within him; and whenever anyone questioned him and sought to define his words, he cried out against them, "You're only trying to mix me up!"

In all the years I knew him, his confusion never ebbed. He was never prey to a single doubt himself, however innumerable the doubters who surrounded him. From the first day when I carried a clock to him and understood him to say that he was God, to the last time I saw him alive over three decades later and heard him speak a little sadly of those who, unlike him, did not know the All-Knowing Spirit that is God, he never had the slightest qualm, never the faintest shadow of a question about his convictions, there was never visible on his features any trace of inner disturbance, save only at such times as he found himself in vain argument with some contentious listener, who might be, and often was a minister, of a profession Louis had come to view with all the dubiety with which others looked upon him when he was in the throes of his obsession.

What he wanted was simply a common denominator in comprehension, and yet he could never understand that for the achievement of this ideal he had begun with an erroneous premise no one could accept; and thus, for lack of anyone's agreement with his semantic confusion about knowing and believing, he made no progress. "If only people could understand each other, there wouldn't be any wars," he frequently said, and with this no one would take issue; but he could not find it possible to learn that his own contribution toward universal understanding was in itself error.

"My mother always said, '*Glauben ist nicht Wissen!*' " he said with the assurance of one who had heard the voice of God. That his mother might not have meant what he understood her to say, he could never admit. She had not been wrong, nor was he wrong —all the ministers who arrayed themselves against him, all the deacons and elders, all the church-going fraternity, men and women alike, all the dictionaries, the encyclopedias, the teachers in the schools—all were wrong, not Louis Karberg. He distressed his wife and daughter; he embarrassed them time after time; they never knew when next they might open their newspapers and find in the *Voice of the People* columns a communication from their husband and father, as esoteric as it was chaotic, a voice crying out in desperation against the bewilderment of his times, striving to hold intact as Peter's rock the security of his knowledge in God.

He was not a man given wholly to this futile quest, however much he dwelt upon it. He was accustomed to taking simple pleasures, and particularly enjoyed riding out into the country. He had a childlike quality of delight in things which never failed him; he could take joy in the sight and sound of things for themselves alone—a bird, a brook, a flower, a tree, sunset or moonrise, a landscape, a quiet pool—any one of them could inspire in him the kind of delight experienced by a child in wonder at its world, or by the pure in heart, by one who had come through the fires of existence untouched by any flame, one who, though his mind was lost at times in the forests of night, possessed a soul which walked always in the green pastures, comely in the eyes of the Lord.

He went from year to year in compulsive search of converts, of someone who might agree with him, and found him not, though he eagerly assailed every listener with his credo, proud and sure of his knowledge, pitying and scornful of all those who were confounded by beliefs instead of knowledge, went his way for almost ninety years, and died in triumph and alone in his security of knowledge he could never successfully implant in any other. And for years after his passing, the streets so empty of him, the shops where he used to stop so free of him, the clocks he had repaired with such loving attention chided those who had known his friendliness and courtesy with their spectral, mnemonic voices chanting his refrain—"*Glauben ist nicht Wissen!* I know that there is an All-Knowing Spirit which is God!"—in the accents of that lonely man who was so profoundly and unshakably convinced that he alone knew beyond doubt, past the shred of any proof, of the living presence of his omniscient God.

✷ ✷ ✷ ✷ ✷

IF there is one winter voice informed with wildness, it is the crow's. Temperature is a matter of moment to him; he sends his challenge over the landscape whenever and wherever he pleases, but in winter he is more in evidence than in other seasons, not alone because his is one of the few voices to be heard in and about Sac Prairie, but because he extends his range in the season of snow and ice, deserting the hills and marshes adjacent to the Wisconsin to fly out over the prairie and the fields beyond, passing over in the company of his fellows, and returning before dark to his roost, secure in his mastery of the heavens.

Being the epitome of wildness, he is canny as well as arrogant, and in every attribute he has, his essential independence of man stands out. Whereas sparrows, robins, starlings, even nighthawks, and a host of lesser birds do not trouble themselves about and often elect the company of mankind, the crow shuns it, mocks it, derides and keeps his distance from even a lone walker in the woods at any season. But winter is peculiarly the crow's season; however more difficult may be his foraging, he seems in this season to come into his own, hurling his challenge from every corner of the grey winter sky, constantly about in all manner of weather.

He is good company, paradoxically better at a distance, for nearby his cries are harsh, forbidding, while at a diminishing range toward the horizon his calls are mellowed by distance and the quality of the air—its dryness or humidity; they are crisp or liquid, with an almost musical quality seldom heard at close quarters. One never doubts, hearing him, that he is the woods' master, the admiral of the snowy wastes where he and his companions command the heavens virtually alone, dark on the grey or sombre blue sky, dark on the white landscape below.

In the sound of his caw is the proof of his wildness. Here clearly is the voice of one who has resisted all the blandishments of civilization, who has defied the best efforts of man to tame or slay him. It is curious to reflect that the crow's voice should comfort a man in his solitude, however much the crow's rascality be known; yet it is so. It is as if this proof of the essential wildness of this black scavenger were an immutable assurance of the persistence of the wilderness, of the continuity of life itself, for there is never any dearth of crows—they survive every season, they escape the most dedicated hunter, they return as inevitably as the seasons themselves.

Early in my teens I went to work for several weeks every summer in the local canning factory, which stood in the south end of Sac Prairie. It was in those years quite new, for only a scant few years before, the old factory had burned down one summer night, and its replacement was as modern for that time as the old one had not been. Apart from odd jobs, there was no other opportunity for work in Sac Prairie. True, a hardy lad could always go to spend his summer as a hired hand on one of the farms which surrounded the village, but few of the younger teen-agers were inclined toward a life of labor from dawn to dusk, though the canning factory often compelled work from before dawn to late at night. This, however, was sporadic; it happened only at the height of the seasons of peas and corn, and never lasted very long.

I was never very enthusiastic about manual labor. I had an unlimited capacity for work, but I wanted to work on my own terms, and I suppose that is one of the reasons I had already then turned to writing, which was not lucrative enough to induce my parents to excuse me from work in the canning factory. I turned a hand at everything—pitching peas, taking hot cans off the line, piling cases in the warehouse—but, very probably because at that time one of my closest friends was Mark Schorer, the son of the factory manager, I was soon put in charge of the brine room, where in two large vats the brine in which the peas were canned was made, one of those jobs which was always held to be a "soft" job—that is, one of more responsibility but at the same time less manual labor, though I considered that hauling hundred-pound bags of sugar up the stairs on my back was as much manual labor as I cared to undertake—and this position I held for most of the decade or more that I worked in the factory.

The brine room was on the second floor of the central building. It commanded the entire yard, had a clear view of the office, and a large part of the south end of the village. Adjacent to it on the west was storage for cans; I used to walk into these rooms to a door that opened on to the west, and looked out to see the Lueders sisters walking to or from their home beyond the cemetery, and to that acreage of maples and arbor vitae and monuments, to which "the best people" of Sac Prairie had reputedly gone, a place which, because of its little red chapel, and its beautiful rows of trees, seemed always one of ineffable repose. A cool breeze always came in by that west door, and I used to stand in it and drink it in between tanks of brine, as it were, resting my soul with the view of the fields and the path along the line fence, where now and then Helen Merk walked to the cemetery, and, far to the west, the line of the hills, a kind of purple or blue-grey against the sky, its colors depending upon the nature of the day.

The view to the east was just as restless as that to the west was restful. Not only was there a constant movement of loads of peas, of farmers standing together to talk while waiting for their turn to unload, but the office was the source of almost incessant movement, not only of people going in and out, but of the manager himself; he might be expected to explode from the office door at any moment—he was always in such haste that simply walking out and back in seemed too slow for him. In a very real sense, the canning factory seemed the personal creation of its manager, and as long as Will Schorer remained its manager, the canning factory was a highly personal operation.

Will Schorer personally attended to every department. Though his ideas of labor-management relationship were rooted in the McKinley years, this did not trouble me nearly so much as his constant appearances to check up on the operation of the brine room. He was likely to burst out of the office and come over to the factory at a fast trot, inspect the capping operation downstairs, then bound up the steps and pop into my room to make sure I had hauled in some sugar, or to proffer me a cap which he thought I ought to wear (I never did), or to produce a change in the formula for the brine. Most of these changes were designed to save a little sugar or salt, and though I gravely assented to the changes, I seldom made any of them; the brine was of good flavor as it was, and I saw no need to change it, though every time Will followed his change with a sampling, and, though the brine was the same as before, he always pronounced it improved.

I have no doubt that his constant supervision did result in improved efficiency, whatever it did to morale; we had no real reason to feel offended, for he treated everyone alike—even his oldest son, Billy, who was for a while called assistant manager, but was maddeningly frustrated in this, for he never knew when, after he had announced a policy, his father might come along and countermand the order he had given. Moreover, the factory attracted part-time workers of a singular variety, and I suppose Will Schorer had some reason to believe that they needed to be kept off balance, quite as if the twenty-five cents an hour we were paid, plus the two and a half cents bonus which might be withheld if we were not faithful to the operation, were not enough to keep us in line. He was also as much harassed as harassing, for there were several foremen who were always plaguing him with trivial details, especially Helen Hahn, who, by virtue of being Will's godmother, assumed that she had first call on his ear, and was forever trotting to the office about something.

These seasons did me no harm, and undoubtedly did me a modicum of good in exposing me to many people I might not otherwise have met, though I was more exposed in the corn season, when I ran a husker next to one run by Hugo Schwenker, and between us we shared a gallery of characters—Rich Monn, who was the Chronic Plaintiff; Hank Knechtges, whom we called Old Sluefoot; young Billy Schorer, who was dubbed the Mandarin Ho-Fat; and Rich Becker, who always had so many ideas to propound to the manager that, quite naturally, he became the Proxy Manager. There were many more, and among them, certainly, we must have attained some status as characters on our own.

All carried on a kind of war with the management; I suppose this was only natural; if we were plagued by unreasonable demands, we became unreasonable in turn. Nothing was more irritating than to be sent home for supper at six o'clock to return at seven for but an hour's work, when we could have worked through. Will Schorer made erratic decisions like this during all his years at the factory, and he always produced some kind of justification for them. Sometimes work was delayed in beginning until almost noon, and then work was protracted into the evening hours, when it could have been done earlier in the day. Sometimes a halt was called that delayed us even more. Perhaps some of these occasions arose from simple bad guesses, but part of the time at least they took rise in mistaken notions of saving money, which I doubt that any of them ever achieved. We avenged these indignities in various ways—the boys on the line deliberately jammed it, the corn-huskers were jammed, machinery failures became more frequent, workers slowed down, and the like, all part of the war with the management. And sometimes, at the end of the pea season, the management hired a bus or two and took all of us on a holiday—which was usually to another factory in the vicinity, one still operating, so that we might compare the efficiency of their workers with our own.

Out of all this, it could not be denied that Will Schorer ran a model factory in those years, and at a steady profit to those who had invested in it. The work was not unpleasant; indeed, the days in the brine room were often so free of work that I could spend time writing there after preparing brine—which troubled Will a little, though he could think of no way to stop it, however much he tried—but the very regularity of it irked me, the loss of so many weeks every summer dismayed me, and in the end I found it impossible to go on there, and one summer did not return. I missed the brine room for a summer or so, but I never regretted my decision to move into that wider world outside.

❋ ❋ ❋ ❋ ❋

I WAIT every April upon the blossoming of the hepaticas in Wright's Valley across the Wisconsin from Sac Prairie, as upon the thrusting up of the windflowers on the adjacent hills, and the first buttercups, stealing as many hours as I can to sit at the top of the valley slope and look down across that sere earth, brown and dry with fallen oak leaves, for oak trees are numerous there, to where the November face of that slope is starred with clusters of short-stemmed flowers, furred against the cold, in purple and deep blue and pastel shades of pink, lavender, blue-white, rose, renewing myself there at a place which was once one of assignation with Margery, a sheltered, secluded valley well back from the river's edge and leading deep into the hills and to fields beyond the hills.

The trees are still leafless; indeed, the aspect of that valley is not of April—save where the hepaticas push up out of the bed of leaves; but the delicate fragrance of the blossoms is always faintly manifest and the air is April's, with the warm sun slanting down the slope to renew the earth as sight of these delicate flowers struggling forth invariably renews me every spring. Only the birch trees crowning the slope betray April in their yellow, pollen-heavy catkins dancing on the wind against the blue heaven with its scudding white clouds.

I used to sit for many afternoons among these flowers, contemplating the beauty they brought to this still wintry slope, sit writing and reading there, opening to the sun as these fragile blossoms and all the earth around opened to it, eternally renewed, knowing that when the hepaticas were done, spring, too, was virtually done, and the long wait beginning again.

Somewhere at the edge of childhood's park pass forever the Widow Buchenau and her daughter, Clara—a tall, gaunt woman who seemed fixed in time, a girl of indeterminate age who, like her mother, seemed older than her years. These two women haunted the vernal evenings of my childhood and youth, always with a wagon bearing a load of wash squeaking its protests between them, for they were poor and took in washing, delivering it of evenings, in that hour between daylight and darkness when the streetlights were lemon flowers on the soft orange and amethystine afterglow, and the village was held in a mist of twilight.

They lived in a house on the western edge of town, a house pressed close to the sidewalk, standing treeless and barren, as barren as the lives of those who lived within its walls. It was said in the village that Clara was a backward child, that she was feebleminded, that she had some defect which made it necessary for her mother always to keep her at her side, to occupy her with work, the monotony of which never altered. In their unlovely, unpainted house, the two women labored from dawn to dusk, washing and ironing; and in the dusk emerged like a pair of moths heralded by the oilless protests of the coaster wagon on which they hauled the wash—Clara drawing the wagon, her silent mother walking gauntly behind.

They never spoke. I used to hear them coming when I stood in the shadows of the Park Hall waiting upon an assignation with Margery, I heard them coming—and going—for blocks. They walked past in a silence all the more profound because of the wagon's voice which bespoke their approach, and told of their passage into town long after they had gone by. Clara always walked with a certain doggedness, for all that her dark eyes were bright and darted here and there, as if she were eager to see as much of life outside the walls of her home as possible on these nightly forays into the wilderness of Sac Prairie. The widow walked with her eyes turned inward; something was deep inside her to hold her mind and heart, something which was a bulwark against the mundane world, an unfathomable mystery integral in her life, and of which no betraying word ever crossed her firm, grimly pursed lips.

They were remote from any social contact, save only the meeting with people for whom they worked, or with shopkeepers of whom they bought their meager supplies. Now and then they visited the widow's sister and brother, less often two other married sisters, and never at all the houseboat-dwelling brother in Upper Sac Prairie, but as, one by one, these sisters and the brothers died, they retreated more completely into their little house at the edge of town. The evening ritual never changed. Though years passed, they continued to wash, to deliver the wash of evenings, to return in darkness to the silent house which stood waiting for them, blinds closed, curtains folded tightly against any curious eye.

Of what their lives were within those walls, not even Miss Minna Schwenker, who lived next door, could say. They owned neither phonograph nor radio; they subscribed to no paper or magazine; they were as isolated from the world in their house as any occupant of a mountain peak in an uncharted land. But there were rare moments of illumination. A new neighbor, passing the house once late at night, heard a bitter quarrel between mother and daughter. Clara complained in a passionately rebellious voice —"You never let me go to a show. You never got me pretty clothes like the other girls. You never let me have a boy friend like they had." This was the burden of other quarrels overheard by passersby, for the house stood so close to the sidewalk that there was no division between the end of the one and the beginning of the other.

Clara's complaint was sadly true. Her widowed mother had bound her close to her from her babyhood on. Perhaps it was because the woman was one of a rather ingrown family, striving to find in her daughter a kind of affection she had never had. Perhaps the Widow Buchenau was simply selfish. Perhaps she disapproved of the progress of what men called civilization and wanted her daughter to have none of it. There was yet one other alternative, which was shrouded in mystery. It was probable that the widow knew more than others suspected of insanity in the Buchenau family, for there was an unsolved mystery lying half a century in the past, when Clara's uncle Hugo, a darkly moody man, had shot himself in an orchard one May morning, scattering his brains among the blossoms, and soon after, Clara's father had sunk into a deep depression and had at last to be taken to Mendota as insane, and there died.

These two events, following so closely one on the other,

aroused a flow of speculation. That Hugo had been mildly deranged, none could gainsay. Had he indeed been beloved of his
sister-in-law? Had some rage of his brother's driven him to his
mortal act? Had, then, his sister-in-law conspired to drive her
husband out of his mind? No one could answer these questions.
The legend grew and lingered to become a part of the inevitable
backwash of small talk in the night life of the village. But if
madness lay among the Buchenaus, then perhaps the widow had a
valid reason for keeping Clara so close to her, aloof from others,
in her fear that in this backward child similar tendencies might
readily develop and grow.

However remote the past, these two women carried with them
the mystery of those years. Something there was that cried aloud
to the unheeding passerby, something that spoke for the futility
of their lives, for the tragedy of their involuntary retreat from the
world, something that brooded over them with the air of the
unfathomable, shrouding and shielding them behind its impene-
trability. It was a tangible aura manifest to all sensitive people,
something that touched one going by, of a piece with the widow's
pursed-lipped silence and her inward-turning eye, one with Clara's
furtive scrutiny of the world beyond her prison.

They were an essential part of the spring evenings in Sac
Prairie, making their pilgrimages almost nightly in this season
from the edge of town into its heart, their coming and their going
announced by the creaking and groaning of the old wagon, which
seemed possessed of the same durability which kept them ever
looking the same, so that the widow looked always fifty or sixty,
and Clara might have been twenty or thirty-five or even forty,
one could not say.

What brooded with them in their little house? Some revenants
of the past, surely. A host of dark memories, a core of darker
knowledge? One felt that though they sat alone to every meal,
there was a shadowy third nearby. Perhaps it was this I felt in

passing them on their journeys into the village. Certainly the ghost of time past walked with them, ate with them, slept with them, more than half claiming them by virtue of the strictures of their existence, the old-fashioned clothes they wore, accoutrements of decades long gone by which bounded their narrow lives.

They lived without change all their lives, the pattern of their ways underwent no alterations. They washed and ironed, delivered wash, took home more clothing to wash. Sometimes they ventured out by day to shop, mother and daughter, or Clara alone. Alone, Clara was apt to be somewhat more communicative than her mother, and spoke in a peculiar speech pattern grown doubtless from inadequate schooling and subsequent solitude, a pattern from the literal German, which had for many years been her only language. People sometimes asked her what she was doing; she usually replied, "Wash—all the time wash!" but on occasion offered this variation, "Make off crass—all the time make off crass." To wash and to mow lawn—she never did more, to judge by any spoken word.

Lives of quiet desperation, indeed! Here, certainly, were two. The widow might be hemmed in by the ghosts of the dead past; Clara was just as surely bound by the circumstances of her life, into which she had gone too far beneath her mother's strictures ever to rise. She might never have been born; she lived so narrow a life she could hardly be said to have lived at all.

But above all else, there was a peculiar harmony about mother and daughter. The taciturn woman, monumental in her silence— the furtive-eyed daughter with her prematurely wizened face, as were she sadly under-nourished, as well she might have been— these two made somehow a unit with two faces. However much Clara might complain about the barrenness of her life in those dark moments of rebellion, her destiny lay with her mother and with no one else.

When at last the widow came to die, Clara's world, pathetically small as it was, was shattered. In its ruins she crawled into her mother's bed, wearing the widow's shoes, as symbol doubtless of that authority past, and lay for hours beside the corpse of the old woman, dead in her eighty-fifth year, refusing to let anyone in until the county sheriff forced his way to where the two women lay, the one dead, the other no less so than she had been all her life.

So, bereft of her mother, Clara bade farewell to the neighbors and went away to another kind of confinement, her poor mind addled and sundered by this catastrophe, her world at an end. She willed herself to die, refusing food and drink, and in a week was dead at fifty-two, and was taken to join the Widow Buchenau beside Hugo and Charlie, the suicide and the strangely dead. The sightless house was left to stand bleakly at the edge of the prairie, and the wagon to fall together after decades of protesting use.

But in the village evenings sometimes still seems to rise the sound of the old wagon, as if somewhere the Buchenau women walked eternally, spending their lives on another plane as bleakly as here their yesterdays were given to a monotony which must have corroded and eaten away both heart and soul.

✤ ✤ ✤ ✤ ✤

THE choir of the frogs is a primal sound without counterpart in nature, like the voice of the earth itself. There is nothing a man could call melody in the hyla chorus, but a man could do without many a melody before dispensing with this choir. It begins with one chill, uncertain note, a hesitant fluting on some chill, uncertain night in March or April, followed by another note, and another, until at last a hundred invisible throats are pulsing with the piping of peepers or the grating rattle of cricket frogs praising the spring evening from a hundred tussocks of grass, from scores of hidden pools.

The evening belongs to them, the dusk and darkness are theirs, and all who pass within hearing know that April has come again, April and life renewed once more. How incredible it is to reflect that there are thousands of human beings who are not stirred by this chorus, who do not even hear it, perhaps, thousands who never shared the privilege of knowing the world at their feet, who may be content to reduce the hyla choir to a simple scientific fact, preliminary to the mating of the batrachia! It stands for so much more than that to the man who is sensitive and alive; it stands for something akin to what is locked within, equally as primal as the choir of the hylidae.

Old Parr drifted into Sac Prairie one day in a battered coupe and set about selling nursery stock with such casualness that most people did not know he was employed at all, and came to accept him as someone who had retired from a small business or a farm somewhere, and elected Sac Prairie as the place of his retirement out of some remote connection, a relative, perhaps. Soon he was a familiar fixture of the post office and all the places where the old men of the village were in the habit of congregating.

He was a short, squat man, somewhat chunky, with a dogged face, distinguished by pale blue eyes with large black pupils out of which he had a habit of glaring at people, and a prognathous chin which gave him a look of singularly determined stubbornness. His hair was usually straggly, and his pockets were bagged out with newspaper clippings. He was not a man who drew the eye; yet there was something about his square face, his broad nose, and a certain ruggedness he had that made one notice him before long.

He had come to Sac Prairie from Indiana, and he never ceased to sing the praises of "Injianny, where I come from." He carried colored postcards of native scenes, though he was partial to oddities, such as a picture of a church steeple out of which a young elm tree had sprouted and grown. "I seen that there myself," he would say. "Ain't that something? Didja ever hear tell of the like?" he would ask with the self-satisfied air of one who knows very well that you had not. But for all his talk of "Injianny," he was best known for his claimed kinship to George Washington. He collared young and old alike and told each one gravely that he was a "descendant" of George Washington, "And you know who he is—the Father of his Country! You got a picture of him in your pocket right now, if you got a dollar bill." Curiously, he looked not unlike Washington, and it was only natural that people should begin to refer to him in good-natured raillery as "George Washington" Parr.

He was constantly bustling about, however seldom he was disposing of nursery stock, sometimes in his little coupe, which he drove with exasperating slowness, or on foot. He had an eye for a particular kind of news, and the clippings he drew from his pockets to display to anyone who paused at his behest were always shown with wide-eyed amazement and tremulous indignation. "Ain't that awful!" he would demand. "They'd ought to take that feller and string him up, that's what they'd ought to do.

Back home in Injianny we'd—we'd—ah, we'd know what to do with the likes a him." Rape, perversion, horror—these subjects fascinated him and, on one occasion, when a little girl had been kidnapped in Wisconsin, old Parr bedeviled the district attorney of the county in which the crime had taken place and the attorney-general of the state with letters purporting to offer "evidence" of the kidnapper's identity, or the place where the girl's body had been concealed though all he had to offer were his own ideas, which were sadly wide of the mark, however much he was incapable of seeing it.

His voice was a high nasal twang, and whenever he grew sufficiently excited, he squeaked. He spoke in something that was a cross between a hoarse whisper and a shrill but muffled and slightly petulant tenor. "Say, d'I ever tell you what we did back home in Injianny?" he would begin, stopping any stranger on the street. "I'm Parr," he would say. "Folks around here call me 'George Washington' Parr. He was a relative of mine." Or he would walk into the stores and approach the proprietors with, "Say, d'you see that there article this morning's paper about that feller killed that girl in the cornfield? Didja ever read the like a that?" His words came pouring out, once he had a listener, with a rush of excitement, made to seem of great urgency by the timbre of his voice, so that it seemed always as if old Parr were communicating secrets of tremendous importance to a chosen confidant.

He was always in need of a shave or wore the appearance of that need. His greying whiskers grew fulsomely, and he managed to convey the impression that he was so concerned with matters of grave seriousness that he had not had time to shave or care for his appearance, which was customarily to the left of neatness, for he was untidy to the point of risking comparison with knights of the road who passed through Sac Prairie now and then, his trousers being baggy and ill-fitting, his coat wrinkled and often of a different color or of several different shades of the same color, as if it had been long exposed to fading sunlight or weather, and his vest was customarily askew, with such spoor upon it that any amateur Sherlock Holmes could usually deduce what old Parr had had for breakfast.

I heard him out many times, recognizing that his wish to be in the limelight was in compensation for his lack; he had a desperate need to be wanted, he needed someone to whom he might seem important, if only for a few fleeting minutes. I gathered that his children had thrust him out, not penniless, and I learned soon that people in town avoided him, not alone because of his interminable and often pointless stories, nor his irritating self-righteousness, but because he fancied himself a sleuth of sorts, and when he was not bothering some district attorney with his theories of local crimes, he was making it his business to appear suddenly before young couples engaged in amorous play on porches or in cars and deliver ultimata and dire warnings of the wrath to come, not so much out of indignation or the desire to emphasize a dying morality as out of an overpowering curiosity and a wish to participate even in so peripheral a way in a pastime in which he himself could no longer indulge.

Unlike so many of his kind, who were most frequently to be seen in the village evenings, he was partial to mornings; he was up and about very early, stopping people on Water Street, particularly tourists who had no knowledge of him and could therefore not know what was to come. Waiting at the post office for the mail to be unpacked afforded him the opportunity to speak to anyone who came in, or to talk with those of his cronies who had come to this meeting place for a similar purpose. People did not recognize his need; shrouded in their own necessities, driven by private wars, they had no time for such as old Parr, though they unwittingly gave him pleasure by addressing him as "George," since this lent him a specious importance, if but for a moment, and he could explain to everyone within hearing his relationship to the nation's first president, without troubling to wait, as he sometimes did, until someone drew a dollar bill from his wallet and calling out in a provocatively shrill voice, "That's a fine picture of my relative you got there!", a gambit which invariably startled those he addressed into giving him the opening he wanted.

He moved from one rooming-house to another in Sac Prairie, always complaining of the way in which he was treated—the food was not good, the other roomers were discourteous, or, if young girls, immoral, his landlady disliked him—his reasons were always the same, though he said nothing of the affronting way in which he adjured young people to obey the conventions of his own youth rather than of theirs, and thus made himself unpopular at one place after another, so that every landlady was delighted to see him go. In time he exhausted rooming-houses in Sac Prairie and had to move on into a neighboring village, where he had an entirely new audience, which doubtless he faced with as much gusto and eagerness as with that hidden pathos of his need to be somebody, to be needed by someone, if only for the fleeting moments which had marked his years in Sac Prairie.

He was a confirmed wanderer, far from his native "Injianny"; what he sought he was not destined to find, because he did not know how to reach his goal, and he no longer had enough time left in which to learn. He was destined for loneliness and isolation and the burden of his need for the rest of the years left to him, wherever he went, from one Sac Prairie to another, a wanderer on the face of the earth.

❋   ❋   ❋   ❋   ❋

OH, the smell of the grass, the wonderful smell of the grass! On a summer night it lies along all the country roads, rising from the drying seedheads as well as from the new green below, the second growth; it fills the air with an unimaginable fragrance *which has a seasonal counterpart, however different, only in the smell of opening leaves in spring, of drying leaves in autumn, in the fresh wonder of falling snow in winter, of mare's tails in September. Men commonly take it for granted, and it is doubtful if most of them are aware of it, or, being aware, know its source. The smell of the grass is the country air in summer nights; there is a kind of basic fragrance in it, as of the earth itself—of rock and soil and stone—not just the grass growing upon it, a kind of exhalation which is sweet because it is so fundamental to existence and to man's being, too, though he may not be cognizant of what he speaks when he says the summer air is good to breathe, a fragrance akin to that of drying hay, but more tenuous, not so concentrated and not so dry, lying in the still air or riding the winds—and the summer winds in Sac Prairie are almost always from the west, tawny and aromatic—like something alive within itself, not belonging to man at all, but willing to be shared by him, knowing it has a greater vitality and immortality than man.*

Lolly Denham was thin and faded at fifty—a stooped woman with pale grey eyes that stared at you earnestly from behind her spectacles. She wore her greying hair drawn severely back and knotted high on her neck, parted in the middle, and on every clouded day, wore overshoes.

She had strange habits.

She used to come into the post office and industriously empty the wastebasket into her handbag. On winter nights during and after snowfalls, she went out and shoveled snow, not only before her own door, but all around the block. Sometimes on autumn nights, she raked leaves as erratically. She stopped people on the street and asked mysteriously what they had done with her "divorce papers." She walked alone at night, talking to herself, and she went through the darkness to lighted windows, moth-like, and looked steadfastly into the lit rooms, as if to satisfy some hunger for life she did not have.

She had come to Sac Prairie from Chicago, an ex-school teacher recuperating from a "nervous breakdown" and now plainly lived in a world of her own, for she paid no attention to the curious watching her empty the post office wastebasket or shoveling snow around the block, lived in a world of wastepaper, leaves, snow, and the night, which belonged to her.

Perhaps night was her last refuge. She avoided eyes by day, and after she had begun one of her strange, irrational conversations, she made an attempt to be rational and often was, until the thread of her conversation broke off and she was lost again in the wilderness of an unexplored country none outside could penetrate. She never spoke of her teaching years; they were locked away somewhere. She never spoke of her brief marriage, or of her husband's faithlessness, which had brought them to divorce and her to the breakdown which had ultimately led to Sac Prairie. Sometimes she talked vaguely of getting a "job"—a mysterious position, somewhere, in a hospital, in civic government, clerking—somewhere "away," but she never went anywhere save from home to town and back again, except on rare occasions when the Parent-Teacher Association or some other local group sponsored a program open to the public, to which she could come to stand unobtrusively in the hall, away from the audience, and listen, usually always to draw away and leave at the first sign of recognition, though she always seemed to respond pleasantly enough when greeted, before her psychic retreat.

There were times when she lingered, drawing closer and closer, but never speaking—as if eager for some more intimate contact, but hesitant, afraid, standing always on the perimeter of the circle, always on the edge, someone wanting desperately to take part in community life, but never quite able to come closer than the rim, within sight and sound—and then swiftly retreated.

Of what went on within her mind no one knew certainly. Her

private world allowed of no invasion, though I often wondered what secret drive she satisfied by her addiction to wastepaper and the work properly to be done by others. Did the circulars and folders, the discarded newspapers and advertisements she found in the post office wastebasket assuage some remote wish for escape? Did the ceaseless nocturnal labor so secretly assumed offer a panacea for inner torment? The wastepaper vanished into her house, and there it was stored in the basement, together with twigs and fragments of wood, as against some need, though there was no necessity for it to heat the house, since there was central heating, and there was nothing in which to burn the paper and twigs she collected but one small range in the kitchen. The paper was never used; the twigs were stacked away until the basement under the house was filled from floor to ceiling with paper and twigs.

If she were observed at her nocturnal work, she never spoke. Sometimes she shoveled every walk; sometimes but a part; sometimes she made a footpath all around the block; on occasion she went but half way and turned back. Now and then she raked leaves into neat piles; other times she carried them home. If she were surprised at someone's window in the night, she fled, most often wordlessly, sometimes with an odd comment about seeing or hearing an owl nearby.

She seldom spoke her name. If someone greeted her, saying, "Lolly," she might reply, "Lolly? Who is that?" or "I knew someone with that name once," as if unwilling to betray the haunter of the dark who was Lolly Denham. With time, she grew to seem increasingly less real by day, existing only by night, as if the black-clad woman with her myopic eyes who appeared from time to time on the mid-day streets or in the post office were an illusion, a strange, haunted creature from an incomplete dream.

Eventually she was taken submissively away and never returned to Sac Prairie.

❊ ❊ ❊ ❊ ❊

WHEN I was a child, the Christmas season in Sac Prairie was always heralded by one event above all others. Even before school was dismissed for the holidays, my sister and I were sent by Mother to borrow the cookie-cutters from old Mrs. Lampertius, who lived in a little corner house just north across the street from the home of my Grandfather Derleth. The house bordered the sidewalk on the west and south; east of it stretched for half a block a tree-arbored garden and lawn reaching all the way to the little shop where Mr. Lampertius repaired shoes, a place where great beds of squills and tulips, hyacinths and narcissi flourished.

The house was a rectangle of one and a half storeys; an intimate little porch made an L of it east of the house. In clement weather Mrs. Lampertius was usually to be found on her porch, which opened off her kitchen, a cozy little room at the north end of the house beyond which I seldom went, for the Lampteriuses were not likely on ordinary days to spend much of their time at the front of the house. In the days of my childhood the house was a gathering place for many women of the village, who came of summer afternoons to sit on the porch and the lawn and enjoy a Kaffeeklatsch; *these were the years of* Gemüthlichkeit, *that easy and gracious way of life that was soon destined to fall victim to the machine age.*

But my sole identification with the Lampertius house was the annual foray for the cookie-cutters. It was something to which my sister and I looked forward, primarily because it inaugurated the holiday season, but also because of the inviting warmth of the Lampertius house and the old people in it. Mr. and Mrs. Lampertius were already then well along in years; all their children were married and living away from Sac Prairie, most of them in Milwaukee, for the second generation of German settlers in Sac Prairie customarily went to German cities like Milwaukee, St. Paul, or St. Louis to live. He was a taciturn, moustached little man, and she was a voluble, dark-skinned little woman, with snapping black or deep brown eyes, and gold hoops in her ears. She always greeted us in so friendly a fashion that I suspect the ritual of the cookie-cutters had as much significance to her as it did to us. Once we had stamped the snow off our feet, we were invited into the kitchen to go through all the formalities of the occasion, which amounted to exchanging news of the mutual health—or otherwise—of our respective families, for, after all, my father had grown up in the Lampertius neighborhood, and the two of them had known him as a boy and therefore had a certain proprietory interest in him. Only when these formalities had been observed were the cookie-cutters brought out and put into a paper sack to be carried home; these cutters were tin forms of various kinds— rabbit, hen, pig, bear, and the like—each with a handle for ease of use. Then came a little gift of cake or candy, and we were once more sent forth into the December weather to make our way northwest four blocks to the house of childhood where Mother waited to make the Christmas cookies—sugar cookies, the fragrance of which, baking, filled the entire house with the most tempting of aromas until later, when they were frosted over with a seven-minute icing, and little colored candies were scattered over the frosting, to make them as much a pleasure to look upon as to eat.

I do not remember that this ritual ever varied—sometimes I went for the cookie-cutters alone, but nothing else was altered—until age and death overtook Mrs. Lampertius; and years after that unhappy event, the cookie-cutters themselves came into my possession for a more extended use. The annual journey for the cookie-cutters was an event that left an unforgettable impression on my childhood; perhaps it was that the Lampertius house was one of the earliest places, apart from the homes of my grandparents, to which I was permitted to go without parental supervision; perhaps it was that a visit to that house was in itself a reward, for an Old World warmth and quaintness held it secure against the assaults of the twentieth century; perhaps it was that the mission was filled with all the promise of the Christmas season's delights, but most likely it was because going for the cookie-cutters was a youthful adventure which somehow touched the borderland of that region of adventurous expectancy which carried through my years.

A dark mystery shrouded Mrs. Opal Kralz. Perhaps it was that she was so seldom seen on the streets of Sac Prairie in her last years, though in her youth she had been about as much as anyone, and in her young widowhood she had chased a young married doctor, creating a scandal, making no secret of her intention to break up his home and marry him. Perhaps her failure cast her into the mould of suppressed fury which seemed always to shine from her hard, dark eyes and linger about the corners of her thin-lipped mouth.

She was a stout, thick-bodied woman, with powerful, well-muscled arms. She had high shoulders and a short, squat neck, upon which her head sat solidly and a little stiffly. She was never loquacious and, indeed, not much given to speech, speaking only when she was spoken to, and then almost always monosyllabically. There was something reptilian about her, something she never made any attempt to dispel. Even when she smiled, her smile seemed a calculated thing, exposing even teeth, with two gold crowns gleaming among them; but I always thought her smile was a kind of concession, and it was never a pleasant smile.

For the last two decades of her life, she lived with her son Norman, a bachelor, and even between them few words passed; each of them seemed to live within a shell of his own making, as if long ago everything that could have been said to each other had been fashioned into speech and neither could any longer bear the incessant repetition of the prosaic words and thoughts they had. Once a day she prepared her son's dinner and then went to stand behind the counter at his drug store while he came home to eat; but this ended when Norman was suddenly taken ill and hospitalized, after which, on his slow, painful recovery, he arranged to sell his business. Thereafter they lived together and were not often apart, save only when he worked now and then for other pharmacists, lived so until her terminal illness bore her to the cemetery in a silence little greater than that which had cloaked her for most of her life.

She had been one of a large family, born on a farm and spending her childhood there. She had had a few years of school, then gone to work, as was the pattern in those years before the turn of the century. She had married well enough—an ambitious young farmer whose eyes turned westward. She and Kralz—as she invariably called him—had gone to stake out a ranch in Wyoming. There she had been unhappy; curiously, though she had seldom shown any affection for the Sac Prairie country of her birth, she developed a hankering to be back, and she wrote letters which were filled with words spelling out her misery, strange words for her. . . .

"I tell Kralz we ought to go home. He says this is home. Maybe it's his home; it's not mine. We could sell the ranch. It's no place to raise a boy. It's all coyotes and wolves and space. The wind blows. It's a lonesome place. No people are here. Ten miles to the nearest. Nobody to talk to. Norman likes it, but he's a boy, he dont know no better. Never been home. Never seen a river like the Wisconsin."

"I tell Kralz to sell."—"I tell Kralz we should go home."—This was the constant refrain of her letters, and to this refrain the sturdy Kralz turned an unlistening ear. He fought the wild country, he tamed it, he grew well-to-do, and all the while Opal wrote home to her brothers and sisters, "I tell Kralz we should sell out, come home. You ought to hear the wind howl here and the snow blow winter nights. A body's got to be afraid he'll never see the sun again once a blizzard comes up. Oh, that Kralz is stubborn! It won't do him any good. It ain't good to be so stubborn. He says he couldn't do as well in Sac Prairie. Maybe he couldn't. But it's where I want to be. That's where I want Norman to grow up."

But Sac Prairie in those years was far away.

Yet Providence had a softness for Opal Kralz—or perhaps Mrs. Kralz had a way with destiny. For Kralz took sick one winter night. "I couldn't get the doctor," she wrote home. "It was so cold. I did what I could." What it was she could do she did not say, what it was she did that left it "too late when the doctor got here." So Kralz was buried, and Opal sold the ranch and everything on it as swiftly as she could, and came hurrying back to Sac Prairie with Norman.

She bought a house not far from Water Street, and for a while she was seldom at home. She haunted Buerki's Fashion Center, where she bought as many as three fur coats in one year; she spent Kralz's money lavishly upon herself and set out in pursuit of Dr. Francis Simon. Perhaps she thought that new dresses and fur coats would make that thick figure with its squat neck attractive to a man like Dr. Simon, who had a young and beautiful wife and a son of his own. She hounded him, but it did no good save to start tongues wagging, tongues that always wagged easily in Sac Prairie without regard for truth.

Without Kralz to work and replenish the funds she lavished upon herself, the money dwindled away like water poured into sand, and as the money went, so Mrs. Kralz retired into her house and herself, embittered, enraged, baffled, and unforgiving. But no word passed her lips. Norman grew up, went to school, began to work in a drug store, and presently went off to study pharmacy so that he could one day have a drug store of his own, and support his mother as once she had supported him. Mrs. Kralz came forth ever more infrequently, save only on occasion to burst from her house and scold careless children who crossed her lawn, and to scream vengefully at their mothers for laxity in care of their young.

The house sat hard upon the sidewalk, dour, too, like Opal Kralz, its shades pulled so that more often than not it wore a sightless appearance, or had the air of a house feigning sleep to look out at passersby from beneath lowered lids, behind which, one fancied, Mrs. Kralz turned upon Sac Prairie eyes masked to conceal the venom she dared not spit forth, if only for the sake of Norman, who hoped to make his living in Sac Prairie. Though she had longed to return to the village, she made little effort to see her sisters and brothers, and they left her much alone, as were there a wall between them.

And, indeed, there was a wall between Opal Kralz and the town, a wall built by Kralz's death followed by her quick return to Sac Prairie, her undisciplined spending, her fruitless harassing of Dr. Simon. What was it Opal had "done" for Kralz that that strong man had died so easily? Lung fever, the doctor had said. Pneumonia. But the whispers that went around Sac Prairie hinted at other reasons for Kralz's death. Who knew? No one. No one but Opal Kralz, who did not speak.

Frugality became her ill. She chafed under it, recalling the years when Kralz's money had brought her everything she wished—save only Dr. Simon. She resented her near poverty, and Norman never brought enough home to please her, not even when he at last owned his own store, to which she went each noon while Norman came home to eat the dinner she had prepared for him, went and learned all about the soporifics and the palliatives, the patent medicines and the cosmetics, learned where the sarsaparilla and the arsenic were kept, and many other things that settled into her dark brain and festered there, stirring the black pool which had come into being there in the long years on the ranch in Wyoming from which she had so long sought to flee, to come back to Sac Prairie.

With Norman's sudden illness, change came once more. He was

found in his drug store in a state of collapse, which made it necessary to rush him to hospital, from which presently the word came that he had unwittingly poisoned himself by careless handling of poisons, absorbing poison through his fingers. At first his life was despaired of, but he came through, though he was in the hospital for a drearily long time, and when he came out he had somehow become discouraged about owning his own store, and sold it, setting out to work by the day as a substitute-pharmacist. Unlike his mother, Norman was a mild, soft-spoken man, with an easily kindled sense of humor, whose blue eyes suggested that his nature was as gentle as his mother's was not. He too retreated into silence in a house of silence, while the whispers began again, the questions rose without ever an answer.

How could it be that he, for twenty years a skilled pharmacist, could have been so careless in handling poisons as to poison himself? And how much arsenic would he need to absorb through his fingers to bring him almost to the point of death? None asked Norman, for he never spoke of his illness. But it was strange how, one day when an insurance agent sold him a new policy, he told the agent, "I'll take two thousand more provided you don't let Mother know I'm taking it." Why? Was it because the dream of money which might come out of Norman's death might drive his mother to some act of madness? Norman never spoke, and Opal Kralz was surrounded by a formidable wall of silence.

A score of unanswered questions clouded about Mrs. Kralz like flies about a placid cow in summer pasture. She heard them not, for none was ever voiced in her hearing. If she dreamed that someone had asked them, there was yet no key to the answers which were possible behind the sphinx-face she presented to the world of Sac Prairie. The years slipped away; Mrs. Kralz did not again have need to go to work for the noon hour behind the counters of a drug store, where she could lay hands on sarsaparilla and toothpaste, oil of bergamotte and arsenic and none be the wiser; she came less and less into the streets of Sac Prairie, but

kept to the dour house in which she had lived since her return
from Wyoming, and when at last she was carried from it in her
coffin, the answers to the questions Sac Prairie asked behind her
back went with her to the grave.

❅   ❅   ❅   ❅   ❅

*WHEN I did not walk into the marshes or the hills around
Sac Prairie—which was seldom, and occurred only in that part of
the summer when mosquitoes made walking unbearable—I often
rode through the hours of evening and night along the country
roads, taking pleasure in the night, in the nocturnal sounds so
common to the summer evenings—the lowing of cattle, the barking
of dogs, the crying of whippoorwills and killdeers, the calling of
frogs, the stridulations of katydids and crickets—and in the perfumes of the darkened countryside—the fragrance of clover and
cut hay, the pungence of mare's tails and other weeds, the cool
exhalation of deep woods, and that strangely fertile musk of corn,
of leaves as well as of bloom, which pervades the air in midsummer
and holds to it for weeks.*

*One could ride for miles with nothing but the smell of corn
broken only occasionally by other odors—of barnyards, a pungent
musk, not unpleasant; of oak groves—a fine, stimulating pungence;
of cedars—sweet yet not without a kind of tingling sharpness; of
alfalfa and clover and drying hay—all fragrant; of newly-cut grain,
sheaved under the moon; of fog, damp and cool and suggestive of
mints and rain in low places; of herbs and blossoms—yarrow,
Queen Anne's lace, bergamotte, late rue, milkweed and Joe-Pye
weed—and then again the overwhelming musk of the corn, given
off by leaf and petal to the summer night in a spreading exhalation
from valley fields and hill-slopes, hundreds of thousands of blooms
and millions of leaves perfuming the night air.*

*In those days there were not yet many cars in Sac Prairie, and
the only one of us fortunate enough to have the use of a car was*

Paul Lachmund. With him I rode out frequently. We used to go every night to Lodi to watch the 10:02 come in out of Chicago on its way to the Twin Cities, watching the train roll by, sometimes making a brief stop at Lodi, myself wondering about the travelers whose lives touched so fleetingly at this place, a wonder akin to the mystery of lit windows over the countryside. We never traveled very far—never past Lodi on the east, and never farther than Mazomanie on the south, and never beyond Plain or Black Hawk, Witwen, Denzer or Leland on the west, or Baraboo on the north—a comparatively small orbit, but our way lay through dark countryside, through strange valleys, past unknown places, and everywhere lamplit windows signified the essential isolation of the human spirit, alone in darkness—not the darkness of human fallibility and ignorance—but of the cosmos and man's relation to it. The farmhouse on the hill or the dwelling in the valley, sometimes surrounded by fog creeping upon it, with the lamplit windows shining pale and distant in the sea of darkness stood for man against the vast, impersonal dark.

No matter what Sam Schroeder had been in the long years of his existence in Sac Prairie, he was always known as a "river rat," for he spent his free hours fishing or boating with an abandon that made him the butt of every joke a fellow-angler could devise. He was one of those happy-go-lucky men who never take to responsibilities; he avoided marriage, he did not much care for work, though he was the village ice-man for decades before the coming of refrigerators, and he discharged this obligation with a sober sense of duty, perhaps because it took him to the river or the adjoining ponds where he could recall with delight even as he worked the fish he had caught of a summer day at the very site where he now cut ice.

Children followed his ice-wagon along the streets on summer days and received portions of ice chips to suck at; he never failed them. But he was seldom at home on the ice-wagon any more than he was in the ice-house, a tall old building redolent of pond water and sawdust which stood, appropriately enough, on the river's shore, though now and then he could be seen lolling on a fender of the truck he got in later years or reclining on the sawdust-covered ice in storage, seemingly relaxed, but actually in an alcoholic torpor.

The river and its environs—sloughs, brooks, marshes—were his first home, but he lived with his strongly religious spinster sister Hannah in a little house on one of the back streets known locally as the "canning-factory street" because the factory lay at its foot. The house was little and old-fashioned, a typical pioneer house of one storey, with a grape arbor, a garden, and several sheds in back of it, along the alley. He very probably looked upon his ice business as a nuisance which kept him too much from the river, for he lamented its every inconvenience, and I used to think he had taken to it solely to discourage Hannah's complaints, for both of them existed on a small competence which was enough for their living; and when at last the ice business dwindled before technological progress, and Sam had the opportunity to sell out, he did so with vast relief and thereafter gave all his time to angling.

He used to haunt the highway bridge, hanging over the railing of the walk along the south side of the bridge with a rod all day long. In winter he wandered into the marshes with pails and a seine after "minnies," with which to fish through the ice for perch or pickerel. He spent hours in a rowboat, though he was extremely wary of canoes, and, for all his love of the Wisconsin, he was not inclined to think kindly of it as a place in which to bathe. When he fished, he took anything, he found a use for any kind of fish which came to his hook.

He was rugged in appearance, though he walked with a pronounced stoop, which, one suspected, was the result of his habit of carrying his hands in the side-pockets of his trousers. His hair was shaggy, sandy in color; his eyebrows jutted forth raggedly;

his chin was often stubbled; and his tanned face was corrugated with deep wrinkles. He preferred toothlessness to plates, and he habitually smoked a pipe, a corncob of ancient vintage, which sometimes hung so far from his lips that it seemed to cling only by some legerdemain. He seldom wore a hat, as if to proclaim that he was a free, untrammeled soul; but when he did, it was a great fur monstrosity, twice as big as his sizable head, which made him look at first glance, what with an ancient and bulky jacket he wore, like a prize exhibit in somebody's home zoo. Despite all his harassed sister could do, he always managed to look as if he had just been put through a washing machine and his clothes had dried on him.

For all that Sam never married and kept largely to the company of a few cronies, he was not a shy man. He talked at length to anyone, and he was a delight to listen to, for he was guilty of more malapropisms than a serious student could have unearthed in years of research. Moreover, he always spoke with such an air of authority that most people were hard put to it to challenge him, whether the subject were international relations or the spawning season of catfish; in his conversation he was equally at home with the homing instincts of pigeons and the most recent news from Downing Street or the Wilhelmstrasse. At the same time, he carried on a torrid and relatively normal affair with a generous Negress in a neighboring city, to which he repaired by bus two or three evenings a week, candidly admitting that he was going to have his "ashes hauled" and returning, time after time, with a venereal disease he ruefully called a "dose." He was accustomed to admitting in later years that he had been "dosed" so often, he didn't "feel natural without it."

He lived with gusto, though his pleasures were simple. He did not like to go to church, which was a cross for Hannah to bear, and she railed at him constantly about this defection from the teachings of his childhood and left him in no doubt that in her daily visits to St. Aloysius she prayed heartily for him until the day of her untimely death, which preceded Sam's and surprised everyone, since Hannah had seemed so well, and he had always looked a wreck, so that people were stirred to observe that her reward for virtue was hardly commensurate with Sam's harvest of a long, wayward life. Perversely enough, Hannah was no sooner in her grave than Sam began to go to church on Sundays with unfailing regularity, if somewhat cagily sitting near one of the side doors so that he could make as rapid an exit as possible once Mass was over.

He was inordinately proud of his success as a fisherman, though he overlooked the fact that he was out so much his catch must be preponderantly larger than anyone else's. But there were occasions on which he had no luck, and some rank amateur did, arousing Sam's curiosity as to how he did it, for he could not believe that anything but a bait secret could be responsible for an amateur's prowess in the face of his own failure, with the result that many a prankster had fun with Sam by pretending to use, with purposely bungled secretiveness, such unheard-of baits as green tomatoes or onions, driving Sam home fully determined to try them himself. And, when he was caught using such futile lures, he answered all his critics with a brash "I used to catch 'em with this when I was a boy," which none could gainsay, none being as old as he.

His joy in the river and its environs was an abiding passion. As long as he could fish, he was happy; whenever he was away from the Wisconsin, he was restless, and if he were long kept from his favorite pastime, he grew morose and argumentative and took issue about anything whatever. There was a deep communion between him and the river, for he was on it night and day. It might have been said of him that life for Sam consisted of days of fishing and loafing on the Wisconsin; he did hunt on occasion, but he was not much given to it. For a good many years he had shared a houseboat with some of his cronies; on this they went all the way down to Prairie du Chien, a trip which could be done leisurely in three days at most by canoe, but which always took a fortnight or more in the houseboat because Sam insisted on stopping to fish at every likely spot along the way. But this houseboat was eventually abandoned as no longer manageable in the increasingly sandy waters of the Wisconsin; it became a barge and eventually came to an inglorious end when an enterprising local carpenter fancied he could improve on the old superstructure and managed to sink the contraption.

Sam was prone to the narration of greatly fabricated and embroidered accounts of his sporting adventures, both on the river and in the woods, as well as in the bordello where he sought surcease from such of his desires as he could not satisfy on the river. He could improve on the best fish story, and any fish he caught grew with astonishing swiftness if it appeared that someone else might have caught a larger one. He talked of his adventures with such marked relish that it was entertaining to listen to him, however seldom he convinced his audience.

Careless of the opinions of others, doggedly determined to lead his own life without apology, firmly convinced of his own rectitude even when he was grandiosely wrong in any argument, which he often was, and quietly sure that nothing else in life offered quite the satisfaction fishing did, he went his way from decade to decade, from fish to fish, as it were, his life one endless round of hunting bait—worms, "minnies," bread, bacon-rind—the catch and sport of it, the pleasure of eating the game he brought to table.

But in his last years, his waywardness caught up with him, as people are accustomed to say, not out of conviction but out of a kind of indulgent self-righteousness, for Sam developed trouble in his eyes and grew slowly blind. He had to wear a black patch over one eye; this lent his rugged figure a certain romance in the eyes of a new generation, for it called to mind the pirates of *Treasure Island*. The other eye, too, was clouded, but not so much as to keep Sam off the streets. However, he fished ever less and less; he could no longer take to boating; and his travels into the environs of the Wisconsin were at an end, for he could not see well enough to permit walking along the railroad tracks or the brooks, and when he could not fish he was disconsolate indeed. He wandered up and down Water Street, more bowed and bent than ever, talking endlessly about his eyes, hopeful of a cure, dreaming of the days when he might go fishing once more, and living ever more in his memories of years gone by.

He was a pathetic, lonely figure in the end—restless, sad, only the shadow of that once proud angler who knew the pools and eddies where fish lurked; his sole consolation lay in the adventures, real or imaginary, he could recall; he lost interest in all else; he was no longer an authority on any subject one wished to mention; he wanted to speak only of his affliction or his lost years. He faded visibly; though his affliction was slow to grow worse, Sam himself continued to flourish, almost as if he were meant to stay alive beyond his time, like a last leaf withering and drying before his increasing age; and, though he grew thinner and carried himself more and more like an old man, he still went around with his hands in trousers pockets, his shaggy head bowed, but otherwise unbent.

His spirit was untouched, though he admitted that his flesh was weak, but more and more in his last years, when he was met on the street, he was less himself, until at last it came to seem that Sam Schroeder was in truth dead, and that this ancient fellow one saw and listened to was only a spectre in Sam's guise, doomed to walk the familiar streets of Sac Prairie, to haunt the river and its environs for time without end.

❊ ❊ ❊ ❊ ❊

SOMETIMES, walking through the marshes, past sloughs and brooks and fingers of the Wisconsin, in those nights of late summer or early autumn when most nocturnal voices are still—the whippoorwills waiting on that last brief period of song before migrating once more, the choir of the frogs virtually silent, and

even the churring of crickets diminished to a subdued rune—I hear
the wood ducks' quiet cree-ee-ee rising not so much like a sound
out of the darkness, but as something fallen into the night, at an
indeterminate distance, with something of the same ventriloquial
quality as a grouse's drumming or a screech owl's song, so that
the precise place of its origin is never quite certain.

It is a pleasant, intimate sound; perhaps its very intimacy is the
most endearing aspect of it, for it is not exactly a melody. It is

all the more intimate at times of duck distress, in those nights after
days during which hunters have scourged the bottomland, for
then there is a constant medley of sounds—duck talk—which is the
summoning together once more of family or flock after the day-
long siege. I have heard this on more than one occasion, heard it
through from where I stood on the railroad tracks, from its beginning to its end, and it never varies.

It begins with one solitary querying note, which falls into the
dusk soon after sundown, and which sounds at intervals until
answers rise, coming from various places in the lowland. There

follows a subdued interchange of query and reply, of call and response, and slowly, almost imperceptibly at first, the sounds draw nearer to the first voice of the evening, converging toward that focal point, and soon it is manifest that there is a soundless movement toward a gathering place which, reached at last, is then the source of a subtly different kind of talk—the querulous notes are gone, and there is a sort of family chattering. Are they taking stock of the day, I often wonder, measuring their losses, discovering which of them has not survived the rapacity of the hunters?

I feel at such times that I am participating in a neighbor's family life, looking in from outside, to be sure, but taking part no less than I take part in the streets and byways of Sac Prairie.

The Lueders sisters were left behind by the nineteenth century, two wizened little old women, perpetually seen in faded blue gingham dresses and enormous sunbonnets, from the depths of which their thin, kindly, resigned faces peered with an odd sort of baffled curiosity. They divided their days and nights between two old houses they owned, one of them referred to as the town house, one as the country house; both of them were very old, and both wore the appearance of imminent collapse; though in time they abandoned the country house entirely, continuing only to work the garden part of the ten acres in which the country house was slowly yielding to the buffetings of time and weather. When I first knew the sisters, Miss Carlotta, the elder, had already lost her mind, and had become a difficult problem for the younger, Miss Augusta, who bore her sister's lapses without a murmur, though her patient eyes often spoke for her.

They were in the habit of walking fifty feet apart, Miss Augusta leading. I do not think their pace ever varied much, nor did the distance between them ever change. Miss Augusta would set out first from the country house, and when she had gone about thirty paces, Miss Carlotta would follow. In this manner they would cross through the cemetery and the fields beyond and come into the town, in the southern end of which their town house stood, like their country house, bowered in trees. Miss Augusta never looked around to assure herself that her older sister was still coming. I often believed there must have been a psychic bond between them, for on two occasions I saw Miss Carlotta halted by traffic on the street, and Miss Augusta, apparently sensing this, turned immediately and plodded back along the walk, not turning first to look for her sister, yet knowing whenever the distance between them widened through no fault of their own.

I used to watch the Lueders sisters from the second floor of the canning factory where I worked during the summer, since the path between their houses led directly toward the factory from the west, and went past it on the north, and was thus in uninterrupted sight from the factory in both directions, both houses being visible from the second floor. In the days when they still lived in their country house, I could see them leave their country house punctually at ten o'clock in the morning, and return from the town house between four and five o'clock in the afternoon. Most often they carried baskets of flowers for transplanting, or small garden tools, for they cultivated flowers and fruits in gardens adjacent to both houses, though most of the fruit was intended for the birds.

The clothes the Lueders sisters wore seemed to belong to the distant past; physically at least the twentieth century left no mark on them. They recognized the present as evidence of the passage of time, they were fully aware of the events of the day, both of them being alert and well educated—(indeed, the sisters and their two brothers—the one dead early in manhood, the other vanished from home in rebellion against his father's dour strictness, and lost to the little family circle forever—were largely self-educated under the tutelage of their father)—given to reading magazines like *The Nation, LaFollette's Magazine, The Atlantic Monthly,* and similar fare, but they did not recognize change. Miss Carlotta's queerness was the only element of change that had come into their lives since the 1890's.

They kept largely to themselves and avoided people, except for the members of the Free Congregation, to which they belonged, and to certain members of founding families like their own. Occasionally I spoke to them on the street, and they replied, in recognition of the mutual bond of ancestral aristocracy that united our families. They were not in the least haughty, they were rather humble, and spoke with shy reserve, though when they were among old friends their reserve dropped from them, withal that they were rather shy, due largely to their unawareness of the world of the village and their having lived so long within themselves.

Miss Carlotta usually paid no attention to conversation, and Miss Augusta always began with an apology for her sister's lapse, always inventing some fantastic reason because she did not like to mention her queerness. Miss Augusta talked with great eagerness, and nothing was so important to her as news about old friends, old families, for there existed in her an innate aristocracy which neither time nor circumstances could destroy, for all that it was principally the aristocracy of intellect. This news was to her like hearing from her own people, which was partly so because the Lueders sisters had but one living relative, a sister-in-law. Throughout conversation, Miss Augusta's eyes would snap and gleam as they peered up into my face; she was all attention, sometimes leaning forward as if she believed she might miss some word by not doing so. Yet there was always present a certain charming shyness evident in the slight droop of her delicate mouth. Miss Carlotta looked at me as if looking through me, her eyes indeed fixed upon something in her memory, though otherwise she was much like Miss Augusta, a little taller, perhaps, and with a wider, firmer mouth.

The two of them were looked upon with some suspicion by

some families in town, partly because their country house was near the cemetery and was shrouded in what was apparently perpetual gloom, what with close-pressing trees of all description planted by their father, who had brought a great shipment of nursery stock from his native Hamburg; a light seldom shone there, and if it had been lit, the many lilac bushes surrounding the house would have concealed its rays. The country house was in reality a charming retreat to which the Lueders sisters arrived each night with relief at escape from the world outside. They seemed to live without any evident means of income, which also troubled some of the villagers; it lent them an air of magic which more superstitious people enhanced in my earlier years with tales of owls and bats seen haunting the ghostly house in great numbers —and it was true, owls abounded in the pines, and bats were at home there, and so were skunks, raccoons, foxes, even deer which came up from the marshes to feed now and then. This kind of distrust on the part of the villagers would have distressed Miss Augusta deeply if she had learned of it, but her friends were careful to keep from her tranquil life anything that might have disturbed her.

Miss Carlotta, of course, was beyond caring. Her mental decay had come slowly, and very probably began with her slow deafening, driving her always deeper and deeper into her own mind and away from the social relationships Miss Augusta still enjoyed —the Sunday afternoons at the Park Hall, the visits to old friends in town, and their visits at the country house. However, her thoughts were busy with strange beliefs about long lost relatives, who, she continually insisted, were coming from Hamburg to visit them. Beyond the fact that these obsessions caused Miss Augusta to do much unnecessary work in preparation for the coming of these fancied relatives, work which Miss Carlotta insisted must be done—baking bread, preparing food, making beds ready—Miss Carlotta's queerness was not greatly disturbing to Miss Augusta. Miss Augusta constantly worried about her sister's chance conversations with others, for on one occasion Miss Carlotta had spoken to an acquaintance in the cemetery about the Hamburg relatives, and had whispered with great gravity that her information had not come by letter, but through her mind.

Miss Carlotta was not always queer; she had lapses. She had many hours of startling sanity, during which she would remember in the minutest detail everything that had passed in her early life. Very often when the sisters were visiting somewhere and she, because of her deafness, pursued her own thoughts, Miss Carlotta would suddenly start recounting episodes from a past long locked away even from her sister, leaving everyone to marvel at the clarity of her memories. She would refer to the town's earliest settlers as if they were still alive. "Mrs. Haraszthy," she would say of a lady long dead before the turn of the century, "has the most beautiful ear-rings. When you go there next time, you must ask after them, they gleam so in the candle-light. Her cousin sent them from Vienna." She would pass from one person to another in a monologue it was difficult to interrupt because it was not so much given to anyone as it was a recital of her thoughts. "Frau Heller has such trouble with that girl who is working there, she told me last week. Such a pity! I said to Augusta we really ought to do something for her, she's so new here in this country, and Augusta thought we might send her our girl for a week or so, just to help out." She would slip from the distant past to the immediate present without a change of tone or expression, and again, almost in the same breath, return to the past, for all time was the present to Miss Carlotta. "The other day as we were crossing the fields Augusta and I had such a scare. We saw a man lying in the field, and we thought for a moment he was a tramp, but of course, it was only a man from the factory resting there. Augusta, you must remind me to give Mrs. Naffz the pattern for that grey dress, which she admired so much," a reference to an incident which had taken place over sixty years before. It was as if in her withdrawal from society, abetted by her deafness and the hardening of her arteries, her entire life flowed through her thoughts in constant flux, occasionally bursting forth in words, and then again retreating into silence.

As they grew older, they were forced to abandon the country house. Their sister-in-law came to live with them in the town house and began to order their lives, unpleasantly for them, in an effort to give them a greater comfort in their old age. Miss Carlotta developed a consuming hatred for her sister-in-law, and had finally to be taken away to the county home, where she died even as I was buying the country house and its ten acres to keep the site untouched save for a new house. Then the sister-in-law, who had embarrassed Miss Augusta by her recitals of the privations her husband had suffered at his father's hands, took sick and died, too, and presently Miss Augusta, now very old, left the town house and went to live with Clara Merkel, who cared for her until she died in her nineties, still clinging to the ideals of her childhood and youth, for all that the world had long since passed her by.

❋ ❋ ❋ ❋ ❋

MANY evenings, following upon the death of his parents, I used to sit in the harness shop and watch Hugo Schwenker ply a trade older than the village, almost as old as the generations of mankind—working with his hands in a creative craft—and "outdated," as he said, "by machines." His grandfather had been a cabinet-maker, just as my great-grandfather had been a silversmith, goldsmith, and locksmith. There were other such craftsmen in Sac Prairie, but time and technological progress left them and their kind behind, so that thousands of the young people of today may never know the dignity and peculiarly fulfilling satisfaction of working with one's hands to fashion objects of utility or art, a loss all the more sad in that the accomplishments of the thousands of unknown and unsung craftsmen of the American countryside were far more durable and aesthetically pleasing than the products of the machines which succeeded them.

Watching Hugo's deft hands working at the leather—not at harness alone, but at sandals, chess boxes, camera cases—I saw him as a last example of a dwindling brotherhood; working in the green-shaded glow over his bench along the north wall, he sat in a pool of light which reflected the narrowing confines of his private world, and the darkness around holds ever fewer and

fewer of those kindred souls who can appreciate creative crafts-manship on an utilitarian plane.

Even the urge to create with one's hands has faded and diminished. Perhaps the multitudinous output of the machines produces a stultifying discouragement. So the ranks of the cabinet-makers, the cobblers, the silversmiths, goldsmiths, the harness-makers and their kind thin year after year. Even the lowlier artisans—the umbrella-menders and the scissors-grinders—are ever fewer in number, the tinkle of their bells is heard seldom on the streets of Sac Prairie.

There is a certain comfort in watching things take shape under someone's fingers, whether it is a leather sandal, a piece of furniture, a silver band—a wholesome assurance that mankind is not yet at the mercy of machines, even if the urge to take part is fading.

For most of her adult life, Ethel Sholl taught the primary grades in Upper Sac Prairie. She was a short, slender woman, very plain of feature. Her hair was dark, as if to complement the duskiness of her skin, but there was nothing about her to cause even the most casual passerby to give her a second glance. If there were one distinction about Ethel Sholl, it lay in that quality she had which made it so easy not to notice her. She cultivated a retiring nature, and happily effaced herself outside of class.

As a teacher she prided herself on being progressive—not in the sense of modern education—but in having a liberal outlook and in being aware of the advances made by science before most of her fellow-citizens learned of them. She was forever confronting her pupils with some new thought—they must eat an orange a day in order to stave off many common illnesses; they must wash with oilless soap to achieve the maximum antiseptic values; they must not season their food too strongly—and the like, all in a day when such ideas were far from common. She mixed such little homilies with her class-work and never ceased to repeat them, day after day, week upon week. But this aspect of her— and the undeniable fact, however vaguely it was put, that Ethel was a "good teacher"—was all her pupils remembered of her. Class after class passed from her charge into the upper grades, went through high school, sometimes went on to college, and ultimately married and settled down—but none of all these children, spanning more than one generation, had any clearer picture of her than as a plain, nondescript little teacher who was a "good teacher" and was forever going on about oranges.

Life had blunted her normal directions even before she got out of her girlhood. She was an only child of poor parents. Her mother took in sewing. Her father was a lazy man who was employed by the day at various jobs, but his laziness was not so hard a cross to bear as his propensity for drink. While she was still a little girl, Ethel was sent time after time to find her father and persuade him to come home; in his cups, he was an obstinate man, and often Ethel had to beg and plead with him for an hour, before she could prevail upon that stubborn man to stagger along at her side. Perhaps her shame at this repeated public display accounted for the conscious striving to efface herself in later life, for she could not have walked unaware of the disgrace of her father's drunkenness, upon which her mother dwelt at length to the growing girl. Only his death at last released her from this indignity, and she was free to develop her small talent for drawing and painting.

This talent, like everything about Ethel Sholl, was in minor key. She was never more than a village dilettante at this art. Unlike others of her inclination, she had no illusions about her ability; she pursued it as a means of private self-expression, meant for no eye but her own, though, inevitably, her small talent was discovered and bruited about by those well-meaning people who only succeed in bringing misery and unhappiness to those whom they intend to exalt out of the vast well-intentioned unkindness of their lack of taste, judgment, and sensitivity.

If you met her on the street, not knowing her, you would sense that aggressiveness, even a modest self-assertion, were not in her nature. As a teacher, she was an adequate mistress of her charges, and her gentle enthusiasm for education was transmitted somehow to her pupils, however little of her reached them because there was so little of her self to go out to anyone. In her effacement, she was negative; she was withdrawn, ingrown, timid, almost shrinking. She was the sort of woman anyone, recounting the persons who were at a tea or a bridge party or any other social

affair, was apt to recall only in an afterthought—"I think Ethel
Sholl was there," or "And, of course, Ethel Sholl," like an impression fleetingly gathered from a patch of fading wallpaper.
Romance seemed forever alien to her. If she quailed before the
glance of the socially elect in Sac Prairie, how she would have
fled before the amorous gaze of some man! But, incredibly, in
her later years, she fell mistily in love with an itinerant preacher,
the Reverend George Fullilove, a plump, balding fellow who, if
ever he had the ear of the Lord, could only have had it at the end
of an interminable long-distance line. Perhaps they were so much
alike that they were inevitably drawn together; he had just
enough self-assertion to hold tremulously on to his ministry despite
the constant encroachment of the world's wickedness in one of his
parishes after another.

Ethel Sholl blossomed for a while, not with the glory of the
rose, but rather with the shyness of a marsh violet, half hidden
in the grass of the village's disapproval, for people, having already
accepted Ethel as one of Sac Prairie's old maids, were reluctant
to disarrange the pigeon-holes in their dusty minds. Her love,
however, was not strongly rooted; it was like a water plant with
such tenuous roots that the first freshet tears it loose; and when
one of her few close friends—like herself, a spinster—made it her
concern to tell Ethel how unseemly her feeling for the Reverend
Fullilove was to the village, Ethel abandoned the struggle without
a murmur of protest.

If she wept alone, none knew. How many tears are shed by
men and women face to face with themselves, without artifice
to conceal them from the ever-prying eyes of others, to whom
their misery is often but so much manna? She resigned herself to
loneliness, to continued spinsterhood, to old age, but in her
desuetude, she assumed a compensatory interest in chiropracty,
and began to haunt chiropractors for relief from all kinds of
fancied pains rooted in her mind, grown out of what could have

been a quality of the despair which must have been her lifelong lot.

As she grew old, she grew dumpy and at the same time more mousy than ever. Though she had given up teaching, she made a conscious attempt to continue some kind of social life. She gave little parties, not far removed in spirit from the parties she had sometimes enjoyed as a little girl in the village, but, with age, she became forgetful, and very often she forgot that she had invited people to lunch or dinner, or, failing this, she forgot some part of the dinner she had prepared, with the result that, days later, she would come upon a salad or a cake in some corner where she had put it. She herself often forgot to eat. She mislaid her mail, her money, papers of some importance, her sewing, and sometimes did not seem to know where she was herself.

This forgetfulness was only the prelude to an enfeebling of her mind. She grew careless of her personal appearance, though she had always been scrupulously neat, and she began to show unmistakable signs of a profound disarrangement of her way of life —she ate when she pleased, instead of at mealtimes, she slept when she liked, she dressed—or undressed—when the fancy struck her. Her mind refused to cling to those little guideposts of memory which alone mark a human being's course through the sea of anonymity which is life; she forgot such pleasant memories as the years of her teaching as well as such unpleasant ones as her long dead father's persistent drinking to excess.

She grew increasingly helpless, though she was only in her middle sixties. Her friends were distressed, but there was no one to help her, and they could not go to her home to rectify a mistake she might make a dozen times a day. They began to fear for her safety, alone in her home, so forgetful, and her mind wandering. She had no close relatives who would take her in and care for her. Was there any other place for her but the county home? She was sent there and forgotten, and in a few years she died quietly there, erased as casually as a pencilled mistake

on a piece of paper, her vagrant spectre left to walk the streets
of Sac Prairie, a faceless, impotent symbol of countless little lives,
which spring into the glory of life and fade, for lack of spiritual
nourishment, almost from the day of their birth.

❀   ❀   ❀   ❀   ❀

*THE ways of snakes are by their nature more secretive
than those of birds or other animals, but I never found them
troubling to me. Bullsnakes, garden or garter snakes, hog-nosed
snakes, blue racers, rattlesnakes and other varieties were to be
met in the marshes and the hills around Sac Prairie, defensive
creatures all, never offensive. I used to come upon a bullsnake
now and then sunning itself in the hilltop dip of the Big Hill near
the wing dam across from Sac Prairie, when I went there to read
in the pasqueflower months, ignored its bluster, and picked it up
to put it away from the place I wished to occupy. Now and then
I picked up a grass snake carelessly and was bitten for my pains,
which I deserved. Sometimes I came upon blue racers in the
ecstasy of mating, a beautiful thing to see, and once, while I sat
on a hillside on a May afternoon, a blue racer which had never
before seen a human being, came up to me unafraid and raised
its beautiful head to sway along my knee where I sat cross-
legged, its tongue darting out and in to impress upon its senses
this creature so strange to it.*

*The Massasaugas in the marshes got out of the way, as snakes
always do if given opportunity, and the rattlesnakes at the Ferry
Bluff gave warning of danger in ample time to enable any walker
to keep his distance while the rattler made its escape. Water snakes
passed by me, swimming in the Wisconsin, as by a fellow habitant
of their element, and little hog-nosed snakes, so frequently called
"spotted adders" by frightened villagers, offered entertainment
when, if touched, their swollen heads and hissing having proved
to no avail, they turned over and played 'possum, disgorging the*

frog or other prey they had but recently caught, and lying for
as long as twenty minutes motionless before daring to look about
and move away. Frequently snakes came to where I lay on the
hills, took the smell of me at their leisure, and moved off, around
me, not afraid.

I never knew the snake that struck out of anything but defense
of its life, or what it felt was its self-defense—unlike the village
serpents who strike out of malice, envy, greed, jealousy and all
those shameful motives to which man is so much more prone than
any other creature on this earth.

I remember Mrs. Mae Bowman best as the woman in the
window of her house near the Freethinkers' Park, sitting at an
old-fashioned corner desk reading her evening paper by the light
of her green-shaded lamp pulled low to make a pool of yellow
glow with her white head bent above. Three decades ago, when
I was younger, I thought her very old, because her white hair
made her seem so. She was in her forties then, a handsome woman,
but already a widow, whose husband had died tragically in his
thirties, and left her with their son. His death was almost mortal
for her, but not quite, for she rallied to give herself to her son;
she put all the affection, all the lost love for her husband into
devotion to her son. But time gave him years, inexorably; he
grew, he flourished, he married and left, and she was alone.

Thereupon began a desperate struggle against loneliness, all
the more poignant for being unrecognized, silent, grim, a private
determination to compensate herself for aspects of life no longer
hers. Clubs, church affairs, social gatherings of all kinds—these
were not enough, these were not to satisfy her need, which was
for intimacy and companionship, however ill-recognized. She
tried them all; all failed her, and with each year she grew more
lonely, living in increasingly terrifying isolation from which she
saw no escape. Her loneliness made itself patent in her need for

conversation with people, however trivial its nature, and drew
her from her house to seek people.

She sat on her front porch steps of an evening or walked along
the streets hailing people, whether she knew them or not, advancing topics of conversation—the weather, ration coupons, the price
of groceries—and went on about them at incredible length,
rambling with almost designed vagueness, striving desperately to
hold attention, as in her later years she pretended to a helplessness which was by no means always hers, not primarily to
enlist sympathy, but to elicit enough interest to gain out of that
sympathetic interest a companion in conversation, quite as if in
conversation lay all her life. Perhaps it did. Perhaps there was
something in this trivial, superficial companionship which filled
her need after the long years of struggling against the loneliness
which was her lot.

She used to stop me on the street or at the post office and,
with an air of great importance, inform me that she had something
of moment to tell me. A query about a new book she said she
wanted to read—which might have been answered by a ready
reference to any book catalog or review, available to her at the
library; an inquiry about a town somewhere up north—"My niece
and her husband stopped off here to visit; they're going there, and
I can't find it on my map."; a dissertation on the cost of living
—"I'm all out of sugar stamps. Whatever am I going to do?" or:
"I can't get any butter. How can I live without butter?" Could
I tell her whither the country was going? Did I know she had
heard from relatives in Illinois who had said, not hearing from
her, they would write to me to ask about her, remembering that
I was in the habit of delivering her mail from time to time? Had
I heard?—she had lost her house key; she had come down town
Sunday morning to shop, forgetting it was Sunday; she had
learned her son was coming for his annual visit—and so on, often
to be repeated and retold a dozen times a week. This kind of
appeasement of the fire that burned within her she could not do

without; it was as necessary to her as food and drink—indeed, it was a different kind of food and drink, as vital in her declining years as any other.

When at last night closed in, she returned to her corner desk and diligently read the paper, page after page, until late, though, since she subscribed to a morning paper, she had had it most of the day. The green-shaded lamp made its yellow pool of light in the two corner windows, one to the north, the other to the west, nightly from late dusk to almost midnight, for many years an integral part of the night in Sac Prairie, seen from far off after all the neighboring houses were long since given over to the enclosing darkness.

❋ ❋ ❋ ❋ ❋

THERE is a time when spring's new leaves are just opened, the grasses are growing to their first tallness, violets—yellow and blue,—cowslips, crowfoots, woodruff, false Solomon's seals are in bloom, the woods are dense against the evening sky, but not yet as dark as in late spring, the time when the evening air echoes with the songs and cries of warblers, thrushes, pewees, and the frogs, with the trilling of toads ringing through the twilight, the time when the evening air in the lowlands is a perfume none other in the year ever equals—the intoxicating perfume of the opening leaves, the essence of leaf and blade, of petal and bud, of ground and water.

The perfume of the spring spreads over the marshes, the hills, the village where these are the wonderful nights belonging to lovers, these nights when every breath of air is permeated with the perfumes of half a dozen flowers which are among the most profuse and fragrant in Sac Prairie—lilacs, lilies-of-the-valley, flowering currant, plum, apple, and syringa—and in these nights the lovers haunt the lanes and byways of Sac Prairie, as once they were to be seen at all hours of darkness in the deep shadows of the Park

*Hall, and the lonely areas of Lover's Lane west of town. It is not
alone the young lovers who walk the streets for there is something
about nights like this that stirs the very wellsprings of being,
arousing restlessness in a wild desire to be up and about, even if
but to roam aimlessly up one street and down another, where
the perfumed air intoxicates the walker in the darkness, every
walker answering some mute appeal of the night, driven by the
secret pulsing of the heart, to be a part of night, as if the night
were an entity to which a sacrificial offering could be made.*

If anyone could be said to haunt the Sac Prairie night, it was
Kate Fleeson. She was a dark woman, hot-eyed, with a skin duskier
than ordinary, a sensuous mouth, and a rather broad nose, not
well-formed. Her hair, too, was very dark. She was not ill-shaped,
though when she smiled or laughed her teeth were revealed as
unnaturally large, and a smile altered the entire character of her
face, which in repose was curiously attractive, for all that it was
essentially coarse, but in any expression of pleasure became oddly
distorted, as were it a sudden caricature upon her true features.
She was in middle age when first I became aware of her—a
married woman with a family, though her children had grown
away from her, married, and moved from Sac Prairie; and she
lived alone with an ailing husband. But in a very real sense, she
had all her life been a creature of night, haunting the shadowed
streets, driven by a nymphoid compulsion. As a young woman,
she had turned early to the sale of her body, and her tragedy lay
in her disinclination to stop after she was married. Wherever she
lived in Sac Prairie, men found her; they made their way to her
house on foot and by car, sometimes more than half a dozen in a
night.
She came from an old family whose members were respected
and not without local dignity, though people were in the habit

of saying that there was a strain of insanity in her family, to which Kate's errant ways were attributed.

Her husband endured her proclivities, perhaps because he himself was a coarse fellow, with a dark, unfavorable appearance, and constantly under the shadow of his illness, which came upon him often without warning, no matter where he might be, so that he was probably impelled to believe that no other woman would have him and, whatever Kate's faults, he must accept them. He used to meet men sometimes on their way to his home, and eventually grew to making crude jokes of Kate's addiction. As her children grew up, she had to abandon her way of nocturnal life for a while, and, almost as if it had been a vital need for her, she began to decline in health thereafter—her face grew drawn, her eyes appeared hollowed and sunken, her mouth, once so full, became somewhat pursed.

I used to meet her here and there of an evening on my way home from the harness shop or the marshes. She would appear as if by some wizardry from the dense shadows of a little-traveled street or path, from behind an old tree along the sidewalk, or from the edge of the park, walking mothlike out to the perimeter of the glow cast by the arc-lights which swung in the wind at the street-corners, and stand there waiting for me to come up, eager for someone to talk to, for in those years she was alone, her husband having been taken to where his illness could undergo some preventive if not curative treatment, and she had begun to fall prey to paranoid delusions of persecution. She was not meant to live alone, who had had all her life so many men around her.

I used to stop and listen to her. It was always the easier course to brush past, to escape what might be unpleasant, to go one's way and turn deaf ears; but even the greatest desperation knows some small alleviation in being allowed to give expression to itself; so I listened to her unburden herself many times, her words coming in an angry torrent, which presently exhausted itself in a diminishing stream of self-pity.

Her complaint seldom varied. She had become convinced that
her neighbors, mother and daughter, abused her, covered her
with invective and vituperation whenever they passed. "You've
no idea the names they call me," she would say. "They holler
at me, 'You old slut, you! Go home, old whore!' " In reality, her
neighbors were only too anxious not to excite her, knowing her
instability. "And that's not the worst of it," she would go on.
"I couldn't repeat the things they say. Oh, it's just awful! What
am I to do? What can I do? I told the marshal and he said he'd
do something, but it just goes right on. Oh, I don't know how
long I can stand it! And they come over and throw stones at my
house all night long."

It was true that on one occasion the son of that household
had stoned her roof—a trivial thing, but one which left a lasting
impression and was converted into nightly attack within the dark
corridors of her mind. The tenor of her delusions spoke for what
must certainly have haunted her, for her delusions were all in one
key—the names she imagined people called her pointed to what
she had done with her body as a young girl, as a young married
woman. It was almost as if now in her last years she were aware
of a delayed remorse or conscience she had successfully suppressed as long as she was still capable of enjoying sexual promis-
cuity. She was sorely troubled by the visions which compelled her
to walk the streets at night, or to sit alone in her house with a
lamp lit in the parlor against the ghosts which rose out of her
past to torment her in the solitude in which she now lived, she
who had once enjoyed the flattery of the men who paid her to lie
with them.

Kate haunted the darkness as much as any ghost from her past
haunted her in the still hours of her days and nights. She wandered
all over town, but was most often seen along those byways where
she had been accustomed to linger in happier days, stepping out
suddenly to startle many a passerby. Few people listened to her;
I knew of no one else, but the village policeman, who heeded her

plea. She went about almost as if somehow she were aware that she was sinking into an isolation darker and more terrible than the loneliness she had known in the years that had just gone before. None could know what went on in her beleaguered mind, other than the delusions to which she gave voice.

Sometimes I saw her from a distance, standing just out of the streetlight's glow, a dark, still figure, and it was as if time had already dwarfed her to fading perspective, time and circumstance combining to bring her to an end for which she might have been predestined. I stood on such occasions and watched her, marking the aimlessness of her movements, false starting away in one direction, the return, the movement in another; she did not know where to go; in one sense, she was lost, but indeed, had she not been lost for all the years of her maturity? Perhaps now the full awareness of being lost was breaking irrevocably in upon her, and she could not bear to resign herself to the ever-growing cruel conditions of her existence, and the restless movements, first up one street, then back and down another, symbolized the confusion of her mind in her vain attempts to escape the circumstances to which time and events had brought her.

It was inevitable that she would at last be driven to seek some redress for the abuse which existed solely in her disordered mind; she took to calling upon all she fancied had insulted her, screaming at them in fury, threatening them with dire vengeance; so she was at last taken away, found to be insane, and locked up in an asylum, where she died soon after. Her little house stood empty for a while, but was soon occupied again.

The streets whose shadowed places she had haunted for so long spoke in their very emptiness for the pathetic tragedy which was her life, and sometimes of a spring evening the wind's hushing in the new-leafed trees made one recall the satin rustle of her clothes, and the gentle touching of limbs and branches reminded me of the way she had often stood wringing her hands in angry despair against all that life, with her connivance, had done to her.

Though she was gone, something of her remained—the memory
of that poor mad woman walking the nocturnal streets in search
of some listening ear, some understanding heart, some sympathetic
passerby who might believe that her impassioned, twisted life
had not been wasted. On many a night the wind had been her
only listener, the wind had borne her words far up along the
leaves where they were lost in the dark, and now the wind alone
remained to sing its rune of the lost and shattered life that was
Kate Fleeson's.

❀ ❀ ❀ ❀ ❀

AMONG the varied voices of the batrachian inhabitants
of the marshes, none is more provocative than that of the common
pond frog. He elects to wait until dark to begin—only after
peepers, cricket frogs, wood frogs, and tree frogs have set up a
suitable background, as it were, does his guttural voice rise out
of the water of slough or pond. Guttural it is; it is also in the
lower register, but it has a range of expression seemingly beyond
that of any other batrachian singer. He chuckles, he is alternately
sinister and bloated with macabre comedy, and he seems always
to carry on conversations with others of his kind.

I have often sat on the Spring Slough Trestle listening to pond
frogs, never many in number in any one place. On the dark side
of twilight, the first pond frog gives voice to the right—a low,
rattling guttural, followed, though not invariably, by a distinct
chuckle. Then silence. And then again, this time a sustained note,
followed by a chortle that is almost a bark. Silence once more.
A variation, then, which is a kind of sucking sound. This continues until another answers from the left, and thereafter call and
answer come steadily, and in the gathering darkness of the spring
night what they have to say seems almost to suggest that he
proposes and she disposes in such a suggestive sequence of
chuckles and audible leers as to fill the night with the very

*tangibility of that primal sexual urge which moves all creatures
in this season.*

*The conversation of the pond frogs—with its sly chuckles, its
guttural innuendos, its muttered curses—continues for hours
against the hyla choir and the barking of wood frogs, the trilling
of toads, filling the darkness with laughter and provocative challenge, and affording a kind of entertainment found nowhere else
in the nocturnal woods.*

A chubby little man with sideburns and a slight goatee, Dr.
Herman Flemburg might have posed for a picture of the village
physician in the 1860's. Not yet fifty, he was a familiar figure in
the lanes and streets of Sac Prairie, hurrying to a patient, or away
from one, his little black satchel swinging from one hand.
Sometimes he carried a bottle of medicine or a stethoscope in the
other. His too large spectacles were never on straight, but slanted
at a rakish angle across his face, so that very often one eye looked
through a glass and the other did not. He was constantly adjusting
them so that both eyes could look through them at once.

Because he had married unhappily, Dr. Flemburg spent most of
his free time with his cronies down town, and with his brother,
who lived on a farm north of the village. He seemed to be an
easygoing man, but he was extremely neurotic, highly irritable,
often jumpy; this he disguised well, usually by excessive joviality.
He was in the habit of telling jokes, which he always attributed
to old Andy Kelster, who was never known to laugh at a joke
in the long life recently ended under Dr. Flemburg's care. He
used to start his stories with "Now, old Andy Kelster told me this
one just before he passed on."

He was, as the villagers were accustomed to say, "not much
of a doctor." For petty ailments Dr. Flemburg gave out pink or
white pills on an unvarying schedule. "Let's see," he would say,

"you had white pills yesterday and you're no better. Guess we'll try the pink ones on you." Both, of course, were harmless sugar pills and did no patient any harm. He was extremely chary of trying anything new; what had been good enough for his patients in the years when he began practice was still good enough for those of his middle years.

He was, according to the villagers, "not much of a man," either. When his brother died, Dr. Flemburg spent more time than ever on the farm, consoling his sister-in-law, to whom he would refer sanctimoniously as "the poor soul." No one would have suspected Dr. Flemburg of enough initiative to lead any kind of *sub rosa* existence if, fourteen months after her husband's death, the poor soul had not exhibited undeniable signs of pregnancy. Apparently she had not been as lonely as Dr. Flemburg had said she was.

When her time came, Dr. Flemburg attended her, but when neighbors called to see the baby, there was none. The doctor told confusing stories of its stillbirth, contradicted himself several times, and finally said there hadn't been a baby at all, only a tumor. There was a good deal of talk about it in Sac Prairie, as there always is, but it would have come to nothing if Dr. Flemburg's ineffectuality had not been compounded by gross stupidity.

Three days after his sister-in-law had been delivered, a box was found floating sôme miles downriver. When it was opened, it was found to contain a baby, dead from suffocation, one newly born. The box had been seen some weeks previously in Dr. Flemburg's tiny office, and, as if this were not enough, it still bore Dr. Flemburg's name and address. After some deliberation, a committee of the village elders called on Dr. Flemburg one night for a quiet little talk.

Next morning Dr. Flemburg was seen going down the street as usual, his little black bag swinging from one hand, his lips moving as if he were talking to himself. There was an umbrella tucked under his arm, for the sky was threatening. He seemed to be on the way to a patient. He went along Water Street, followed the lane into the country, crossed a stile, and was lost to sight beyond a curve in the road to westward.

He was never seen again.

❀   ❀   ❀   ❀   ❀

THERE are afternoons in late autumn or early winter, during that recessive period of the year when the sun is low in the southern sky, when a special kind of light lies on the face of the familiar marshes. Snow has not yet fallen, or has thawed and gone, the land is brown, dun-colored, grey, with every vestige of the vernal seasons vanished save only for the tight buds on the maples. But in this very drabness—relieved only by osiers' red, the mustard of willows, and the many-colored lichens, and here and there in a sheltered nook, a sturdy green blade—which maintains wherever the eye courses, the sunlight lingers; it falls at an angle which invests every blade and seed-head with a life it has at no other time, for sunlight gleams from the blades of the dry rushes and the grasses, it shines off the twigs and limbs of willows and osiers, it glows supernally from the seed-heads of goldenrod, wild clematis, milkweed and dogbane, the dying cattails and the thistles, and off the climbing false buckwheat seed-pods it sheds a mellow tan effulgence, so that for a few hours of every afternoon, warm or cold, the meadows and the marshes seem endowed with a special kind of sentience in the soft siena haze which holds to everything as were it the tangibility of sunlight itself. And through the middle of it the rails of the roadbed reflect the sun more brightly than anything else, leading away in the direction of the sun itself, through the meadows, past the ponds, sloughs, grassy regions and rush-grown hummocks, past brook and leaning maple, past willow grove and silky cornel, as if to mark the only possible direction through this unreality which

*cloaks the familiar scenes of spring and summer with an iri-
descence which holds within it not alone the certainty of winter,
but also the assurance of spring once more.*

A half-seen face, a wispy, spectral hand, the flirt of a shawl, a
draggle of hair—these were old Mrs. Miles Keysar, locked in her
proud house high above the river, leading a ghostly existence
in that great empty dwelling, which had once rung with the cries
of children, where the life of a happy family had been carried on.
She had come to Sac Prairie from the east, a proud, vain woman,
the second wife of Miles Keysar, who had put up this magnificent house and furnished it with imported rugs, with French
wallpaper, with hangings from Marshall Field, for the young wife
who had given him three frail children and then died.

She had come into this house, the second Mrs. Keysar, cold
to the rooms occupied by Miles's first wife, colder still to the
village with the wilderness at its doors, so different from Boston,
coldest of all to the children of her husband's first wife. A proud
woman, not unattractive by any standard, one accustomed to
being indulged, to having her way in all things, a woman who
wanted to mould her house, her husband, her step-children into
patterns she devised.

She tried, but none would mould—not her husband, whose
business commanded all his attention and time, nor her step-
children, who silently resented and distrusted her, not even the
house, which, despite all she could do to its beautiful gumwood
panels and its teak and mahogany, remained the house Miles
Keysar had built for that delicate, lovely being who had lived
in it only long enough to possess it utterly before dying and
making room for the girl from Boston. Her resentment answered
the children's, her coldness increased, she grew unkind to her
husband and his children, and one by one the acquaintances she

had made in Sac Prairie excused themselves from seeing her, making their little pretences to conceal their uneasiness in her presence.

Miles and the children drew away from her, and one after another, with horrifying implacability, they withdrew forever—Miles dying first, and then the children, one after the other—and she was left finally and irrevocably alone. The handsome stairs no longer sounded with the footsteps she could not abide, and soon now came to long for; Miles's booming voice no longer rose to her distaste for his lack of gentility, and now she wanted to hear it again and again; the house no longer echoed with the children's cries which she had always sought to subdue and now would have given anything to hear once more.

She could not leave Sac Prairie; there was no place she could go. Her relatives in the east had died; old friends she had none. And in Sac Prairie, where nothing is ever secret in the long rolling over of time, she was resented and disliked, every unkindness she had inflicted upon the children was remembered and kept alive. She was alone and left alone, with all the ghosts of her own creation to keep her unwelcome company, with the knowledge that no one in the community cared in his heart whether she lived or died, alone in the house which still reflected that long dead first wife and the husband she had lost and the children, a house that was her mausoleum, waiting grimly for her to languish and die.

There she stayed with her bitter destiny, unsought, unwanted, forgotten. The house, people said, was haunted, and indeed it was—haunted by the mistakes she had made, the unkind words she had spoken, the spiteful deeds which could never be recalled but existed as long as she herself remained alive to be reminded of them, in one room and another, in attic, gables, along the handsome staircase, in the vestibules, the words and deeds of the world she had spurned and lost, like living entities intended to punish her with each passing moment. Haunted it was, certainly, by the ghosts of those who had died, those for whom the house had come

into existence, that little family group to which Mrs. Miles Keysar
had never really belonged because she had never tried to become
one of them but always held herself aloof and superior until time
had made her position at once secure and bitterly irrevocable.

I saw no more of her than a face at the window, the oddly
half-real flash of life, almost spectral, almost on the edge of belief,
so that one could not be quite sure that someone lived behind the
bland windows, that one had really seen evidence of life within
those mute walls. She came out only by night, as if she recognized
that night and darkness were her only friends, to walk around
her house and down the sweeping length of lawn to Water Street
along the Wisconsin which gleamed below, beneath the lights of
the houses under the hills on the river's east shore and the stars
high overhead, and retreated again into the silent house.

No one strove to assuage her bitter loneliness; if neighbors called
to offer her coffeecake or bread in a gesture of friendship, her
haggard isolation rebuffed them, or her terrible self-pity and self-
censure and her cry, "Oh, if only I could hear a child's voice
again in this house!" frightened them and sent them in shame
away. She lived in this dreadful loneliness in such desperation that
at last the very house itself, which had been so cold to her, took
on something of her solitude and became a house of darkness,
beholden to night, speaking mutely of a despairing isolation which
shut it away from life, a house on the borderland between living
and dying, between the quick and the dead, waiting upon the same
consummation as its lone habitant, the obliteration of a fruitless
life, passed by, unwanted and half forgotten before at last death
released Mrs. Miles Keysar from her Gethsemane.

Even then the house in which she had mouldered in spirit spoke
of her, taking her into itself. For years after she had been carried
away to lie beside Miles, his first wife and their children, the dark
wraith of that unhappy woman was seen by the imaginative on
her nocturnal walk about the house and grounds which were her

limbo and her inferno, crying voicelessly still the loneliness and haunted isolation of the woman who had lingered out her childless life and died there.

✶ ✶ ✶ ✶ ✶

THE essence of autumn is in the soft October evenings, mellow and hazed with pungent smoke, deriving, old-timers say, from cranberry marshes or forests burning somewhere up north

—never from any certain source, evenings lit with leaf fires here and there, and echoing with the honking of geese flying south, following the great bend of the Wisconsin at Sac Prairie and confused by the diffused glow of the lights from the village, circling blindly overhead, hour after hour, deep into night. Something is in such evenings that touches upon man's racial experience, that reaches far back into the ancestry of mankind and forges a link to today and tomorrow.

Smoke and haze, pungence and musk, darkness and bonfire

glow—and from overhead the troubled crying of the geese, briefly lost—the geese which are no small part of the night's intimacy or of that dark mystery which carries the very exhalation of the autumn earth to the sensitive and sentient among men—all are symbolic of flight from the moment, the escape from self which seems to everyone sometimes so necessary, so desirable. Perhaps these migrant birds represent the passage of man himself from birth to death, the continuity of which every man is in his own way aware throughout his existence. Bird and man, each in his cycle, obeys his own dark laws.

Even in her seventies, Meta Meyer still kept traces of that singular beauty of her youth when she had been the belle of Sac Prairie. She had aged more gracefully than most beautiful women, save that her body went to that weight so common to the women of her mother's German pioneer generation, when women's figures were Junoesque. For almost fifteen years she had reigned virtually unchallenged as the prettiest girl in Sac Prairie, in those carefree years of the turn of the century, the only surviving child of a pioneer couple who were proprietors of the United States Hotel, the mecca of every drummer who came to town for two weeks or more to ride out of town and call upon the country storekeepers with their wares. Her sister Ida had died at fifteen, when Meta was but six, and thereafter every doting care was lavished on Meta.

Soon after Ida's death, Fred Meyer died, too, leaving his buxom wife and Meta to manage the hotel, with its bar-room and dancefloor, a task of such magnitude for the two of them that the new century was not yet very old when they yielded to the blandishments of a smooth-talking salesman they had known for years and traded their hotel for a Dakota farm, which proved on belated examination to be worth but one-sixth of what the hotel was worth. They were thus lowered from the status of being well-to-do to that of genteel poverty; they moved into a little house just south of the hotel they had so foolishly lost; and Meta began to clerk in a drygoods store a block up Water Street from the hotel, supporting her mother until the old lady died.

Her youth gone, Meta left Sac Prairie. She went to Milwaukee and again found work as a clerk in a store, to Chicago to clerk in The Tailored Woman. But she was soon prey to homesickness; she began to come back to Sac Prairie at every opportunity; when she was prevented from doing so, she telephoned her cousins, her friends, and was loath to leave the wire, loath to sever this slender bond to the years of her triumph in the home town, to the years she remembered with steadily growing warmth, the years of country picnics, sleighing and ice-skating parties, *Kaffeeklatsches*, dances, boating parties, those years when young people of the community did not yet go to the cities for entertainment but found it within the village and its environs.

With every year away from Sac Prairie, she grew more homesick for the village, and eventually, comforted by a dream that her Dakota farm land, which yielded her a small rental, might some day provide her with ample wealth if oil could be found on it, she retired from clerking and came back to Sac Prairie to live. That she had no visible means of support excited comment among the industrious in the village and speculation about whether she had been kept by one or other of the men she had known; her early years were resurrected and re-examined; but of all this Meta was happily oblivious. She plunged into a round of card-parties, she was always to be found at her cousin Emmy Littel's Christmas Eve gathering, renewing the old years, and she sought in many small ways to recapture the gayety of the years at the turn of the century, as if unaware that this was a way of life which had gone. Though she lived in various places, she finally came to rest in a second-floor apartment just down the street from the old hotel which had been turned into a city hall, and from this apartment she sallied forth on trips to Milwaukee or Chicago or St.

Paul, and from here she came into the village on every pretext—to buy a stamp or a newspaper, to lunch, to mail a letter, to pay a call on someone.

Before infirmities bound her to her apartment, she could be met on the streets of Sac Prairie at almost any time of the day or evening. Her thin-lipped mouth broke into ready smiles, her roguish eyes danced at sight of a friend, old or young, and a kind of infectious gayety came easily to her, so that it was always a pleasure to meet and talk with her, to listen to her, though there lurked always in the distance, somewhere behind her laughter, the sadness of her decline into old age, as were it one with the ghosts of those halcyon years gone by, ghosts with which she spent her solitary hours in that apartment looking north to the site of the triumphs of her girlhood and youth, up Water Street past the home where she had long lived, past the hotel her parents had once owned, and the house from which she had set forth many a night on the arm of a young squire.

At the time of her return to Sac Prairie, there were still many houses which were a kind of second home to her, not alone those of her cousins, but those of such friends of her girlhood who had married and still lived in the village, some of them widowed now, where she was always welcome because she so successfully assuaged someone else's loneliness or nostalgia; but these, in the unslowed passage of time, were one by one closed to her, as her friends died or went away, and so her world, which had always been circumscribed, grew grimly more narrow, year upon year. "The world falls away in such little pieces," she was in the habit of saying, "one at a time."

Yet, with a certain defiance which was wholly admirable, she clung firmly to life, she kept up her round of parties as if time were still destined to unravel before her toward limitless horizons, even as it had seemed to her in the days when her beauty excited the envy of the girls and the breathless admiration of the young fellows of Sac Prairie. In this, she was indefatigable, she was not to be beaten, though she knew that inevitably life must win this unequal struggle, and she, too, must go down to death; yet there was never a sign of this knowledge in her eyes, and you felt that Meta would meet death, too, with the same steadfast smile, and the same dancing eyes which concealed the fact that, for all the vaunted beauty of her youth, she had had so pitifully little of the very life she most wanted.

What had she done? Where had she been?—she whose beauty and youth had held such promise for her future. She had endured one disappointing romance after another. She had taken one never-to-be-forgotten trip to Europe, on which she had met other happy travelers who had been delighted with her gayety—but of this trip all her friends and relatives had heard scores of times—the same tales, the same accounts, told with an insistence that betrayed the exaggerated importance this one event of her life had to her, none of her bored listeners ever realizing that Meta returned to this happy escape from the burden of her memories and her failures in life as a drowning person clings to the last spar of his disintegrating ship, and their failure to do so prompted their impatience and often their rudeness, for their own memory of Meta's remarkable beauty still aroused their envy, and it was out of this envy that they passed judgment on her.

Little complaint crossed her lips. Of regret she spoke once or twice, and perhaps an edge of fear betrayed itself now and then, fear of what life might yet do to her before it had done with her. She regretted the lost romances, not always with conviction. Once she said, quite frankly, that she would rather have married and had a dozen children, than be a spinster, but it was equally evident that whatever she said, she was often quite as well satisfied that she had not married some of the men who had taken her about, the gay blades who had squired her along the streets of the village where now every lane and byway had its own meaning for her, each tree in the vicinity of her old home, each walk conveyed sweet memories to her whenever her eyes fell upon them in her daily walks.

But if she had no regret of consequence, she was no less lonely for all that. She lived in a shell of loneliness, however much she dissimulated. The walls of her apartment were decorated with old photographs—of her mother, her mother's friends, of herself as a girl, of her friends, of old houses, people, now old, remembered fondly only because they were a part, however trivial, of that happy girlhood when there was not another girl in all Sac Prairie who could match her beauty and popularity. And her very activity was the key to her loneliness. She came up Water Street primarily to find someone to talk to; she kept on her rounds so that she might put off as long as possible that hour when she must return to her little apartment, which, however comfortable and attractive it was—for it was in a house as old as she herself was— was nevertheless the abode of all the spectres of her past years, and at the same time the cemetery in which her hopes and dreams were buried, and however it rang with gayety from time to time when Meta entertained, untenanted, it was far from the quarters where she had lived in the house just up the street, or the hotel which had been alight day and night in those memorable days when the drummers came and went from the red brick building, and when their coming always meant a good time for Meta, men who for years thereafter thought of her as that "dear old girl" of many a dream, many a summer afternoon at Lodde's Millpond or Ferry Bluff, many a moonlit evening along the river roads in a hired rig from the livery stable just west of the hotel.

In a sense, she was more alone than most of her friends. She lived with the impatience of her relatives, some of them unable to resist a little gloating pleasure at what they imagined was her coming down from the eminence of her girlhood, seeing always before their minds' eyes the beauty she had been, superimposed, as it were, upon this heavy woman, envying to the end her ability to be gay and cheerful in the face of every adversity. Having never had other than friends close to her after her mother's death, she watched them marry and move away, or die, until the circle which had once seemed so large, had shrunk to nothingness, and in her last years she was forced to look to more recent friends, who were as much drawn to her cheerfulness as the friends of her youth had been. Yet no weariness ever escaped from behind her smile; she might on occasion be tired or peevish, but she was resilient and soon recovered her buoyancy and good spirits. No matter how alone she was in the world, she was determined to make the best of it before the eyes of all who knew her.

Of what went on in the solitude of her quarters, no one knew. Did she retire into that halcyon past among the photographs which brought memory to reality before her eyes?—the books of her girlhood?—the mementos of those earlier years, the knick-knacks and old things each of which belonged to some happy incident of that past which, at least here in her rooms, lived still, however spectrally? Did she come back each night to walk into a living past, to sit at her windows looking up the street to see there the old hotel, still, though remodeled now, lit up for the dances given in the hall that was part of the hotel, or the trade that was part of the tavern below the street level, to see there herself, young again, the belle of Sac Prairie, off on a sleigh-ride or an ice-skating party, back once more in 1900 or 1910, when "the girls" were in the bloom of their youth and all the world was young?

She was inextricably associated with the warp and woof of romance in Sac Prairie. The men and women of her generation whispered half-told tales of her great popularity, of her love for a young doctor, which came to naught, of her romances with other men, tales in which she was variously pursued and pursuer; they speculated about her life apart from them, of the years she spent in the cities—whose sweetheart had she been there?—never dreaming that her life in the city might have been as prosaic as her existence in the village. When, at a time when she was already in her fifties, she became the heroine of *Any Day Now*, one of her friends said of her that she bought many copies of that issue of *Redbook* in which she was presented recognizably as a glamorous if unhappy young woman in a fictionized version of the romance with the young doctor, and sent them to all her city friends, representing that the novella offered the true story of her life. And perhaps in a sense it did, though none could imagine that this might be so, that the kind of denial which diminished her happiness in fiction might well have done so in life. And it was possible, too, that this very act was one of desperation; perhaps she wanted terribly to believe in this story which was so plainly drawn from her life, perhaps this tale served for a little while as tangible proof that the events in it were true, as she had always believed them to be true.

Though she held her own among her friends and could be indignant as well as anyone else, she was invariably thoughtful of people; it was in her nature to be. She was disposed to kindliness and, recognizing that the loneliest people are the very old or the young, she intuitively turned to them, to please them, flattering with some little attention, building upon their self-esteem for a little while; and if this favor were not returned, no matter, she had taken such pleasure in the doing that she needed nothing more, though sometimes the spite and envy of little people in her own circle of friends wounded her deeply. Yet she always recovered, perhaps because her acquaintance with the slings and arrows was of lifelong duration.

I met her quite often on the streets—sometimes when the mail came in, though she was too impatient ever to stand waiting for the mail at her call-box while mail was being distributed behind the closed windows of the post office; sometimes in the hot summer afternoons, under a parasol; sometimes late at night on her slow way home from a card-party, some of which lasted into the small hours of the morning—a heavy woman who rolled a little from side to side as she walked, unconsciously, with her greying hair cut short and pulled back in what was called a "bob" some years before—and I always felt that of all the men or women who were to be discovered in Sac Prairie's streets and lanes at any hour, none had a greater right to be there than she, for in her was embodied all the romance of Sac Prairie's middle years, when the village had passed beyond the boundaries of the pioneer settlement it was, when it had become a prosperous, German agricultural village in the Wisconsin of the elder La Follette, an awakening, forward-looking town; she was an anachronism, perhaps, someone belonging neither to the distant past nor to the present, but very tangibly to a span between.

In the end, after much travail as the result of an accident on a Milwaukee street, she fell victim to cancer, and for well over a year she bore the ravages of the disease with admirable stoicism, refusing to admit for a long time that she might not recover—a vibrant woman, brimming over with life. Even in her illness her great warmth and color shone through—and her essential loneliness was betrayed only by her reluctance to bid her visitors goodbye, or to leave the telephone when someone called in those months when she was confined to her apartment; and later, when she was taken to the hospital in the terminal stages of her illness, her spirit did not flag—she rose on her elbows one day after an old friend had visited her and said to a cousin at her bedside, "Oh, I love men—old men, young men—I love them all!"

When she died in her late seventies, a curious factor in her illness answered her detractors in the village. Because a cancerous growth had taken root in her jowl, her face had remained well fleshed, as a result of which the face of the woman who lay in the casket was that of one of forty or less, smooth, without lines, full, unmistakably the face of a beautiful woman.

✽ ✽ ✽ ✽ ✽

WHAT is it about hawks that strikes the note of kinship with which I am always moved at sight of them—a feeling amounting almost to the conviction of sharing the hawk's solitude as well as its ecstasy in flight, which enables me to float aloft while I am prone upon a hilltop, watching that magnificent bird ride the air currents invisible to any human eye, high up, remote in heaven? Surely the hawk is master of all it sees—as much king of this domain as its majesty implies!

It soars, it floats, it circles, turns, vaults, dives—it makes all sky and cloud, wind and air, all earth its own. The hawk which thus for these hours belongs to me, also claims me for its own without more than a cursory awareness of my existence. The keen, discerning eye takes in heaven and earth, scans ground and water, and knows the habitants of that upper air—osprey and swallows, all others are below its range.

Its scream drifts down the buttes of heaven, its shadow crosses slopes, plain, river, village, so small a cross of darkness on the land, so small a mark of darkness in the sky where it goes by with a rare beauty which has within it all the lost beauty of the wilderness that was America.

Often of May evenings I used to meet young Nicholas Kenyon walking as I walked along the railroad tracks through the marshes, listening for the voices of frogs and the songs of birds, and inquiring of the night so filled with the sights and sounds of nature's renewal what meaning it had. A tall, well-built young man, almost athletic in appearance, with a pleasant smile and intense eyes, which betrayed the uncertainty of his quest and the lack of self-assurance in his being. He was rather long in his legs, but not unseemly in this; his hands were big and looked capable; and, though he was reputed as given to outbursts of defensive temper if teased or tormented long enough by his schoolmates, he was always gentle and complaisant in all that I knew of him.

He was by nature a solitary. If there were such a human being as a "born solitary," it was surely Nickie Kenyon, for he shunned people—they made him "uneasy," as he explained it, "I never know how to act around people," and he chose to be by himself as much of the time as possible, though he was not a misanthrope. His schoolmates did not invite his confidences; he was too shy to make overtures to girls, though he showed no inclination toward misogyny; and the boys he knew well had little to offer his restless, inquiring mind. He was said to be "bright" and a little "strange," which is to say he did not do conventional things, he did not go out for football or basketball, he did not care for the amusements most of his classmates liked, he made no effort to be one of a crowd, but always remained Nickie Kenyon.

His errant mother had left their household many years before with a casualness that bespoke neither love nor responsibility for her children. He and a younger brother lived with his father, an unhappily improvident man, who was always pursuing some dream of fortune which promised to deliver riches and lifelong comfort and, like a will-o-the-wisp vanished under the clear light of reason, which Nickie alone had. He was poles apart from his father, but he was nevertheless in the grip of filial obligations which he could not water down or break. Perhaps there was, too, an element of shame because he felt that his father was so different from most fathers, though this faded when at last he realized that he too was different in the sense that he could never bind himself submissively to the conventional existence led by most of his fellowmen in Sac Prairie.

I never met him but I was keenly aware of his yearning for answers to the questions which thronged within him, all of which resolved into a tormented demand for enlightenment, for an explanation to existence, not only his own, but the universe's. What did it all mean? What was the significance of human life upon the planet? Often I stood at his side where he gazed up at the stars, tracing the constellations, marking the planetary courses, and I listened to him speak of his own shortcomings, as seen by so many of the villagers, of whose opinion he was painfully aware. He was troubled by his inability and lack of desire to conform, by his shyness, by his feelings about his father, by his tendency to withdraw into himself, by his self-consciousness, and he talked broodingly about the fears and tribulations which beset him.

In part his need was for love, something of that intimate affection he should have had from his mother and did not know; in part it was the lack of the security always to be found in a closely-knit family; but in essence it was something more. For a while in his high school years he kept a journal in which he set down his observations and revealed his mental alertness and discernment, together with his awareness of his "difference" and his comparative isolation from his fellows; his brief paragraphs gave evidence of that almost invariable compensation of the sensitive, intelligent mind for its own lack, in the heightened sensibilities of the solitary who, taking pleasure in no company, yet is able to weigh and assess the people of his milieu, not with retaliatory bitterness but with a wisdom and a judgment not commonly the lot of a gregarious man.

He was not ill-favored in looks, and he was well toward the head of his class, but year after year, through his high school term and his university years, he walked the same paths, asking himself and the stars the same questions, in different words, perhaps, but in all else the same. Before nature he was unafraid; he was not shy; he had no fear of snake or ivy, of bog or brook, of woods or hills; he walked in the darkness of the forest or the marshes with the assurance of a wild creature in its home country, for the wilderness of animals troubled him not at all and the wildernesses of human minds stirred him profoundly to a kind of fearful rebellion, as if he were afraid he could not remain strong before the vast and spreading infection of the commonplace.

What did it all mean?—life and the stars, the planet and its inhabitants, the mores and ethics of man, his religious beliefs? Was
there a pattern? Was it God's or had it some other source? He
read voraciously of philosophy, psychology, of logic, ethics, and
the arts, of anthropology and biology, but no light was thrown
upon the problems that troubled him, and he went on, year after
year, challenging his ideals, trying to adjust to an existence in
which, increasingly, there was less and less room for his kind. It
was as if he had some foreknowledge of failure in his quest for the
meaning of existence, for he pressed it all the more despite its
futility, and he was always exasperated at my refusal to join his
quest, at my answering all his questions with "Yesterday I was not.
Today I am. Tomorrow I will not be."

He used to stand so earnestly under heaven and the stars, en-
raptured by the smells and sounds of the night, taking pleasure in
the songs of frogs and the cries of nocturnal birds, listening to the
music of earth in its passage through eternity; but in none of what
gave him such profundity of satisfaction and delight lay answers
to the questions propounded by his mind and heart. That these
were locked within himself for his discovery alone he did not
know or believe; so he walked out into the beneficent countryside, one with frogs and birds, one with the wind's hushing in the
trees and the night sounds of aquatic dwellers in ponds and
sloughs, one with the fragrance of flowers and grasses, with the
musk of decay.

He never saw me but he propounded some problem, but every
problem was an allegory for his central puzzle, the wonder at the
meaning of it all, of living and dying, of being. And, once begun,
he spoke with animation, setting forth his credos, outlining his
plans, his hopes, his dreams, with an exuberance which did not
permit of doubt or uncertainty, however strongly these loomed
behind his dreams. He would not hear that the answers to the
questions he asked lay only within him, and none could give him

the power to see. He was gravely earnest; his eyes when he spoke were fixed upon the essence of his problem suspended in infinity; he seemed half aware that no answer could be found, half in hope that what he wanted to know lay just at his fingertips if only he could find the right avenue to its exploration.

In time he went away from Sac Prairie to work in Madison. A young woman took an interest in him, his ties to his father were weakened, his life opened toward new horizons, and he found himself conforming ever a little more to please the young woman whose affection he so sorely needed, partly perhaps as a substitute for that maternal love he had never known, however little he recognized this need; and slowly the young man and his inquiry into life's meaning was pushed back, slowly locked away with childhood and youth, until all that was left of him was the reve-nant met now and then in the old places along the railroad tracks, still looking as in his prison of flesh it must still look, still asking, as in his secret places he must ask, to know the meaning of it all, or that young man, who, visiting Sac Prairie now and then, walked of an evening into the marshes along the familiar railroad tracks, listening to the long-known voices of birds and frogs, and search-ing mutely for something that once was, something lost.

❅   ❅   ❅   ❅   ❅

SOMETIMES of evenings there is in the air a quality which makes for the temporary illusion of timelessness. A subtle transference is effected by a fragrance, a scene, a familiar face, a pattern of light and shade, so that the present falls away and seems to merge into those aspects of the past first associated with awareness. Usually it is a fragrance related to change which effects this reversion—the smoke of burning leaves marking the turn of autumn to winter, the indescribable musk of thawing snow, presaging the spring, on which turns the experience of walking into the past.

I have known this illusion many times—who has not? It is one which is perhaps peculiar to long familiar places—of walking down toward Water Street on a night of thaw and of suddenly seeming to be once more an adolescent on the way to the Electric Theatre where I was sure to meet the object of my first affections beyond the home circle: the trees, houses, walk, road, the lights in the windows, the pervasive smell of thawing snow, all are the same, and for a few moments the illusion is the reality—but then today intrudes in the absence of the outside lights of the long-abandoned theatre, the illusion falls away, yesterday returns to its proper perspective;—of walking through a smoky October evening homewards, and seeming briefly once again on the way to Grandfather Derleth's house with the evening paper, the mind's eye recreating that familiar scene of the two old people sitting together at the table under the green-shaded light in that long-known kitchen—once again trees, houses, even the voices of passersby, the cries of children on bicycles, the sweet pungence of burning leaves, all are the same, and time is not a dimension but a state of mind.

One expects at such times the very physical presence of those who have peopled the past—that first girl in all her shy loveliness; the grandparents who were once thought to be the fount of wisdom—that first girl who became a tired, complaining housewife, forever lost to the girl she had been; the grandparents who divided into a lonely, ill woman, and a weakening old man, betraying himself by his fear of loneliness. One expects even more— the recreation of the exact scene, a projection of the mind's eye from the near past or the remote years: the ill-lit post office becoming once again that magic place from which one might receive, after the evening mail was in, a treasured letter from that first girl; the depot where the evening train came in, with old Mike and Beau Wardler waiting at the station platform, and the mischievous boys, as always, troubling them, with the angular agent himself pushing and pulling expresswagons and carts around, shouting at the boys before the locomotive's whistle sounded at the bridge; the supper table at home, under the yellow lamplight's glow, with father and mother and sister restored as at first the child's groping awareness recognized them for his haven and his security from the cold, physical and spiritual, outside.

Perhaps these moments are integral in an existence close to the familiar scenes of childhood and youth, wherever there is a continuity of living. They do not occur with nostalgia, they come without warning; suddenly the chance of the moment, the place, the scene, the familiar sensual experience combine, and the present becomes fleetingly once more the past—time, in effect, ceases to exist, despite the unalterable clock. It is a kind of meeting with one's self, a meeting and passing by, the man meeting the boy he once was, meeting once more the scenes and the people of that boyhood, an experience that is an essential part of life in any long known place. The owl that keens softly in the summer evening park is the owl of childhood and youth; the arc-light swinging at the corner is the light of adolescent years; the children playing in the park are the companions of one's own childhood; the long street of arc-lights yellow on the western afterglow of April evenings still opens on the promise of adventurous expectancy; and every corner, every turning, offers still the same adventure, the identical expectancy of something beyond the commonplace, something waiting to be created in the country of the mind and translated, however inarticulately, into the familiar face, the long-known tree, the ancient house, into the eternal afterglow, new moon and evening star.

Perhaps it is the subconscious yearning for past time, for a time of irresponsibility, which lays traps for the unwary, the longing for a return to the dark, enclosing place, the intimacy of being lost to alien eyes, of being secret and alone, which may be another expression of the desire to be merged with all things, with earth itself, an awareness not of timelessness as such, but of the ob-

literation which is both death and the merging into time, the moment behind is the moment that has died, as were it knowledge that death always lurks behind, and before, the unknown, and beyond the unknown somewhere death at full circle, life and death being one.